Rural Route 8 Part 2:

Unrequited Love

Rural Route 8 Part 2:

Unrequited Love

E. Raye Turonek

www.urbanbooks.net

Urban Books, LLC
300 Farmingdale Road, N.Y.-Route 109
Farmingdale, NY 11735

Rural Route 8 Part 2: Unrequited Love

ISBN 13: 978-1-64556-401-0
ISBN 10: 1-64556-401-0

First Trade Paperback Printing December 2022
Printed in the United States of America

10 9 8 7 6 5 4 3 2 1

Distributed by Kensington Publishing Corp.
Submit Orders to:
Customer Service
400 Hahn Road
Westminster, MD 21157-4627
Phone: 1-800-733-3000
Fax: 1-800-659-2436

Rural Route 8 Part 2:

Unrequited Love

by

E. Raye Turonek

In loving memory of my grandmother Patricia Turonek.
You will forever be held in our hearts.

The Beginning of the End

At 7:00 p.m. Evelyn couldn't bring herself to leave the office until she'd completed the arduous goal she had set out to accomplish. She leaned back in the black leather chair that sat behind the massive mahogany desk in his corner office. Though a lingering frigidness permeated the air outside, her view of the city of Detroit from the sixty-first floor of the Renaissance Center was breathtaking. A wave of passion overwhelmed Evelyn as she stared out at the star-riddled night sky, wondering if Colin was looking out at the sky at that very moment. Oh, how she missed him. The statuesque woman with the gleaming white teeth and mocha skin was utterly enamored with Colin—and was ready and willing to fulfill his every desire if he so beckoned.

Colin's chiseled physique complemented his kind smile, deep dimples, and intoxicating dark brown eyes, easily garnering him the attention of any woman in his vicinity. Sometimes Evelyn couldn't manage to keep her focus, as thoughts of Colin would race through her mind. She would envision his strong, capable caramel hands coming at her from the rear, then traveling up her torso to meet at her breasts. He would hold them firmly while nibbling at the nape of her neck. At the thought of this now, Evelyn's heart raced. She began to sweat, and the scent of coconut escaped her pores. With her Ferragamo flats on, she was just tall enough for her ponytail to brush across his nostrils. In her mind, he breathed in deep the aroma of her curls as she closed her eyes, giving in to tingling she felt in her core. Evelyn's stockings grew damp between her thighs—the daydream feeling more real this time than it ever had.

The sound of a black Ferragamo tote bag hitting the mahogany desk startled Evelyn, ripping her from her daydream. Her eyes sprang open to the sight of Jocelyn. She was gorgeous. Her straight jet-black hair traveled down to the middle of her back, and her turquoise eyes matched the peacoat she was wearing. Jocelyn stood five feet, nine inches tall once she'd kicked off her heels. Evelyn was at a loss for words. She wasn't expecting to see Jocelyn there.

"What the fuck are you doing in my husband's office!" Jocelyn rested one hand on her hip.

"Calm down. I was going to go over the checks and balances for the audit. Plus, I wanted to drop off Colin's birthday gift."

"Bitch! You don't work here anymore. What about *fired* don't you understand? You're not even supposed to be in this building. How did you get up here, anyway?"

Before Evelyn could furnish a reply, Jocelyn added, "You know what? It doesn't matter. You need to leave. Now!" She snatched up the gift bag Evelyn had placed on the desk then slung it across the room. "Get your shit and get out."

Evelyn kept her cool as she rose from the chair to collect her belongings. "Fine. There's no need to get upset or call the police. I'll leave."

The smirk on Evelyn's face as she got up from the chair left a sick feeling in the pit of Jocelyn's stomach.

"I'll be seeing you around," Evelyn sang, gift bag and purse in hand, as she pranced by Jocelyn to exit the office.

"Evelyn!"

Evelyn turned to see what Jocelyn wanted now. At that very moment, Jocelyn got a firm grip on the keyboard she had snatched up from the desktop and swung it at Evelyn. The keyboard cracked in half when it collided with Evelyn's face. The blow caught her by surprise. Blood instantly began to leak from her nose. It ran down her chin and stained her silver blouse. Anger that simmered in her belly had reached the boiling point. With a jolt of fury, Evelyn lunged at Jocelyn and wrapped her hands around her throat. Evelyn's plan was to choke the life from the other woman right then and there, but Jocelyn's swift kick to her abdomen sent Evelyn backward and onto her bottom.

Jocelyn grabbed a paperweight off the desk and headed straight for her nemesis. "I've been waiting to do this for far too long," she snarled as she closed in.

As Jocelyn approached, Evelyn grabbed a Taser from her purse, which she'd somehow managed to hold on to, then zapped her in the leg before Jocelyn could exact her revenge. The surge of electricity brought Jocelyn to her knees. Evelyn didn't waste any time; she sat up all the way and jabbed the Taser into Jocelyn's side, delivering another jolt of electricity. Jocelyn's body jerked involuntarily. The five seconds it took for Evelyn to relent felt like hours to her debilitated opponent.

Finally, Evelyn stood, attempting to wipe the blood from her shirt with her hand and smearing it instead. Regardless, she refrained from losing the cool she'd regained upon getting the upper hand. It wasn't until she walked over and picked the gift bag up off the floor that her sanity waned. Hearing the shattered pieces of what was once Colin's birthday gift as they shifted around in the bag caused Evelyn to snap. Her eyes bulged. "Now look what you've done! It's broken! You selfish, spoiled little bitch. You're gonna pay for this." She released the bag from her clutches, allowing it to drop to the floor.

I can imagine you're wondering how this came to be. Come then . . . Allow me to take you back months prior to the start of it all.

Chapter 1

Routines Change

The time on the stove read 3:31 a.m. It was time for Evelyn to head to work.

"Honey, I made you a cup of coffee!" Erick called out as he twisted the cap down on her thermos.

Evelyn crept up behind him, ran her hand up, then down his back again before wrapping her arms around his abdomen. The embrace was one they shared every morning. Evelyn loved her doting husband, and he loved her just as much in return. He turned to her, and his hazel eyes bored into her soul. She pushed his shoulder-length blond hair back behind his ears as he leaned in to taste her lips. Evelyn rubbed her hands down the sides of his face, then tugged on his beard a little as she planted three tender kisses upon his thin strawberry lips. As her tongue moved down his neck, her right hand moved to his genitals and fondled him through his boxer briefs.

"Oh, you want more, huh?" His eyes lit up with excitement.

Evelyn glanced over at the time displayed on the stove, giving his proposition a second thought. It was already 3:33 a.m. Evelyn was scheduled to clock in at 0400 hours. Opening up the post office before the first of several mail trucks pulled in to unload mail was her first duty every morning.

"How about we postpone this until I get home?" she replied.

"Then I want you naked as soon as you come in the door, 'cause Daddy's gonna take you to pound town."

Evelyn blushed and giggled at her husband's admission. After over a decade of marriage, he still had the ability to make her burn with intense desire and feel bashful at the same time.

"You know I have to take my nap before I run errands and the kids get out of school."

"It's okay. Daddy's gonna put you to sleep and take care of dinner."

"Ohh . . . Daddy, I like that." Evelyn smooched the side of his neck.

"You sure you don't want me to bend you over right now?"

"All right. All right. Let me stop, before I'm late for work." Evelyn backed off.

Erick reached over and grabbed her thermos off the granite countertop. "Here. Don't forget your coffee." He handed it over to her.

"Thank you, baby."

"You're welcome, my love." He followed his wife through the mudroom, then out into their garage, where her SUV was parked next to his Harley. Erick opened her driver's side door and allowed his wife to climb into her Yukon before shutting it behind her. "Now, lock it." He made a downward motion with his finger.

Evelyn pressed the door lock, then gave her husband a thumbs-up. "I'll call you on my lunch break," she said, loud enough that he could hear through the raised window, as she pushed the button atop her sun visor to lift the garage door.

After getting a thumbs-up in return from Erick, she started the engine, then turned on the radio. A compilation of classical melodies would be her music choice for her ride to work, as it was on many occasions. The drive to work was a time to clear her mind of any confusion before she'd have to worry about a mass of mail, followed by kids, T-ball practice, gymnastics, chores, and a multitude of other priorities. She pulled out of the garage and onto the street, then made her way through the dark to the two-lane highway she traveled for twenty miles to make it to the Clarkston post office. The rural area where she and her family resided had an abundance of cornfields and cow pastures among acres of open land. Evelyn held her breath as she passed by the pet cemetery on the left and the town's traditional cemetery for people directly across the street. She was superstitious like that. Her belief was that if you neglected to hold your breath when passing by a graveyard, an evil spirit or someone who'd recently passed on would have the opportunity to inhabit your body. No matter how absurd the notion, no one could convince Evelyn otherwise.

She glanced over at the time displayed on the dashboard. It was 3:45 a.m., and she was about seven minutes away from her destination. Evelyn appreciated her job and took her duties seriously, so getting there on time was of great importance to her. Her route to the Clarkston post office was an easy one to drive. She would only ever see a few cars on the road during those wee hours of the morning, which made the trip much more pleasant than the one she took during the lunch hour rush, when she made her way home. After she crossed over Interstate 75, Evelyn relaxed, knowing that the Clarkston post office was only a couple of miles ahead. She turned up the volume on the radio. Beethoven's "Moonlight Sonata," one of her favorites, blared from the car speakers.

As Evelyn turned off the road in front of the post office, her headlamps illuminated the thick chain that blocked the entrance to the parking lot. She came to a stop, shifted the gear into park, let her car window down, then hopped out to unlatch the chain. Once that was done, she got behind the wheel and drove through the parking lot, past mail trucks on both sides, to make it to the dimly lit employee parking in back. An American flag strung to a pole flapped overhead in a gentle breeze from the west. She parked the Yukon, got out once more, then pulled at a cord tied to a belt loop on her shorts. Her keys were attached to one end. Evelyn kept the building's keys strapped to a belt loop to avoid losing them. She often worried that they'd one day slip from her grasp, then fall through a space in the sewer grate in the employee parking area. Paranoia, much of the time unwarranted, pushed her to take extra precautions.

After getting the metal gate in front of the post office's back door unlocked, Evelyn slid one side of the gate back as far as it could go, then turned and did the same to the other side. As she headed back to her vehicle in the dim light to retrieve her thermos and her purse, she thought she saw movement in her peripheral vision. She squinted in an effort to sharpen her vision and saw what appeared to be a masked assailant, dressed in all black, running full speed in her direction. Evelyn's eyes bulged from a mixture of shock and disbelief at what was taking place. A jolt of panic surged through her, spurring her to move fast. She reached her vehicle and prayed that by the time she was able to get in, her assailant wouldn't already have her in his grasp. Acting fast, she opened the car door just as the assailant reached her. The open door separating them gave Evelyn the time she needed to dart off between the mail trucks.

"Oh my God . . . Oh my God," she uttered, her voice barely audible. The last thing she wanted to do was alert her attacker as to her whereabouts. *I can't believe this is happening to me. What the fuck am I going to do?* she asked herself. Evelyn hadn't noticed a weapon in the assailant's hand when he'd rushed toward her. Maybe this person was just trying to scare her, she hoped. Evelyn told herself to calm down. *It's only a person. One that bleeds, just like me,* she assured herself. Dim lighting in the parking area allowed her to see the assailant's shadow moving across the asphalt as he approached. Evelyn climbed under an LLV, lay flat on the pavement, and stared at the assailant's feet as he was about to pass by. But black combat boots stopped right in front of her. Suddenly, he turned, then rushed back to Evelyn's vehicle. He hopped into the driver's seat, somehow started the Yukon, then shifted the gear into drive and sped deeper into the parking lot.

Evelyn scooched along the pavement until she was able to stand. She ducked and weaved through the trucks, using them for cover, as she tried to pinpoint her attacker's location. She thought about running out into the open but abandoned the idea, assuming he was faster than she was. She looked down at her wristwatch. It was 3:58 a.m. *All I have to do is wait a couple more minutes. The semi carrying today's mail will be pulling up soon,* she thought, clinging tight to hope.

That's when a gloved hand reached out of the darkness and gained a strong grip on the back of her neck. Another hand pressed down on the joint between her neck and left shoulder, bringing her to her knees.

"Ahhh! Get the fuck off me!" Evelyn yelled as she forced her body forward and to the ground before quickly rolling onto her back. The swift kick she delivered to her assailant's groin took his breath away and at the same time confirmed that she had guessed right as to his gender. The heel of her shoe stabbed his scrotum not once, but two more times before she crawled backward, then hopped up to run out into the open while he attempted to catch his breath.

The truck driver who was pulling into the lot at that very moment neglected to see her, but he felt a bump when Evelyn's body slammed against the grill of his semi.

"Oh my God." The driver's boot collided with the brake pedal. By the time he jumped down out of the cab, her assailant had already crept off into the darkness to nurse his wounds.

Within five minutes of the call, police and paramedics were on the scene. Two paramedics loaded an unconscious Evelyn into the back of the ambulance. Colin, the more experienced of the two paramedics, rode in back with Evelyn. Blood streamed from an open wound on her forehead, painting her face crimson. Colin soaked it up with gauze as it seeped down into her eyes. Evelyn's lids sprang open once she got a whiff of the ammonia inhalant he waved under her nose. She came to in a panic, as if she was still battling her attacker. She slapped, scratched, even clawed at Colin, attempting to fight him off.

"Whoa. Whoa. Whoa. Calm down."

She didn't let up, and her arm badge flew onto the floor amid the commotion.

"Please, calm down. I'm not going to hurt you. I promise." Colin could tell she was frightened and confused.

Unable to keep fighting, Evelyn stopped moving, then slipped from consciousness.

Ten minutes later, the gurney carrying her body burst through double doors at the local hospital's emergency room.

"Try to stay with me, ma'am. Please, stay with me," the paramedic said calmly, trying to keep Evelyn awake.

She'd been slipping in and out of consciousness since he'd waved the ammonia inhalant under her nostrils. "You're gonna be okay."

"Don't . . . Don't leave me," she whispered, staring into his big, deep brown eyes.

"I'm right here. Everything is going to be okay."

A vision of Colin remained in the dazed mail clerk's mind before she fainted yet again.

"We'll take it from here," a doctor announced as he took control at the head of the gurney and the rest of his medical team moved in along its sides. "We've got an injury to the frontal lobe. Patient has been suffering multiple bouts of syncope."

Colin watched as the gurney plowed through a second set of double doors, then completely disappeared from view. He turned and headed back outside.

Once he got back to the ambulance, he went to close the back doors and noticed Evelyn's postal badge on the floor of the vehicle. He picked it up and tapped it on the palm of his hand, contemplating his next move. *I should take this back inside to her*, he thought. *I wouldn't mind checking on her later, though. It's not as if she'll need it for work tomorrow. I'll bring it to her in a couple of days.* Colin shut the ambulance doors, ready to end his shift for the day.

Days had passed. Erick had been by Evelyn's side for three days now, waiting for her to open her big brown eyes. On the fourth morning he sat at Evelyn's bedside, clutching her limp hand. Rays from the rising sun peeked in through the vertical blinds that covered her hospital room window. Bandages covered her head wound, and gauze had been taped over bruises on her face. Seventy-two hours had gone by since she was last conscious. A team of medical staff huddled in a corner of the room, discussing Evelyn's recent CAT scan. Her husband's belief that she would awaken remained resolute, despite the pessimistic attitude of the surgeon who'd closed the wound at the front of her skull.

Erick whispered to her, "Wake up, my love. It's time to wake up now. I can't do this without you. I need you. The kids need you. You've gotta fight this thing. You're stronger than this, baby. Please, just wake up. Just open your eyes for me."

Evelyn didn't move a muscle. A tube that plumbed the depths of her esophagus at one end and protruded from her mouth at the other looked more painful than helpful. Until yesterday it had weakened Erick at his very core to see her in such a feeble state. The fact that there was nothing he could do to help her had made him feel useless. He was her protector. At least, he fancied himself that. But his will to be strong had crumbled, and his wanting had turned to wishing, but only for a day or two. On the third day of Evelyn's hospitalization, Erick had gone to the hospital's chapel and, on his knees, had prayed for God to restore her to health. He'd vowed that no hell would be worse than losing his companion for life. In that chapel, his faith had triumphed over his will, and he had determined that God would return Evelyn to him.

Later that day Colin peeked into Evelyn's hospital room. It was nearly empty, the doctors having all dispersed. He pushed through the door and approached the bed, a small bouquet of yellow lilies attached to a teddy bear in his hand. Colin had hung the postal arm badge Evelyn had dropped in the ambulance around the teddy bear's neck.

"I know you don't know me, but I just wanted to check on you, make sure you made it," he told Evelyn as she lay still in bed, her eyes closed. "I, uh . . . I also wanted to bring this back to you." He sat the gift atop the white blanket covering her legs. "You dropped it in the ambulance. You probably can't even hear me, can you? I had an aunt who was in a coma once. She swore up and down she could hear the family when they came to visit. My mom didn't believe her. She would always say, 'Aunt Raye sure could weave a tale.'" Colin placed his hand atop hers. "Well . . . whether you can or can't hear me, I'm sorry this happened to you, and I hope you wake up soon."

Just as he was about to turn and walk away, Evelyn's hand clutched Colin's. She opened her eyes, and he looked directly into her wild, wide-eyed stare. It was her first time *really* seeing him.

"You're awake," he whispered softly.

"What's going on here?" Erick asked as he rushed into the room. He had peeked in on Evelyn, and the sight of their clasped hands had taken him completely by surprise.

Evelyn loosened her grip, and Colin pulled his hand away.

"Who are you?" Erick's brows wrinkled with concern as he approached.

"Hi. I'm Colin." He extended his hand for a proper greeting.

Erick accepted. "I'm Erick, Evelyn's husband. Is there something I can help you with, Colin?"

"I'm one of the paramedics that brought your wife here. She dropped her work badge on the floor of the ambulance. I figured I'd return it and look in on her to see how she was doing."

Erick's face relaxed as his worries eased. "Thank you. That was very thoughtful of you. And thank you for getting my wife here so quickly. She could have died if it weren't for you," he responded, closing the gap between himself and Evelyn. By then her eyes had closed again. Erick hadn't even noticed that she'd regained consciousness.

"You're welcome. That's what I'm here for. It's actually just a part-time gig. I don't know how long I'm going to keep doing it. I've seen some pretty horrible things over the past year. I'm just glad she made it. Some aren't so lucky."

"I'm glad she made it too. I don't know what I'd do without her. The kids miss their mother more than ever. Hopefully, she'll be coming home soon."

"I'll say a prayer for you guys," Colin said. "I should be going. My wife is probably wondering where I am."

"Thanks again for stopping by."

"No problem. Take care." Colin exited the room.

Chapter 2

Mommy's Home

One week later . . .

Her hands trembled as Erick guided her across the threshold into their chateau-style log cabin home. It had been built from the ground up. Everything they'd envisioned together as a couple, they had poured into the design of this house. Those had been happier times. Back when Evelyn had remembered the love she and her husband shared.

"You're shaking." Erick ran his hands down the sides of her vibrating arms as they stood in the foyer. "What's wrong, baby? Are you cold?" He stared fixedly at his weary wife.

"I'm sorry. I just can't remember." Her eyes toggled left, then right, taking in the scenery. "Everything is so beautiful."

"Of course it's beautiful. You decorated it yourself," he responded emphatically.

Her eyes widened with disbelief. "I did all of this?" Evelyn couldn't understand where she'd gotten the talent to do such a thing. Nothing her gaze settled on resonated with her—not even the truffle-colored drapes or the Egyptian valances that matched.

Erick released his grip, allowing her to step forward from the foyer into their great room. A crystal chandelier attached to the vaulted ceiling sparkled like new diamonds.

"How can we afford all of this? I'm just a postal worker," Evelyn said as she stared at the chandelier.

"Lucky for you, your husband has his own construction company."

"I see," she remarked in a hushed tone. Evelyn moved to the fireplace, where family photos were lined up neatly in their frames. Unable to recognize anyone in the pictures, she turned to him. "Who are these children? Are they all mine?"

"They are all ours, my love. All three of them."

"They look so happy."

"They are happy. And once they find out you're home, they'll be even happier." Erick was ecstatic to finally have his wife back, but he was also secretly nervous about how she'd adjust to the children. It wasn't their fault their mother had lost her memory. Nonetheless, they'd have to bear the brunt of the tragic event that had taken place.

"I'm a good mother," she proclaimed, although subconsciously she questioned whether this was true. How could she really be a good mother if she couldn't even remember giving birth to the children? Just that fast, the moment became more stressful than she could handle. Weariness washed over Evelyn, and she said, "I need to sit down. I just can't." She allowed herself to flop down on the plush leather sofa.

"Baby, are you okay?" Erick rushed to her side.

"This is just a lot to take in at once, I think. Maybe I should lie down."

"Okay. Let's get you into bed."

The doctors had assured Erick that his wife was able to return home and she would fully regain her strength, yet it seemed that coming home would prove more difficult for Evelyn than they'd anticipated. Erick wouldn't dare complain. He was determined to make it work. Having his family whole again was all he'd dreamed of over the past several weeks. The doting husband helped his wife up from the sofa, then led her down the hall and into their bedroom. Their bedroom was spacious, as were the walk-in closet and the en suite bathroom.

Mentally exhausted, Evelyn stretched out on the bed and rested her head atop the black satin pillow, wondering where she'd go from here. Her children would be home soon and would expect to find the doting mother they'd become accustomed to. What would she say to them? How would she explain the fact that they were indeed strangers to her? The skin between her eyebrows wrinkled as she furrowed her brow. Erick noticed the worry splayed across his wife's face.

"Everything's gonna be fine, baby. I promise. Just get some sleep. A nap is probably just what you need. I'll take care of the kids. They'll be getting off the bus in a few hours. If you're feeling up to it, maybe they can visit with you?"

"I don't know what to say."

"Don't worry. They know exactly what to say. You're their mother," Erick replied, intent on dissolving her concerns. He hoped that seeing the children would spark her memory.

Evelyn brandished a fleeting smile, masking the remaining uneasiness she felt and at the same time squelching her husband's.

"If you need anything, I'll be in the kitchen, getting something ready to eat for the kids," he announced before leaving the bedroom.

The moment he was gone, Evelyn shut her eyes, and images of Colin flooded her mind. He was the one. Every part of her body told her so, from the warmth she felt in her belly to the dampness she felt between her legs at the very notion of him laying hands on her skin. Evelyn wanted him. She wanted Colin's lips pressed against hers, their tongues intertwined and, even more so, their bodies interlocked. In that moment finding the object of her intense desires was all that mattered, not the husband and children she'd yet to remember having.

Colin traveled a path through the woods on his ten-acre property. In the distance, he could see the greenhouse, where his wife, Jocelyn, was busy tending to their plants. She had a passion for all things natural: fruits, vegetables, even cannabis. All of these had their place in the enormous structure. Colin had used every cent of the money he'd made as a part-time paramedic to purchase the structure. It was the best birthday present he'd ever given the love of his life.

A five-hundred-yard hike brought him to the glass doors of their greenhouse. "How's it coming?" he called as he open the doors and stepped inside.

"I think we're gonna need some help." Jocelyn pulled gardening gloves from her hands. This crop has turned out much better than I thought it would. Check it out." She moved her nose in closer to the marijuana plant she'd been trimming, then took a whiff of its aroma. "Smells just like nature intended."

Colin eased up beside her to sniff one of the buds. "Wow! That's potent! Great job, baby."

"I told you I could do it. My green thumb knows no bounds." Jocelyn tilted her head in his direction for a kiss.

Colin happily obliged, planting a long, passionate kiss upon her lips while at the same time copping a feel. His large hand squeezed her firm rump, causing her to yelp.

"Mr. Ravish, the greens making you a bit horny, aye?"

"Not at all. It's Mrs. Ravish that's making me horny. You've got the fans going. Your hair is blowing in the wind. All you have to do is take off this flannel shirt and slide those jogging pants down."

"What's the matter? Don't like my outfit?" Jocelyn teased.

"Let's just say, I like it better off than on." Colin assisted his wife out of the restrictive garments, eager to have his way with her.

Back at the Todd residence, the doorbell chimed, waking Evelyn from her slumber. She got out of bed, then peeked through the curtains to get a view of their visitor. Although she had no idea who the man was, Erick, on the other hand, knew exactly who'd stopped by to put a damper on their day. Their next-door neighbor frequently paid them a visit to address his concerns. Erick and Evelyn had recently added an in-ground swimming pool to their yard, and their neighbor was not at all happy about it. He'd stopped by every week since it was installed to lodge a complaint with the Todds.

The stumpy, overweight middle-aged man with the receding hairline pounded at their door after ringing the bell a few more times. Once Erick's desire to let him stew had been fulfilled, he answered the door, his calm, collected demeanor intact. "Mr. Fuboi, how can I help you?"

"Your son's dog messed in my yard again! And I know it was him. My Dalila never messes in the front yard. I fully expect you to come over there and clean it up. I don't care which one of you does it. Just as long as it's cleaned up by the time I get home from work," he barked, his face as red as a beet.

"Mr. Fuboi, I apologize for Sheba's mess. My son must have turned off her electronic collar somehow—"

"I don't want to hear your excuses," he interrupted, halting Erick's reply. "You always seem to have one ready and waiting. Just get over there and clean it up!" The frustrated man turned, then stomped down the porch stairs.

"Who was that?" Evelyn asked, having emerged from the safety of her bedroom and made her way to the foyer.

Erick closed the front door. "It's just our neighbor. What are you doing out of bed?"

"I'm feeling better now. I think I should try looking at some pictures. Maybe that will jog my memory."

"We've got plenty of photo albums stored in the attic. I can go get them, if you'd like."

"Please . . . if you wouldn't mind?"

"No problem, my love. I'll be right back." Erick took several steps and then trotted up the stairs just off the foyer to fulfill his wife's request.

A loud grumbling sound erupted. Evelyn rubbed her hand across her tummy, attempting to tame the hunger she felt. *I'm starving*, she thought. *As big as this house is, we ought to have some food around here.* She made her way to the kitchen, which was just off the great room. Evelyn was so famished she felt as if she could eat a feast fit for ten men, but once she entered the kitchen, something caught her eye that caused her to forget about her voracious appetite. She spied him walking across their backyard. It was their neighbor Mr. Fuboi. *Not him again*, she complained silently. "What are you up to?" she said aloud.

Evelyn watched intently as Mr. Fuboi headed straight for their in-ground swimming pool. His poodle's toy lay in the center of the blue tarp that covered the water. There was no way he could reach his faithful pooch's toy to retrieve it. He had to find a way to get it out without getting his dress suit wet. A long pole with a net attached answered his query. He lifted it from the ground, then stepped to the edge of the pool. Leaning in, feet teetering on the edge, he stretched his arms as far as he could and attempted to pull the toy toward him with the net.

That was when Erick noticed him from the attic window. "What the hell is he up to now?" As he peered down at Mr. Fuboi, Erick found it humorous to see the man stretching his stumpy arms as far as they could go to accomplish his goal. That was until their robotic lawn mower started to move around the yard. At first, it spun round in circles, as if it had some sort of malfunction, but then it took a straight path toward their neighbor. "What the hell?" Erick watched in disbelief as the mower slammed into the man. His footing already unstable, Mr. Fuboi toppled over onto the tarp upon impact.

"Ahhh!" Mr. Fuboi flailed his arms.

Erick snickered as he watched his neighbor struggle. Bolts drilled into the cement did their job of holding the tarp's cords in place. Mr. Fuboi wasn't in imminent danger, so Erick saw no need to rush to his aid. *I'll let him ride the wave for a while*, Erick reckoned as he went back to his task of retrieving photo albums.

Mr. Fuboi hollered upon seeing the lady of the house exit through the sliding glass doors that overlooked the backyard. "Help me! I need some help here, dammit!"

Evelyn didn't rush to the pool to assist. Her eyes toggled left, then right as she cased the scene.

"I said, 'Hurry up, dammit!' I'm getting all wet."

The small pockets of water that had collected atop the tarp were nothing to panic about, but of course, Mr. Fuboi didn't see it that way.

Evelyn paused nearby to watch him struggle. "It could be a lot worse, ya know? Here, I'll show you." Evelyn proceeded to undo one of the tarp cords attached to the secured bolts.

"Mrs. Todd, what are you doing!" he screamed, a look of sheer panic in his eyes.

"I'm helping," Evelyn assured him as she moved to the other end of the pool and loosened yet another cord.

"I can't swim!" Mr. Fuboi revealed as he thrashed around in the water. Five minutes later, exhausted from the effort, he sank to the bottom of the pool like a sack of stones.

Evelyn brandished the evilest of grins. She didn't care whether their neighbor could swim or not. Some lessons had to be taught the hard way.

"Knock, knock . . . Who's there? No one now," Evelyn remarked wickedly as she turned to go back inside the house.

Erick gathered up the five photo albums he'd found, then headed over to the window to see if Mr. Fuboi had made his way out of the pool. "Oh my God!" Erick was horrified at the sight of his neighbor submerged in the water. "What have I done?" Gripped with fear, Erick bolted from the attic, then down the stairs.

"Too late," Evelyn whispered as her husband blew by her, then dashed out the sliding glass doors.

Erick thought he'd heard her remark, but he just didn't want to believe his wife had said it. He'd even noticed the remote to the robotic lawn mower sitting on their kitchen table. However, Erick refused to entertain the notion that his wife had caused Mr. Fuboi's demise, and he certainly wouldn't question his wife's motives. It was the start of a pattern of denial that would threaten the fabric of their seemingly perfect life.

Ten minutes, which felt like an eternity, passed as Erick watched his neighbor floating lifeless face down in their pool before first responders finally arrived. He could hear sirens blaring as the ambulance and the authorities sped up the block. Nervousness simmered in his belly. He couldn't help but feel at fault. After all, he'd noticed his neighbor struggling in the pool, yet he hadn't as much as lifted a finger to assist him. Had Erick rushed to Mr. Fuboi's aid when he saw him struggling on the tarp, he'd still be alive. It was a truth he dared not reveal to the authorities. There was no way he could. Who'd take care of his wife and children should they decide to lock him up? Erick couldn't risk it. The appearance of a police officer in the backyard snapped him out of his reverie.

"Are you the one who called the police?" Officer Jan Fackender blurted as she hastily approached the pool. The diminutive woman, who was with the Oakland County Sheriff's Office, was always the first on the scene, ready to solve the case at hand.

Erick turned to address the officer. "I am."

"Oh, my Lord!" Her eyes had settled on the floating corpse. "What happened? Why didn't you try pulling him out?"

Erick shook his head, then lowered it in despair. "I was in the attic, rummaging through boxes, when I looked out the window and noticed him floating there." He offered up the excuse with a generous amount of regret.

"So, you assumed he couldn't be saved?"

"It takes less than a minute to drown, and he was already floating when I saw him. By the time I got downstairs from the attic and ran into the yard, he'd already been underwater for much longer than that."

"What is your relation to the victim, sir?"

"He's my neighbor." Erick went on to explain as two paramedics rushed into the backyard to retrieve the body from the pool. "I think he must have been trying to retrieve his dog's toy from the center of our pool. His weight was too much for the tarp to hold."

Picking at her pastel purple fingernails, an anxious Evelyn watched intently from the great room window, hoping one of the paramedics who had arrived on the scene was Colin. She pouted at the sight of two strangers pushing a gurney through her yard. Unfortunately, the object of her desires wasn't on duty that day.

Chapter 3

Rewriting the Rules

A couple of weeks went by, during which Evelyn slowly gathered her strength. She used the time to get to know her children again, which pleased her husband. His guilt over allowing his neighbor to drown subsided. Everything was looking up for them. Although she couldn't remember much of anything, Evelyn had taken the initiative to get back to normal. In addition to reacquainting herself with her children, she drove around town with a map, so that she could know where she was at all times. And dropping their eight-year-old son Bryson, the youngest of the bunch, off at school not only cemented their bond but also helped her to learn her way around.

Erick wasn't exactly comfortable with his wife driving aimlessly around Clarkston, but he didn't really have a say in the matter. Evelyn was adamant when it came to asserting her independence. She was proud of the progress she'd made all on her own. Now that she was all healed up, on top of looking better than ever, Evelyn decided she would soon go back to work, so she made the necessary arrangements with the post office. She couldn't remember the number scheme for the street addresses to process letters, but she could complete other duties, like scanning and tossing parcels.

"Are you excited about the Scholastic Book Fair at school today?" she asked, staring at Bryson in the rear-view mirror as she cruised down Main Street a few days later. Her first day back to work was fast approaching, so she was spending as much time with the children as possible.

The pale little boy with the short brown curls lowered his gaze, then let out a long sigh. "Yes, Mama."

"What's wrong, Bryson? You have the money I gave you, right?"

"Yes, I have it."

"You should be able to pick out a nice book with twenty dollars. Don't you think?"

"I guess so, Mama," he answered, the pitiful look on his face unchanged.

"Bryson, tell Mama what's wrong. I can't fix it if I don't know what's wrong."

Initially, Bryson held out, for fear of being called a tattletale. But the foreboding look in his mother's eyes when he glanced up at her pushed him to spill the beans. "I won't be able to buy anything, anyway."

"Why not? You have the money."

"Every time I bring money to school, this kid named Domonic takes it from me."

Evelyn's heart pounded, an anger she'd never felt before brewing inside of her. "Why haven't you told the teacher, Bryson? You can't just allow people to pick on you like that. If you let them get by with an inch, they'll try to take a mile."

"What?" The little boy had a puzzled expression on his face. He had no idea what his mother meant.

"If you let someone pick on you once, Bryson, they'll continue to do it, and more often. Understand?"

"Yes, Mama. I understand."

"So, what are you going to do about it?"

"I don't know. He's a lot bigger than me. It's his second time in second grade, so he's bigger than all the other kids. He picks on everybody. Not just me."

"Well, seems I need to set up a conference with his parents. Get some things sorted out . . ."

"She's a big, fat, mean lady, too," Bryson blurted.

"It's okay, Bryson. The biggest ones fall the hardest."

Evelyn pulled into the school lot, then parked in the back, as opposed to the front, where she'd normally drop Bryson off.

"Where are you going, Mama?"

"I'm coming inside with you, and you're going to show me this Domonic character you're talking about."

Just then a black minivan rounded the corner, its tires screeching and painting the asphalt black, and pulled into the school parking lot. Bryson's big brown eyes widened. "That's them," he announced, alerted by the sound of screaming rubber.

"Who?"

"In the black car." He pointed in the direction of the black minivan. "That's Domonic and his dad."

"Stay inside." Evelyn exited her SUV to confront the boy's father.

The impatient father barked his demands from the front seat as Dominic rushed to gather up his things. "Hurry up! Get your coat on and grab your book bag. I've got things to do before work, boy."

"But, Dad, you're supposed to drop me off in front of the school," countered the chubby boy with the spiky mohawk.

"I'm not waiting in line for ten minutes just to drop you off. You're a big boy. You can walk to the front if you have to. Now stop whining like a little girl and get out of here."

A knock on the driver's side window snatched his stern gaze from the rearview mirror. His eyebrows wrinkled at the sight of Evelyn standing alongside his vehicle. She was cloaked in a peach one-piece silk pantsuit. He had no idea whether she was a parent or a school faculty member. The man allowed his beady gray eyes to travel the length of Evelyn's body, attempting to surmise who she was, as he lowered his window.

He offered up an excuse before she even had a chance to introduce herself. "I'm just dropping off my kid. I'll be out of the way in a second."

Evelyn brandished a fleeting grin, attempting to mask the disgust she felt at the sight of his disheveled minivan. It was filled with junk; empty soda bottles and bags of trash from various fast-food restaurants were scattered about the floorboards. Although a mound of cigarette butts overloaded the ashtray, it was the smell of liquor that filled her nostrils once the window came down that made her turn up her nose at him. The fortysomething father was scrawny, wrinkled, and overly tanned. Evelyn had noticed the missing molars in his mouth when he'd offered up his excuse.

"Not a problem. I actually wanted to talk to you about your son, Domonic." Her attention turned to the boy in the back seat, who was attempting to zip his jacket over the rolls of fat that made up his muffin top. "Good morning, Domonic," Evelyn uttered in the nicest voice she could summon. In reality, she wanted to rip him from the vehicle and give him the spanking he so rightly deserved.

Domonic kept quiet. He had a feeling Evelyn wasn't there to compliment him on his exemplary behavior.

"Well, what do you want, lady? I don't have all day. Some of us do have jobs, ya know?"

"Yes. Well paying, I see," Evelyn replied, throwing in slight shade. "From what my son has told me, Domonic has been taking his money. In fact, he's been bullying Bryson for quite some time now."

"My son doesn't have to take money from nobody." He turned to his boy. "Right, son?"

"No, sir. I sure don't."

"See, I think you must be mistaken, lady. Sounds to me like your boy is just a pushover. You should teach him to have a backbone. Then maybe he wouldn't have to make up lies about my son taking his money."

Evelyn's heart pounded. Not out of fear but out of fury. Her initial thought was to stab the key to her truck straight through his eye socket. The calm demeanor she maintained was solely for the sake of her son. "First off, the name is Evelyn, not lady." All softness had drained from her tone. "I hate to put a damper on your trashy parenting, but if your son so much as blinks at my son wrong, you'll feel the full extent of the repercussions."

"Oh . . . what are you gonna do? Call the PTA? Set up a meeting? Your threats don't scare me in the slightest, lady. Go home and tell your husband to teach your son how to be a man. If you even have one."

Evelyn's brow lifted on one end. She couldn't believe he had the audacity to argue the issue and rouse her anger. "My hopes of you having some sort of class went out the window at the sight of the inside of your vehicle. Still, I figured I'd give it a try. I see now that you don't heed verbal warnings. My mistake . . . It won't happen again." Evelyn turned, then headed back to her truck.

"Good talk! I'm glad I made myself clear!" he hollered out his window, then lowered his tone for a final insult. "You uppity, bitch." He hawked up the fattest glob of mucus he could rip from his sinuses, then spit it out onto the pavement as he watched Evelyn climb into her SUV. "Domonic, you better not even think about caving in for that rich brat and his uppity mother. You hear me?" He turned abruptly and stared the boy down.

"I'm no wimp, Dad."

"Damn right. Now get out of here and get to class."

"What happened, Mama?" Bryson inquired as Evelyn sat in the front seat, ruminating over what had just taken place. He could see the frustration splayed across her face: the frown lines across her forehead were deeper.

"Nothing Mama can't fix, son. Don't you worry." She started the engine, then pulled off.

"Where are we going?"

"I'm dropping you off in the front, and I'll be here to pick you up afterward."

"I don't have to ride the bus home?" he asked excitedly.

"Not today, Bryson. And if that boy so much as looks at you wrong, you'd better tell me."

"I will, Mama."

"Promise me. No more secrets . . ." She focused on him in the rearview mirror.

"I promise, Mama. No more secrets . . ." He reached for the door handle to exit the Yukon.

"Bryson?"

"Yes, Mama . . .?"

"One last thing . . . Would you happen to know Domonic's last name?"

He offered up a response without haste. "Danielson. His name is Domonic Danielson. Everyone knows it. He gets called to the office at least once a day. Why? Are you going to tell the principal what he did?"

"Mama doesn't need the principal, Bryson. If the school was going to do something about Domonic's behavior, they would have done it a long time ago. You go on and get to class. Let Mama worry about this."

"Okay. I'll see you after school, right?"

"Yup. I'll be here waiting for you."

Bryson flashed a wide smile. He was elated that his doting mother was finally back home. "You're the best. I love you, Mama."

"I love you too, Bryson."

Words that should have warmed her heart had a dull effect. Regardless of that fact, she knew Bryson was her offspring. As a mother, it was her duty to protect him, at all costs. The mama bear sticker displayed on her bumper had reminded her of that, and she assumed it was an accurate reflection of her past self.

Chapter 4

Rules Get Implemented

Evelyn cruised south along Dixie Highway, her mind preoccupied with how she'd go about exacting her revenge on Mr. Danielson. Should the punishment be meted out solely to him, or should she include his unsuspecting wife as well? As vile a human being as Mr. Danielson seemed to be, his significant other had to be just as bad, Evelyn concluded. That was when a vital piece of her plan presented itself. She pulled over to the side of the road, then hopped out of her vehicle, eyes fixed on one thing. It was the telephone book hanging at the end of a narrow chain inside the pay-phone booth on the corner. All Evelyn needed was one page. That would lead her directly to the Danielsons' residence.

There can't be that many people with the last name Danielson in Clarkston, she told herself silently as she lifted the book to peruse its contents. Evelyn flipped through it, found the page she was seeking, and ran her index finger down it, to where the last name Danielson could be read. There were five of them listed. None offered her a clue as to their identity, so with one swift motion, she ripped the whole page from the telephone book. To Evelyn, it was worth checking each residence one by one to find him. If only she knew Colin's last name. The thought crossed her mind as she exited the booth to head back to her SUV.

Evelyn had everything she'd need at her disposal. The postal shirt and the pair of slacks that hung neatly on a hanger in the rear of her truck would come in handy. She'd hung them there since she was scheduled to see the postmistress in several hours for an interview to assess her ability to return to work after the tragedy she'd endured. Looking official would make the job of spying on each residence a breeze. She drove to the nearest fast-food restaurant, parked, grabbed her postal uniform, and headed into the restaurant. After finding the restroom, she changed into the collared postal shirt and casual blue slacks.

Evelyn headed out of the restaurant, determined to right the wrongs her child had suffered at the hands of Domonic Danielson. She climbed inside the Yukon, then grabbed her local map of Clarkston from the center console. Evelyn had already marked off the location of each residence that might be home to the ruffian father and son. All she had to do was find the right one. Her eyes scanned the map. One location in particular stood out. It was a mobile home park.

"The trailer park . . . how fitting," she muttered, concluding it had to be the residence she was looking for.

A heavyset woman with a curly red mullet huffed as she pulled handfuls of garments from the dryer and dropped them into a plaid laundry bag. Huge breasts dangled free under the purple muumuu she was wearing for the third day in a row. Beads of sweat that covered her forehead dripped down the sides of her face, soaking into her sideburns. It didn't help that the compact laundry room was smoldering, on top of barely having enough room to fit her large frame. Mrs. Danielson couldn't wait to get off her swollen feet and ankles. House chores had become a daunting daily task, and most times they went unaccomplished. This fact contributed to Mr. Danielson's peevishness, which only compounded her depression and lack of self-confidence.

Mrs. Danielson herself was no picnic to be around, as she refused to fight her addiction to painkillers and whiskey, let alone admit she had one. Most days, by the time Mr. Danielson got home, she'd already be drunk and well into burning the evening's dinner. Be that as it may, the couple had stuck by one another, infecting Domonic with their misery. Arguments were a regular occurrence in the home. Yet no matter how bad they got, neither parent would leave. Both of them often wondered if it was love or a lack of finances that kept them together.

By the time Mrs. Danielson lugged the bag of laundry through the double-wide trailer, then into the living room, she was nearly out of breath. Drained of energy, she plopped down on the sunken area at the center of the frayed green sofa. The woman's eyes toggled from the bag of clothes to the 750-milliliter bottle of Jack Daniel's atop the glass coffee table. An ashtray nearby housed a burning cigarette, while a cube of ice melted in a double shot of whiskey in the small glass alongside it. *I'll just have a few sips while I finish this episode of* The Price Is Right *before I get started folding*, she told herself. Mrs. Danielson grabbed the remote from the cushion beside her and turned up the volume on her floor-model television. "Eight hundred and one dollars!" she yelled, guessing the price of the showcase being offered up, as if she herself were a contestant on the game show.

Moments later Mr. Danielson pushed through the front door and marched straight through the living room on his way to the kitchen, blocking the television as he scurried by, arms weighed down by bags full of groceries.

"I thought you were heading straight to work?" Mrs. Danielson blurted, caught off guard by her husband's presence. She concealed her glass of whiskey underneath the table, then began pulling handfuls of clothing from the laundry bag to create the illusion that she was using her time wisely.

Their entire kitchen was outdated, from the peeling green-and-white wallpaper to the cracked tile flooring. Mr. Danielson glanced over at their grease-coated stove, which had long ago lost its glowing white luster. His shoulders sank in despair. She'd even left the empty ice tray out on the counter.

"Drinking already, I see," he said loudly, so that she would hear, as he placed the grocery bags atop the cheap laminate countertop. Secretly, he wanted something to go off on her about, as the recent tragic death of his half-brother weighed heavily on his heart. It had all happened so suddenly: his brother Randy had been shot just after he'd been suspended from his route at the Clarkston post office.

"Shit." She realized she'd been found out. She attempted to explain her addiction away as she quickly folded a few towels and piled them on the sofa, one atop another. "I was just having a sip while I finished up the laundry, that's all."

"You know what, June?" Mr. Danielson stood in the doorway between the kitchen and the living room. He couldn't wait to start in on her. The berating he was about to bestow on his wife would surely compound her insecurities and lingering self-doubt, as had happened on numerous occasions. But, of course, she'd sit there and take it, and then she'd release her own frustrations on Domonic once he returned home.

He went on. "Don't act like you're gonna clean the kitchen. This sink has been piled high with dishes for the past three days. You probably won't even get that entire load of laundry folded. Is this what you do all day? Sit around getting drunk and watching daytime TV? I'm so sick of this shit!"

She held back the tears threatening to escape her eyes and picked up her glass for a few more sips.

Evelyn whistled the tune to "Moonlight Sonata" as she walked through the mobile home park, a mail sack hanging over her shoulder. She'd even pulled a stack of envelopes from one of the mailboxes she'd come upon to make her presence there more convincing.

One of the residents called out to her as he checked his box for the day's mail. "Good day to you."

Evelyn waved hello but continued on her way through the park. Five minutes later she caught sight of Mr. Danielson's minivan, parked right in his driveway. A wry grin formed about her lips. "I've got you now." Evelyn approached the trailer and could hear Mr. Danielson tearing into his wife through the single-pane window. "What an asshole," she muttered in a low voice.

She crept back to the driveway and walked up to the garage. When she pulled open the garage door, she was surprised by what she found. The space was set up like a man cave. *This must be where he goes to ignore his family*, she thought. The man cave was even heated by a large propane unit in a corner of the room. A couch nearby was fitted with a blanket and a pillow for sleeping. Mr. Danielson even had a big-screen television of his own, decorated with bobblehead Red Wings hockey players, which were lined up on the top.

Inside the trailer, the verbal abuse continued. Mr. Danielson refused to let up on his mentally battered wife.

"Oh, now you want to cry!" he barked.

Mrs. Danielson didn't utter a word in her defense.

"You weren't crying when you were pushing your favorite poison down your throat. I swear, you're nothing but a big waste of space. Look at you! You can barely walk without having to sit down. Do you think I want to come home to this shit every day? You suck as a wife. You suck as a mother. You suck as a lover. You just plain suck. As a matter of fact, now that I think about it, you suck at everything! Now I have to go to work after you've successfully ruined my day."

He'd gotten himself so worked up that a stinging feeling shot through his chest just then. He moaned, his hand over his heart. "I swear, you'll be the death of me. Just get these groceries put up," he said, a little calmer now. "I don't want to see any of this mess when I get home, or there will be hell to pay. I assure you of that."

Mr. Danielson walked toward his weeping wife, but instead of showing her some compassion, which she so desperately needed, he grabbed the lit cigarette from the ashtray to finish it off. Then he tore out of their trailer and into the yard to fetch something from his man cave. By the time he reached the garage, the cigarette had dwindled down to a mere butt. That was when he pulled another cigarette and a lighter from the breast pocket of his button-up flannel shirt, placing the cigarette between his lips.

Mr. Danielson opened the garage door as he flicked the lighter's flint wheel. Instantly a spark ignited, and the fumes escaping from the propane tank caught fire. The garage exploded, red flames shooting in all directions. His eyes had just enough time to bulge in their sockets before his body was blown down the driveway, bloddy limbs flailing. He crashed through the windshield of his minivan and ended up on the dashboard, his body battered and bloody.

Evelyn could see her handiwork from the driver's seat of her truck, which was parked a good distance away from their property, its engine on. The loud boom and the fierce blaze sent other residents pouring out of the neighboring trailers to see what the commotion was all about. "Talk about knocking it out of the park," Evelyn said as she admired the scene.

A few minutes later, she shifted her truck into drive, then slowly cruised back up the street, watching the blaze in her rearview. A feeling of contentment washed over her as she exited the mobile home park and pulled out onto the main road.

Two hours later Evelyn stared up at the analog clock on the wall above the postmistress's office door. She sat in one of the chairs arranged in front of the desk, her legs pressed firmly together and her hands clutching a black leather portfolio atop her lap. The resolute facade Evelyn attempted to present would have worked had she not been biting at the skin of her lips for the past five minutes.

"Are you okay?" Postmistress Hilary Osborne stared fixedly at Evelyn, who'd apparently drifted from reality.

Evelyn quickly shifted her gaze to the postmistress in response to her inquiry. "I'm feeling much better. Why do you ask?"

Hilary leaned back in her leather chair, pushing her bobbed brown hair behind one ear, as she studied Evelyn further. It was said that her beady blue eyes could bore a hole in your brain to extract the truth of any matter. At least Hilary thought as much of her power and authority. "You just seem a little out of it today. Are you sure you're ready to come back to work?"

"I'd say that was a silly question. But taking into account what they say happened to me, I can understand your concerns. I appreciate you considering my health and well-being. Fortunately, the doctors have that covered." Evelyn opened the portfolio and removed an official-looking document. "Here is my release from the doctor." She handed it over to the postmistress.

Hilary looked it over. The document was indeed official. Either way, she wouldn't give in so easily. "They say you can't remember anything about the past."

"It's true. I'm still trying to recover my memories. So, I guess that means I'll require a bit of training."

"You'll have to study the scheme again, in order to case letters. You can't just go back to your old position without proving you can do it, you know?"

"I'm not asking for any favors. I'm fully capable of learning the scheme." Evelyn figured if she'd done it before, she could surely do it again.

"Good. I'm glad to hear that. In the meantime, Elise will be your trainer. Report to work tomorrow at four a.m. It's good to have you back, Evelyn."

"Thanks. It's great to be back. The new me is certainly up for the challenge."

Chapter 5

Living the Illusion

Elsewhere about town, a yellow backhoe dug into loose soil, scooping up piles one by one before dropping them off on the opposite side of the dig, creating a separate mound of dirt. The clatter from drills, saws, and other machinery running inside the hollow cement structure made it difficult for the construction workers to hear one another as they shouted commands and responses necessary to keep their operation running smoothly.

"This room will serve as the media room! They're going to need several outlets along this wall!" Erick pointed it out to Joe, his right-hand man, who was working alongside him.

"Where the hell is that new kid you hired? What's his name? Harry? Where's Harry?" Joe removed his hard hat and scanned the area with his eyes. He found the new hire. "Hey, kid! What are we paying you for? To relax? Get over here!" He kept his sights set firmly on the lanky chocolate fellow.

The fellow was twenty-two years old and was at least six feet, four inches tall. Yet his demeanor was timid and aloof, and this caused most of the other men there to treat him as if he were their little brother, as opposed to a grown man with an electrician's degree. He had a neatly trimmed medium-length high-top fade. Coke-bottle glasses enhanced his bulging brown eyes, and his collared, long-sleeve shirt was buttoned up to a protruding Adam's apple.

Talking to people in general pushed Harry out of his comfort zone. The muscular, overly tanned, bald guy barking demands at him caused him to retreat into himself. Harry kept his head down as he peered at blueprints spread out in front of him on a wooden table.

"What the hell is up with this kid?" Joe muttered. "Where did you get him from? The Boys and Girls Club?"

"Go easy on him, Joe. It's his first job as an electrician. You've got to ease him into it," Erick advised.

"I'll ease him into it, all right." Joe rushed Harry's way to grab his attention. "Come on, kid. Allow an old dog to show you a few new tricks." Joe steered Harry back over to the wall on which they intended to work, then pulled a stud finder from a pocket in his work vest to demonstrate its use. "You run this stud finder across the area in question. Once it detects a stud, you'll hear a beep."

Harry nodded in agreement, waiting for Joe to give it a try.

Joe took his time running the stud finder across the wall. Then, after a few seconds, he hovered it over his abdomen. "Beep . . ." He imitated the sound it made, implying that he was the stud it found.

"Really?" Harry shook his head, but only until he realized that Joe had made a corny joke. "That was pretty good," he admitted.

"You can even use it as a pickup line. I told you this old dog was gonna show you some new tricks," Joe remarked.

"Now that I'm prepared to secure a dinner date, how about some tricks that'll help me get behind this wall . . . in the right spot."

***

Over at the Todd residence, a famished Evelyn stood in front of the open refrigerator, a cordless phone pressed to her ear. She had just dialed Erick.

"Hello, my love," Erick said when he answered the call. "How did the interview go?"

"Hi, honey. Oh, my goodness. Why is it so noisy in the background?"

"I own a construction company, remember?"

"Oh yeah . . . It must have slipped my mind." Evelyn paused, contemplating what to say next.

Erick stuck his index finger in the opposite ear so he could hear her better. "Honey, are you still there?"

Evelyn spoke up. "I'm actually standing here, staring into the fridge."

"How about I pick you up? We can get some lunch and talk about how your interview went."

"Okay." She closed the nearly empty refrigerator. "You sure you want to pick me up? I could just meet you somewhere."

"It's not a problem. I can come get you."

"You are so good to me." Evelyn felt lucky to have such a dedicated and compassionate husband.

"I was thinking about doing something that would be therapeutic for you," her doting husband continued.

"What did you have in mind?"

"I kept a logbook outside your hospital room so that everyone who came to see you while you were in the hospital could sign it. I figured you'd like to express your thanks by sending them a little card. I left the book and some cards on the table in the kitchen. You should start on those today. Maybe seeing some of the names will stir up some memories."

"What a great idea, baby. I'll start on those while I'm waiting for you to get here."

"Give me about a half an hour or so."

"Okay."

"I love you."

"I love you too, baby. See you soon." She disconnected the call, headed straight for the book of names. The sight of the logbook triggered a memory, and Evelyn was transported back to the day her passion for Colin was ignited.

Colin placed his hand atop hers. "Well, whether you can or can't hear me, I'm sorry this happened to you, and I hope you wake up soon."

Just as he was about to turn and walk away, Evelyn's hand clutched Colin's. She opened her eyes, and he looked directly into her wild, wide-eyed stare. It was her first time really seeing him.

Evelyn suddenly snapped back to reality, with one thing on her mind. Colin. His name had to be in that logbook, she thought. She lifted back the hard front cover, then began flipping through the pages, hoping to find his name. After she turned three pages, there it was, printed in black ink: Colin Ravish. Her heart felt as if it skipped a beat. Evelyn breathed deeply. *This has to be a sign*, she decided, further deluding herself. Evelyn, a supposedly happily married woman, had tried to stop thinking about him, but she just couldn't, and numerous times throughout her day, he came to mind. Now she had a full name to put to the face that filled her fantasies. At last, there was nothing standing in the way of her finding the object of her desire.

Her doting husband stared at Evelyn from the opposite side of the booth they shared at a local diner.

"What's going on, my love?" he asked, concern in his voice. "Black beans are your favorite. You've barely touched your burrito. Is something wrong?"

"No. Nothing's wrong. I just have a lot on my mind."

He extended his hand across the table in a silent request for hers. "You know you can tell me anything."

Evelyn placed her hand in his. "I'm just worried I won't be able to keep up at work," Evelyn told him, offering the same lame excuse, knowing there was no way she could admit that she missed the company of another man.

"Look at me, Evelyn." Erick's warm hazel eyes stared intensely into hers. "You can do anything you put your mind to. I know you don't remember much, but I can tell you with all certainty that you are not a quitter. In no way, shape, form, or fashion. You've never given up on a thing since I've known you. So, don't you worry . . . Everything will be fine."

"You know what? I think you're right, baby. Things are looking up. Everything . . ." Evelyn paused abruptly, as she suddenly believed that all her dreams had come true. She got up from her seat in the booth, her hand sliding from her husband's grip, then headed straight for the tall caramel-complected man strutting across the diner. He had an innocent swag. It was effortless. Colin just had it. And whatever it was he had, Evelyn wanted it badly.

"Honey, where are you going?" Erick called out to her, totally perplexed.

Evelyn ignored her husband's question, licked her lips, then put a twist in her strut. Nothing would stand in her way. At least she thought as much until she saw Jocelyn sitting in the very booth her dream man was headed for. Her pace slowed once she realized Colin wasn't there alone. She noticed they were both wearing wedding rings and realized that theirs was a serious relationship. Evelyn had never even allowed the concept to enter her mind. At that point she had to rethink things.

Jocelyn was beautiful. Her shiny jet-black hair flowed down her naked back, between her shoulder blades and beyond. Evelyn studied the way Jocelyn caressed Colin's broad shoulders when he leaned in to greet her with a kiss. As she snatched up the ketchup bottle on an empty table nearby, Evelyn breathed in deep, taking in the aroma of his cologne. His scent flooded her nostrils, then filled her lungs, before feeding the hunger she harbored for him. He was intoxicating. She'd get more, but some other time, she vowed, turning back to head to the booth she shared with her husband. A frown was frozen on Erick's face, until he saw the ketchup bottle in her hand.

"I was wondering where you were going. Why did you just walk off like that? You could have called the wait-ress." He was a bit angsty about her ignoring him the way she had.

Evelyn sat down and said in a demure voice, "I'm sorry. I couldn't remember her name, and I didn't want to be embarrassed by asking again." She hung her head low.

"Oh honey, I'm so sorry. I didn't think . . ." Erick paused, not having the words. He felt bad for having made her feel inept. "Hey, you know you're still healing. You shouldn't be so hard on yourself. It's a process, my love. I'm here for you every step of the way." As Erick expressed his dying devotion, he had no idea about the train wreck in the making.

While they enjoyed the rest of their lunch, Evelyn stole peeks at Colin from across the room. Jealousy got a grip on her when Colin took his wife's hand across the table and caressed it. *She doesn't deserve a man like him*, Evelyn told herself in an effort to convince herself this was true.

Erick took note of how distant Evelyn seemed, yet he had no doubt that he could restore their connection. "So, tomorrow is the day, right? You report to work at four a.m."

"Yup, four a.m. sharp."

"I don't know if I like you going to work that early anymore. It's still dark outside. And considering what happened, I just don't feel like it's the safest option."

"How about you take me to work? Just until you feel comfortable with me going alone . . ."

"I could do that. I'm awake when you leave for work, anyway."

"Problem solved, then."

"Is there anything else I can help you with?" the waitress announced as she approached their table.

"I think we'll take a few items to go. The kids will be out of school in just a few hours," Erick answered.

As Erick rattled off his request to their waitress, Evelyn took the opportunity to watch the unsuspecting couple across the room. Colin and Jocelyn got up, ready to head out of the restaurant. He assisted his wife in putting on her peacoat, and then they headed for the door. Then, just as Evelyn had hoped, Colin's gaze traveled across the room and found hers. Their eyes locked for a brief moment. Her stare was so intense, it was as if she had willed him to look her way. Evelyn was beautiful indeed. As it turned out, Colin didn't recognize her with her gauze and bandages off. He flashed her a soft smile, being the gentleman he was, then quickly turned to open the door for his wife. Colin noticed Evelyn watching him as he exited, a fact that merely stroked his ego. Of course, he would never dream of acting on this brief interaction.

Unfortunately, his pleasant stares conveyed a message to Evelyn that was completely at odds with his intent. *He saw me. He really saw me*, she exclaimed silently, relishing the thought.

Chapter 6

Back to Work

The next day at the Clarkston post office seemed like something altogether new for Evelyn. It was quiet for most of the morning, and only she and two of her coworkers were at the post office. Elise was busy training Evelyn, while Daniel cased magazines on the other side of the building. The open-floor plan allowed the workers to see one another clear across the room. In the center of the room were baskets of parcels, and that was where Elise and Evelyn were hard at work.

"So, you really can't remember anything?" Elise, a petite, strawberry-blond woman, busied herself by scanning in boxes on a pallet with a hand scanner. According to office policy, they could chat as long as they kept the operation going at the same pace.

"Nope." Evelyn's voice sounded tranquil, as she was preoccupied by the image of Colin in her mind. She reminisced about how handsome he had looked in his wheat-colored peacoat as they locked eyes in the diner.

"You don't even remember being attacked?"

"Nope. No recollection of it."

"Do you wanna try to remember?"

"I don't know, Elise. How would I even go about doing that?"

"Do you want me to show you where they found you that morning? The bloodstain is still there. The postmistress has been trying to get maintenance to clean that bloodstain off the pavement for weeks. So, do you wanna see it?"

"You seem pretty eager to show it to me. You must really think it'll trigger my memory or something."

"Wouldn't hurt to try." Elise shrugged.

"Okay. Let's go. It's light enough outside now."

"Really?" Elise's eyes lit up with surprise. She didn't think Evelyn would agree to this.

The women placed their hand scanners atop a pallet of packages, then headed on their way. Once they had exited the building through the swinging green double doors near the parking lot, Evelyn's breathing sped up. Holding it together as she navigated the sidewalk behind the line of LLVs took more effort than she'd anticipated, but she didn't understand why. Not one memory had surfaced to justify her emotions. Even so, as she rounded the back corner of an LLV to view the blood-stained pavement, the hairs on the back of her neck stood at attention.

"There it is. That's where they found you, all bloody and battered. Hell . . . you were nearly dead." Elise offered up the play-by-play with a nonchalant nod of her head.

Evelyn stepped out into the open and inched closer to the crime scene. That was when the bright headlights of a vehicle pulling into the lot blinded her momentarily, startling her so much that she suddenly remembered snippets of that fateful morning.

Evelyn remembered the blinding beams of light that had obstructed her vision just before the mail truck collided with her body. "Oh my God." Her hands flew to her mouth and perched there, covering her parted lips.

Elise crept up beside her. "You remember something, don't you?"

"I do."

"Well . . . what is it? Do you remember who tried to kill you?"

"No. I can't remember. I can't remember who it was. I can only remember the truck hitting me."

"I bet I can help you remember more. You should come by my house tonight. I've got a few tricks up my sleeve."

"Okay. I will." Evelyn had no idea what she would tell Erick when she left the house that night, but she was confident she'd figure something out.

"We should get back inside and finish scanning. The carriers are starting to arrive, and we're not even close to having the mail up," Elise told her.

"Whatever you say." Evelyn thought Elise was kind of bossy, but she needed her help in recalling her past. As much as Evelyn desired to pursue Colin, her quest for vengeance on the one who had attacked her and placed her in such a precarious situation took precedence. For now, she'd play nice and follow Elise's instructions to the letter.

That evening all the Todds sat at the neatly set kitchen table. Together Erick and Evelyn had prepared dinner, which was seafood mostaccioli. They passed around a wicker basket filled with garlic bread sticks, and each of them took a turn at grabbing a couple.

"So, Bryson, how was school today?" Erick inquired, with a mouth full of the evening's vittles.

"It was great, thanks to Mama." Bryson flashed his mother the biggest grin.

"I'm just lucky to have such a wonderful son. Two wonderful sons and one gorgeous daughter, in fact," Evelyn said.

Evelyn's flattering words went unacknowledged by her sixteen-year-old son, Michael, and her seventeen-year-old daughter, Diana, who both happened to be wearing earbuds under their full heads of long, curly sandy-brown hair. Normally, Michael's would be braided neatly in cornrows bound together behind his head. Unfortunately, because Evelyn had lost her ability to braid along with her memory, Michael's hair looked as if it were a lion's mane much of the time. Ignoring the rest of the family had become a normal practice for the two teenagers. It seemed nothing could tear them away from their precious devices, not even an intimate dinner with their mother, who had recently returned home. Evelyn didn't see it as a slight. It actually made her more comfortable that they didn't crowd her. She needed time to get accustomed to being back at home.

"I was thinking maybe we should take a little trip. Maybe we could take you guys down to the zoo. I heard they added a new part to the arctic structure. What do you think, Bryson? That sounds like fun, right?" Erick waited for feedback.

His suggestion excited Bryson. "That sounds great. I'd love to go. So, when can we go? How about tomorrow?"

Erick shook his head. "Whoa . . . not so fast, buddy. Your mom and I will have to check our schedules. I'm thinking this weekend would be better."

"I'm sure my calendar is free this weekend," Evelyn interjected.

"It's a date, then. We'll go to the zoo this weekend."

After dinner, Evelyn and Erick washed the dishes while the teenagers did their homework and Bryson prepared for bed.

"Honey?"

Erick finished drying a cast-iron skillet then hung it on the rack above the island at the center of the kitchen. "Yes, my love?"

"I know it's really short notice, but some of the girls from work are getting together this evening for a few drinks to welcome me back to work. I really want to go. Show my appreciation, ya know?"

"But you don't even drink."

"I don't have to drink to have fun with the girls."

"I guess that's a good thing. I don't see any reason why you shouldn't be able to have a little fun. Go on. I'll finish up here."

"Are you sure, baby?" Evelyn moved in for a kiss on the cheek. That was when Erick turned his head for a full-on lip-lock. Their lips met, and the passionate kiss ended only when they heard Bryson's outcry.

"Ew . . . Is that what you guys do all day when you're alone?"

Erick sighed. "You're supposed to be taking a shower and getting ready for bed."

"I wanted to take a bath, but I couldn't get the water to stay in the tub. Can you fix it?"

"Yes, I'll come help you." Erick turned back to his wife and gave her neck a few pecks. "I want you to leave the address of where you'll be, just in case something happens. Okay?"

"Of course I will." Evelyn smiled softly.

"I love you. You know that, right?"

"I do. You show me how much every day. I love you, Erick. I just hope I can live up to the woman I once was."

"You're doing great so far, my love."

Chapter 7

Friend or Foe

When Evelyn pulled up to Elise's residence, she could see the lit tiki torches in the backyard. A shadow emerged from the darkness out back, then motioned for her to come over. It was Elise, wineglass in hand. Evelyn shut off her engine, then hopped down out of her SUV and approached Elise.

Elise greeted her with a tone that was more upbeat than usual. "Hey, girl."

Evelyn assumed it was the alcohol. "Hey, Elise."

"So, are you ready to get this thing started?"

"Just how do you plan on getting it started?" Evelyn had her doubts.

"I'm going to hypnotize you and then instruct you to remember your past."

Skeptical, Evelyn chuckled at the idea. "I really doubt that I can be hypnotized."

"That's what everyone says, until I hypnotize them."

"Okay, I'm game. Let's see what you've got."

"Come on. Let's go get started, then."

Trailing closely behind, Evelyn followed Elise to the back door of her three-bedroom bungalow. The solid oak door scraped the floor, producing a squeaking sound, as Elise pushed it open. They stepped onto a platform at the top of the steep, narrow, dimly lit stairwell, then began decending the creaking wooden steps. Evelyn tightly gripped the railing, until they reached a wide-open space down below. The basement was cold and damp, thanks to its unfinished cement walls. Evelyn eyeballed the copper pipes that ran the entire length of the ceiling.

Then she surveyed the scant furnishings. A worn plaid sofa that sat in the center of the basement was riddled with so many holes that the foam in each of its cushions protruded. A triangular metal pendulum with a swinging brass bob sat on the wooden coffee table nearby. Evelyn assumed it was what Elise would use to work her so-called magic.

"Wow . . . I love your chateau," Evelyn commented.

"Don't be a smart-ass. Not all of us can snag a hunk with a construction company."

Evelyn walked over to the sofa, plopped down on it, then made herself comfortable. "Maybe you're not trying hard enough," she countered, reaching over to give the pendulum a nudge with her index finger.

"Hey, that's *my* job." Elise quickly marched over and halted the swinging of the pendulum's bob with her finger before sitting down at the other end of the sofa.

"You're pretty testy. What's got you in such a funk?"

"You just basically told me that my house is not up to par, and neither is my significant other."

"I guess I didn't look at it like that."

"I'm not surprised. You never did before," Elise informed her. "To be quite honest, you've always been kind of uppity, but your cheery persona always seemed to paint a pretty picture for those on the outside looking in."

"So basically, you're saying I was a bitch."

"A fake-ass bitch, actually."

Evelyn shot Elise a seething stare, not taking too kindly to being referred to in this way.

Evelyn's stare felt unfamiliar to Elise. She'd never seen Evelyn so blatantly display her disgust. In fact, her unwavering stare made Elise a little uncomfortable. She searched for signs that Evelyn was just playing around but she found none. "Wow. No snappy comeback, huh?" she said. Elise paused for a moment to reflect, then added, "That accident really did change you."

"Now you're going to try to change me back, right?" Evelyn asked. Her question broke the tension in the room.

"And not a moment too soon, I imagine," Elise blurted before she could stop herself.

Evelyn wasn't quite sure how to take that. "What's that supposed to mean?"

Elise came up with a plausible response without batting an eyelash. "I can imagine your children and husband miss you. You know, the old you . . ."

"Then I guess we should get started. What do you want me to do? Should I break into a ridiculous chant now?"

"Listen, Evelyn. You've gotta have an open mind for this to work. Just relax. Take a deep breath in and then exhale slowly." Elise watched closely to ensure Evelyn's breathing pattern slowed, as this would aid in what she called "the manifestation." "That's it. Nice and steady," she coached.

Evelyn gazed at Elise in silence.

"I want you to look at the light," Elise instructed as she clicked on a light at the center of the triangular pendulum's base. "Really focus on it. I'm going to count backward from fifty. Soon you'll be back to what was once familiar to you."

Elise began counting. "Fifty, forty-nine, forty-eight, forty-seven . . ." By the time she reached forty, Evelyn's eyes had closed. Elise's voice remained strong, but the scenery looked much different to Evelyn now.

In Evelyn's mind she was back home, in the kitchen. Somewhat confused, she stood idly by, watching as the recollected version of herself turned her gaze from the patio's sliding glass doors to the remote control on the kitchen table and then grabbed the remote. Mr. Fuboi had just rushed by, intent on retrieving his dog's precious toy. Evelyn's gaze became transformed. She admired herself, and as she did so, the wrinkles about her brow smoothed out as the edges of her mouth turned upward. She felt accomplished as she watched herself loosen the cords at the corners of the tarp, ultimately causing Mr. Fuboi to fall from grace. His body sank like a rock to the bottom of her swimming pool. It wasn't until Evelyn heard a tirade of insults that the scenery changed.

"You weren't crying when you were pushing your favorite poison down your throat. I swear, you're nothing but a big waste of space. Look at you! You can barely walk without having to sit down."

Evelyn saw herself peeking in the window of the mobile home. She had a front-row seat to the lives of the Danielsons. Every insult he'd hurled at his mentally battered wife was justification to Evelyn as she watched herself snatch loose a tube that safely restricted the flow of gas from the propane tank in a corner of the Danielsons' garage. The blaze, which she saw in the reflection in her big brown eyes as the garage went up in flames, pulled her into a separate memory. Back into the path of headlights that stunned her before the truck crashed into her. The instant wave of pain that washed over Evelyn tore her from the hypnotic trance.

When Evelyn's eyes sprung open, Elise's palms were resting atop her shoulders. Elise stared intently at her in an effort to garner her full attention. "What's wrong? Are you okay? Do you remember anything?" she quizzed, hounding her now lucid coworker. "Tell me. Did it work? What did you see?"

Evelyn pulled away from her grip. "I didn't see anything. Just the headlights of the truck before it hit me," she replied, conveniently omitting her recollection of the murders she'd carried out.

"You couldn't see his face? Maybe we should try again."

Evelyn abruptly forced out a hard no. But realizing her reply was a bit abrasive, she softened her tone. "I just can't handle any more tonight. I didn't even think it was going to work in the first place, but where it took me, I'm not sure I want to return there. All I could feel was pain when the truck hit me." The memory frightened her for more reasons than one. What if she'd mistakenly revealed something damaging to her reputation while she was under hypnosis? It was a risk Evelyn was unwilling to take again. There was no way she was letting Elise put her under again. "Let's call it a night. I should probably get home. We have work early tomorrow."

"Yeah, I guess you're right." Elise stood up from the sofa. "I'll walk you out."

The intense thumping radiating from Evelyn's chest seemed to ease as the soles of her sneakers touched the back porch of Elise's house and the night's breeze flowed through her nostrils. That could've been bad, she silently told herself.

Chapter 8

A Different Perspective

Home, sweet home . . . Evelyn crept into her dimly lit bedroom, hoping not to wake her husband. She figured if she just kept the light off, he'd remain in his slumber. Little did she know, Erick had not yet fallen asleep.

"So, how'd your welcome back party go?" he asked when he heard the sound of hangers being moved in their walk-in closet. It was dark in the bedroom, but soft lighting radiated from inside the closet, enough for him to see Evelyn's purse resting atop the glass and chrome dresser near the closet door.

Silence.

"Cat got your tongue?" He sat up and leaned against his pillow, waiting for her reply.

Evelyn spoke as she emerged from the closet, cloaked in a silver nightgown that reached her passion-purple toenails. "It was nice."

"You're nice," Erick replied, referring to the way her curves were showcased by the nightgown's delicate material.

Evelyn snickered, flattered by her husband's compliment. "Are you always like this?"

"Am I always like what?"

Evelyn climbed into bed. "Always so funny, upbeat, compassionate, and thoughtful?"

"I am. But so are you . . . What can I say? We're happy people. At least we used to be. You used to be."

"What makes you think I'm not happy?"

"I don't know. I mean, can you really be happy if you can't even remember the things that make you happy, and why it is they make you feel that way? That's what I ask myself when I'm tempted to feel slighted because you don't seem as happy as I'd like you to be. I realize it's not my burden to make you happy. You have to figure out what it is that brings you contentment. I'm learning to love the new you as you are. So, what do you think? How am I doing so far?"

"Wow . . ." Evelyn shook her head in awe of the man she'd married. *He's a complete pushover*, she thought. *What have I done to deserve such a saintly man?* "You're unbelievably perfect."

"Well, you better believe it. I'm as good as it gets, my love. I suppose that's why you married me."

"Can I be honest with you?"

"Of course you can be honest with me. You don't ever have to hide anything from me. We're best friends."

"I think I'm ready to drive myself to work. I may not remember much of anything, but . . . I just don't feel like I'm being true to who I really am. Everything in me screams for the independence that I've yet to embrace."

"I completely understand, my love. You were always a very independent woman. I won't stop you if you want to drive to work. Just do me a favor first."

"What's that?"

"I want to show you how to defend yourself. I bought a Taser for you. How about after work tomorrow I'll show you some techniques? Then you can start driving yourself to work."

"I think that's a great idea. It would definitely make me feel more secure."

"Good. I want you to feel safe."

"Erick?"

"Yes, my love?"

"Can you tell me more about myself? I mean, about the woman I was?" Evelyn pulled the comforter up to her scantily exposed breasts, then leaned back against the leather headboard, ready to immerse herself into whichever story Erick chose to regale her with.

"Okay. I've got a story for you. Something to illustrate how patient and forgiving a person you are." Erick sat back farther, reminiscing about their past. "You said you had a good time at your welcome back party, right?"

"I did. It was enlightening, to say the least."

"Well, allow me to enlighten you further. You know your coworker, Elise?"

"What about Elise?"

"You and Elise used to be friends back in high school. You guys would always go tit for tat, back and forth, with a playful yet mildly offensive banter. There wasn't one thing you two didn't compete against one another for, including me."

Evelyn's neck twisted, and a look of disbelief appeared on her face. "What do you mean, you?"

"When Elise found out you were going to be married before her, she tried everything to ruin our plans. She stopped at nothing short of trying to seduce me. The woman did anything she could dream up to make sure you didn't win. After several failed attempts, she finally gave up. She claimed your friendship was more important than winning. You forgave her, her indiscretions, she got a job at the post office with you, and you guys have been two peas in a post office ever since."

"Nice. Was that supposed to be a play on two peas in a pod?"

"I thought the story could use a tad bit of humor. The look on your face was starting to worry me. It could get stuck like that, you know?"

"Honey, it's my memory that's lacking, not my common sense."

"It was worth a try." Erick shrugged.

"You're completely serious about this Elise business?"

"I'm being one hundred percent truthful. I always wondered how it was you forgave her after the things she'd done. If you ask me, I don't much care for her, but if you choose to hang out with her in your spare time, that's up to you. Just watch your back, is all I'm saying." Erick fluffed his pillow before lying down to rest his head. "You should get some sleep, my love. You've got only a few hours before you have to be up for work."

Evelyn fluffed her pillow, then followed suit, yet her mind remained fixated on the truths Erick had revealed. Evelyn decided that her longtime friend was never to be trusted. When the wee hours of morning arrived, sleep still evaded her. Evelyn reached the conclusion that Elise was out to get her. She thought about the events she'd recalled during her hypnosis. All were revelations that would destroy her life if they somehow surfaced . . . *What have I done?* she asked herself, worried. Evelyn tossed and turned until her alarm clock sounded at 2:30 a.m. The time to get ready for work had come.

She rose from the bed and trudged into the bathroom. After washing her face, she peered at herself in the vanity mirror. Bags encircled her tired eyes and enhanced the fine wrinkles at their corners. Despite being tired, she had to show up for work. It would only be her second day back on the job. Plus, she wanted to get a feel for Elise's attitude since their hypnosis session. Evelyn turned on the shower. Once steam began filling the bathroom, she stepped under the warm stream of water and enjoyed the comfort it provided.

By the time Erick finished the thirty-minute cruise down the two-lane highway and pulled into the parking lot at the Clarkston post office, Evelyn had spoken less than two sentences to him. At first, he had assumed she was resting, so he had chosen not to disturb her, but when she sprang to attention when he put the car in park, he became concerned.

"I thought you were sleeping," he said.

"I was awake the whole time. What makes you think I was sleeping?"

"You didn't say a word the entire ride here. Are you okay?"

"You didn't, either. Are you?" she countered.

"I guess that's a fair question. I didn't say anything because I assumed you were sleeping, and I didn't want to wake you. What's your excuse?"

"I couldn't think of anything to talk about. In my defense, I don't remember much."

"We don't have to talk only about the past. Next time, I'll have a plethora of stories ready to entertain you."

"Oh joy . . ."

Erick felt offended by the snarky response. "Whoa. Somebody woke up on the cold side of the pillow this morning."

"I'm sorry. I guess I didn't get much sleep. I don't mean to take it out on you."

"I understand, my love. When you get home, you can get some sleep before the kids get out of school."

"I appreciate you being so understanding."

"I only want what's best for you, Evelyn."

"I know you do." She leaned toward him for a kiss goodbye.

Her doting husband complied, planting three tender kisses on her puckered lips. "Have a great day at work, my love."

"I'll certainly do my best." Evelyn gave him a fleeting grin.

Chapter 9

To Forgive or Not

The mad rush to scan each package had begun. The time clock read 0800 hours. A group of clerks had congregated around the makeshift rolling table under the PASS machine, where they scanned the thousands of parcels due to be delivered by mail carriers that day. Daniel, Elise, Evelyn, and Christian all shared the duty of completing the morning's scans as they immersed themselves in chatty conversation to pass the hours. The women kept up a rapid pace as they scanned Clarkston residents' packages, while Daniel took his good old time, as he always did. "A fair day's work for a fair day's pay" was his motto. The mildly attractive, fifty-something mail clerk with salt-and-pepper hair rushed for no man. He grinned, showcasing his small, cavity-riddled teeth, as he strutted to and fro, with his chin held high and his chest protruding so that it looked twice its normal size. Anyone could see he thought highly of himself. His solid, round belly took nothing away from his brooding self-confidence.

"Talk, talk, talk—it's all you women like to do," he joked.

Christian flipped her long dark brown mane over her shoulder before batting her baby blue eyes. "Yet we still manage to get more work done than you, Daniel. Imagine how that works out." The middle-aged woman, the nicest of them all by far, always made her opinion known in the subtlest of ways. Her passive-aggressive nature allowed her to fly under the radar and stay on good terms with her coworkers. Many saw her as a working family woman, intent on staying at the level she'd reached at the post office. So others could most certainly scratch her off the list of people who would stab you in the back for a career boost.

"A fair day's work for a fair day's pay is all they're getting from me," Daniel insisted. "If one of us dropped dead today, they would have our position listed as available the next day. You've got to care about yourself more than they do. I'm not wrecking my body for nobody's nine to five."

Daniel's reply made perfect sense to Evelyn. So much so that she had slowed her pace. Evelyn studied Elise, wondering if she'd seen the truth in his statement. To her surprise, Elise kept up her pace, every so often stealing glances at their postmistress, who stood nearby in fear of a revolt. There was no way Elise would blemish her reputation. Her plan to soon join management remained of the utmost importance. Evelyn silently took note of this.

"Speaking of the dead, Evelyn, you made a miraculous recovery," Daniel commented. "For a moment there, we didn't think you were going to make it—"

"I was in a car accident once. It put me in the hospital for over a week," Elise interrupted.

Daniel rolled his eyes, irritated by her interruption. "I said Evelyn, not *Elise*."

The slight caused Elise's lips to tighten. One would think she'd think twice before speaking again, but that just wasn't Elise's style. She never shied away from a little strife. "I know what you said, Daniel."

Evelyn spoke up, with the intention of easing the tension between them. "What can I say? I'm hard to kill."

"I know, right?" Elise chuckled.

The others frowned at the awkwardness of her reply.

"What? I mean, you did actually flatline for a moment there," Elise said, trying to explain her response.

"I know, right? It is funny how I came back," Evelyn retorted.

Elise quickly caught on to her sarcasm. "I was just agreeing with you. But, of course, make me out to be the bad guy. I'm always the bad guy."

Christian chimed in, "You said it, not us."

Later that morning, once they had gotten the numerous mail carriers off on their routes, Evelyn stood staring at a mail case where she used to sort incoming mail. She snatched one letter at a time from the stack in her left hand and put it in the correct route slot with her right. At least she hoped so. Evelyn had been studying the scheme for only about a week, and much of it remained a blur.

A wave of motivation took hold. "You can do it, Evelyn. You went over this yesterday. Just focus," she coached herself out loud as she glanced down at a letter and read the addressee's name. "Do it for Jane on Bird Road." Her memory kicked in. "That's route four." She cased the piece of mail before moving on to the next. "Do it for Matthew on Mary Sue Avenue." Right away, she recollected where it belonged. "That's city route one." Aaron on Fir Street was her next successful guess. "Aaron, you live on route sixteen. Oh my gosh . . . I'm on a roll," she proclaimed, a wide grin on her face. "Colin on Thendara," she read nonchalantly. *Colin . . . ?* She peered down at the addressee's full name. "Colin Ravish . . . ," she read. Her heart fluttered. "It's you. I knew I'd find you somehow."

"What are you over here whispering about?" Elise peeked over her shoulder and read the addressee's name on the letter. "The Ravishes live on route one."

"You know them?"

"I do. The wife is super nice. They have a post office box across the street, and she always brings us doughnuts or pastries. We always feel so relaxed after a visit from Mrs. Ravish. Something about her is just so calming."

"His wife?" Evelyn repeated the only part of Elise's statement that mattered, realizing her suspicions were confirmed.

"She's definitely a triple threat. The woman is thoughtful, beautiful, and she cooks."

Elise's proclamation about the woman Jocelyn was ate at Evelyn's confidence and compounded her jealousy. "Well, she's a lucky woman to have such a wonderful husband," Evelyn mused in response.

"I didn't think you knew them."

"He was the paramedic who saved my life."

"Oh, that Colin," Elise exclaimed, realizing where else she had heard the name.

"I don't remember telling you about him."

"You've mentioned him a time or two," Elise assured her suspicious coworker.

Evelyn couldn't imagine herself willingly offering information about Colin. She started to wonder what else she'd told Elise. She had allowed Elise to hypnotize her, not knowing the past they shared. Evelyn was left asking herself if Elise would take the newfound information and use it against her. *She will surely be able to beat me in this so-called game of life if she is privy to my secrets*, Evelyn fretted. And just that fast, Elise was added to her list of assumed threats.

And for the very first time, she heard a voice in her head. *We should try again tonight*, it said to her.

Evelyn took heed and turned to Elise. "Maybe we should try again tonight."

"Try what?"

"Hypnotizing me again . . . I'm ready to dig deeper. Aren't you?"

"I thought you'd never ask." Elise brandished a sly grin, utterly oblivious to the trap she had just stepped into.

Chapter 10

Claiming Her Spot

Meanwhile over at the Todds, Jocelyn had been pruning plants in their greenhouse all day. It was nearly time to hang the last batches of their crop. Jocelyn inched forward atop the milk crate she was perched on, arched her back, then leaned in to prune a marijuana plant. It was a feat to angle her torso in such a way that she could complete the work comfortably. Jocelyn worried whether she would be able to keep up with the demands of her husband's lucrative side project. Regardless, she had put her best foot forward to ensure its success.

"What a beauty you are," she remarked, clipping the purple bud attached to the branch she had pulled closer to begin trimming. After a few snips here and there, a tingling feeling crept up the fingers of her right hand. Hoping more than assuming the glove she wore was the cause, she ripped it off. But the numbness traveled up her arm. Jocelyn sprang up off the crate. A minute later, the numbness had engulfed the entire right side of her body. "Not again." She pouted from the misfortune she'd been dealt. The multiple sclerosis that plagued her central nervous system had become more persistent in recent months. "I'm just so sick of this!"

She hobbled along, dragging her motionless right leg, through rows of plants. Jocelyn only had to make it to her Jeep out front. But Jocelyn's symptoms seemed to worsen with every step she took. Her vision became blurry, and she wondered how she would make it to the house. Her impaired vision caused her to trip over a bucket blocking the door to the greenhouse. As she was propelled forward, she felt a strong hand grab her and prevent her from falling, which immediately quelled Jocelyn's panic. It was her knight in shining armor, so to speak. Colin had saved the day by catching his ailing wife before she tumbled to the ground.

"Baby, what happened? Are you all right?" Colin held her close.

"I guess I bit off a bit more than I could chew." Jocelyn leaned into the safety of her husband's arms.

"I'm sorry, baby. This is all my fault. I should have known this was too much for you to handle. I'll take care of it. I promise. Let's get you up to the house. You've done enough today."

Colin carried Jocelyn several yards, then helped her climb atop his ATV. He got on and took the dirt trail back up to their house. As he drew closer, he noticed a woman pacing the grounds in front of their porch. Her attention turned their way once she heard the sputtering of the ATV's engine. She had a bright, unassuming smile.

"Can I help you?" Colin asked as he pulled alongside the woman.

"I certainly hope so." She batted her eyelashes.

"Tell you what, I'll help you if you can give me a hand," he replied.

"Seems fair enough . . . ," she agreed, with a nod.

"I need to get my wife into the house. She's not feeling too well—"

"I'm fine, Colin," Jocelyn interrupted. "There's no need to fuss over me."

"I beg to differ. As your husband, it's his job to fuss over you," the woman commented.

Jocelyn couldn't make out much of the woman's face, due to her impaired vision, but what she could make out of the woman's attire put her at ease. She could see the postal emblem on the lapel of the woman's shirt. "I'll be fine. I just need a little rest."

"Come on, honey. Let's get you inside." Colin lifted his wife from the ATV and climbed the porch, the woman right behind him.

"Can you get the door for me?" He glanced over at the stranger with the radiant smile.

"That I can do." She turned the brass knob, pushed open the front door, and let herself in. She came to a stop on the far side of the foyer and gazed around, in awe. The home had a sharp, sophisticated, state-of-the-art feel to it, from the glass-encased waterfall that separated the living room from the kitchen to the floating transparent staircase that led to the second level of the white stone structure.

"I'm going to get my wife into bed. I'll be right back," Colin told their awestruck visitor.

"What a beautiful house," she uttered, her admiration sincere.

Only a few minutes passed before Colin dashed back into the foyer, ready to tackle whatever issue she presented. "So, how can I help you?"

"I'm stuck. I got a flat tire on the main road. This was the closest house. I was wondering if you could help me change it."

"Well, that seems pretty simple."

"I'm assuming that's a yes?"

"That's definitely a yes, ma'am."

She cringed when Colin addressed her as ma'am. "Please. Call me Evelyn."

"Evelyn," Colin repeated. He uttered her name one more time as he pondered why she seemed familiar to him. "Do I know you, Evelyn?"

"I'm not sure. I mean, I wouldn't know."

"That's kinda strange. Don't you think?"

"It's the cards I was dealt." She shrugged.

"What do you mean?"

"I can't remember anything from my past due to an accident. A blow to my frontal lobe washed my memories of the past away."

"Oh my God, I *do* know you. How coincidental is this," Colin remarked with delight. "I was one of the paramedics that got you to the hospital the night of the accident. I came to visit you at the hospital too. You really don't remember anything?"

"I don't see how I could possibly forget a man as handsome as you, but apparently, I have. My apologies."

"Don't apologize. It's not your fault. You've been through quite an ordeal. I'm happy to see you've recovered. You look so different than you did in the hospital."

"I clean up pretty good," Evelyn said, her demeanor innocent.

"You do." Colin agreed as his eyes admired curves hugged by black spandex leggings. He allowed his thoughts to take him to places his mind had no business wandering, but only for a second, as his better judgment seemed to kick in. He cleared his throat. "Eh, em . . . I guess we should go take a look at your tire, yes?"

Evelyn smiled. Like a lioness, she could smell her prey. The way he studied her body told her that her deepest desires could be fulfilled. *All in due time . . .* , she thought, calming impulses that yearned to be satisfied. "I'll lead the way." Evelyn turned, then sashayed to the door, adding a sultry twist to her hips, confident he'd admire the view.

Other than his initial glance at her caboose, Colin remained a gentleman, keeping his eyes on the path ahead. He opened the front door for her, and they stepped out on the porch.

"We can take my four-wheeler back up to the main road . . . as long as you don't mind riding as a passenger," he said as they descended the porch steps.

"And your wife wouldn't mind me riding along with you? I wouldn't want to cause any trouble."

"Jocelyn isn't like that. She's secure with herself and the sanctity of our marriage. She knows I'd never risk losing her by doing something foolish." Colin climbed aboard the ATV.

"In that case, I welcome the ride." Evelyn hopped on behind him, allowing the insides of her thighs to rest along the outsides of his. "Be gentle with me." She wrapped her arms around his waist.

"Of course." Colin snickered, having noticed the increased seduction in her tone. It wasn't his intention to entertain her subtle advances, yet Colin couldn't deny Evelyn's compliments stroked his ego. He started up the all-terrain vehicle, then headed up a path to the main dirt road, where Evelyn's truck sat disabled.

"Your back tire looks completely flat," Colin commented as they approached the Yukon.

"I have a spare underneath."

"Okay. You wait here. I'll take care of it," he said as he dismounted.

"Are you sure? I can help."

"I appreciate the offer, but I wasn't raised to watch a woman change her tire."

"In that case, I don't mind watching."

Colin removed his gray hooded sweater, which matched his sweatpants. "The wife will kill me if I get this dirty. She bought it for my birthday last year." His pants came down next, revealing the pair of basketball shorts he wore underneath. Lust surged through her core. His strong caramel pecs under his white V-neck T-shirt seemed to invite her tongue to explore.

"Is that all?" she asked as he laid the clothes on his seat.

"If you're referring to my getting undressed, yes. I think I'm safe if I get my shorts and T-shirt dirty."

"So, what made you want to become a paramedic?" Evelyn stood nearby as Colin proceeded to repair her flat.

"I needed the extra money. Plus, I figured it would be exciting."

"So, you like the adrenaline rush?"

"I guess you could say I'm sort of an adrenaline junkie. Fortunately, I made the extra money I needed, so I'm no longer chasing the ambulance high."

"Oh, you quit?"

"I did. I have several endeavors on the side I dabble in."

"Is that why you smell like marijuana?"

"What? You can actually smell it on me?"

"I could smell it even more on your wife. At first, I thought it was something else, but then I noticed all the drug paraphernalia scattered around your house."

"Maybe it's time for me to do some reorganizing. It hasn't been easy with Jocelyn being sick. I'm left to do quite a bit when she has setbacks."

"I'm sorry to hear that," Evelyn lied, then followed this up with the actual truth. "I wish there was something I could do to help you."

"Do you know how to prune plants?"

"If I do, I certainly don't remember."

"Of course. I forgot."

"But that doesn't mean I can't learn," she said quickly, not willing to miss out on an opportunity to get closer to Colin. "I really wouldn't mind helping out. Besides, I hear gardening can be therapeutic."

"That really would be a big help. Wow . . . It's as if the angels answered my prayer before I even had the opportunity to tell them what I needed." Colin yanked off the flat tire, having removed the lug nuts.

"Amazing how that works out."

"I can afford to pay you about twenty bucks an hour. Do you think you could work for about five hours a day? It would just be for a few days out of the week."

"I can definitely work that out."

Colin placed the spare into position, then wiped his brow free of perspiration. "Your husband won't mind us stealing you away?"

His question caught Evelyn off guard. "How did you know I was married?"

"I visited you in the hospital, remember?"

"Oh yeah . . ." Evelyn paused in recollection.

"He won't be upset, will he?"

"Erick be upset . . . ? Not at all. He's much too nice for that."

"Good. Then I'll see you tomorrow around . . . What time is okay for you?"

"You can expect to see me no later than one o'clock."

"I won't be home until about three p.m., but Jocelyn will be here. You can meet her down at the greenhouse, and she'll show you how everything works." Colin twisted on the last of the lug nuts, then tightened it with the tire iron to ensure the tire's stability.

"Sounds like a plan."

Evelyn's plan was coming together beautifully. The man of her dreams was nearly hers. Only one thing stood in the way of her fulfilling her aspiration to bed Colin, and it wasn't Jocelyn. Evelyn didn't see her as a threat in the slightest, and she was confident in her ability to seduce Colin when the time came. It was Elise whom she planned to remove from the equation. *But how?*

Chapter 11

Tying Up Loose Ends

A cigarette hanging from the edges of her lips, Elise pushed a vacuum cleaner back and forth across the worn brown shag carpeting in her living room. Out of nowhere, the doorbell chimed, causing her to pause. She wasn't expecting anyone. "Damned Jehovah's Witnesses." She'd seen them traveling around her block as she pulled into the driveway upon returning home. Elise kicked her foot upward against the lever to shut down the vacuum cleaner. "Maybe they'll just go away if I stay quiet," she said aloud to herself.

To her disappointment, the bell chimed again. "Damn it. They heard the vacuum cleaner." Elise concluded she had no other choice than to answer the door. Besides, her Volkswagen was parked right outside, an indication that she was home, not to mention the fact that the missionaries had watched her pull into the driveway. "I might as well just get it over with." She pulled the front door open to greet them, cigarette still dangling from her lips. "Oh, it's you!" Elise removed the teetering cigarette from her mouth.

Evelyn smiled. "You said we could try again today."

"I did. But I thought you'd be coming in the evening."

"I figured it would be better to get it over with before the kids get out of school. I'd like to keep my evening open for the family, ya know? I'm sure you and yours have things to do tonight."

"Well, to be quite honest with you, it's just me and my two boys. Greg left several months back. One minute he's a family man, and the next he decides he wants to be kid free. I'll tell you one thing, though. I can assure you he won't be child-support free."

Evelyn kept quiet, not knowing exactly how she should respond. Everything in her told her she had been personally acquainted with Elise's ex-husband, but what advice could she really give? Evelyn was in the process of stealing Jocelyn's husband away, so how could she possibly empathize with Elise?

Elise could tell that Evelyn was engaged in an internal struggle by the look on her face, and so she decided to move on from the topic of marital betrayal. "Okay. Well, let's head out back." This was the opportunity she had been waiting for, as she wanted to get more dirt on Evelyn. The fact that she'd already heard several disturbing admissions directly from Evelyn's lips had done nothing to thwart her plans. In fact, the revelations had accomplished quite the opposite. Elise had become convinced she would be the ultimate victor in the battle the two women waged once all was said and done.

As they were about to leave the house, Elise came to an abrupt stop. "Hold on. On second thought, let me grab my recorder. I have thought of a few things we should do after the last time we tried it. Maybe if you could hear a playback of yourself recounting the events, it'll help jog your memory outside of hypnosis." Elise darted to the back of her three-bedroom bungalow to retrieve her recorder.

That was when Evelyn saw it, a newspaper clipping on the oak coffee table in front of the sofa. The clipping was an article that detailed the fatal drowning of her neighbor

Mr. Fuboi. The drowning was front-page news in yes-terday's paper, yet Elise hadn't mentioned a thing about it. Evelyn found that rather strange. Why wouldn't Elise have mentioned it? Maybe she'd already known about his drowning, Evelyn mused. And then she convinced herself that this was the case.

As Evelyn's paranoia intensified, the pair stepped outside and headed in the direction of the bungalow's back door.

Out of nowhere the voice in Evelyn's head spoke up. *Now's our chance.* Evelyn heard it loud and clear. For a moment, she looked around, sure someone had spoken, but there was no one but Elise present.

"You can't get to your basement from the inside of your house?" Evelyn asked.

"The stairs aren't safe, so to prevent someone from get-ting hurt, we don't use them. We rarely use the basement at all because of the flooding during spring. My eldest boy plans on snaking it out for me next year. Hopefully, we can get the problem fixed before I have to worry about being up to my ankles in water come April." Elise pushed the sturdy oak door. Its squeaking echoed in the small space as they stepped inside.

As Elise paused at the top of the stairs, Evelyn peered over her shoulder, then squinted and exclaimed, "What is that at the bottom of the stairs?"

Elise's eyelids nearly met as she squinted to catch a glimpse of whatever Evelyn was looking at. But darkness engulfed the basement below. "Some light would help," she remarked as she tried to capture with her fingers the string that hung from a dingy yellow bulb in the ceiling of the top of the staircase. Suddenly Evelyn gave her a swift kick in the tailbone. The impact sent Elise catapulting forward into the darkness. Evelyn, her eyes accustomed now to the darkness, could see her hand searching frantically for the railing on the way down, but to no avail. The snapping of bones could be heard each time her body slammed against the stairs. Evelyn found the string, yanked it, and the bulb cast a dim light down the staircase. A long rusted nail protruding from the bottom step appeared to have been painted crimson. It had pierced the back of Elise's skull before she crashed, facedown, on the cement floor.

"Oh my . . . That was easier than I thought." Evelyn pulled a cell phone from the pocket of her spandex jacket and used the camera's flash to brighten the staircase. She slowly tackled each step. It wasn't until she saw the crimson puddle forming beneath Elise's head that she halted her steps. "Dead as a doornail," she noted nonchalantly. Evelyn trekked back up the stairs, leaving the scene of her crime.

Elise had become embroiled in a dangerous game. A game in which she'd drastically underestimated her opponent, her *new* opponent. The old Evelyn was no more. A more formidable foe had emerged. And she was playing to win, by any means necessary.

The closing bell chimed mid-afternoon, sending a flood of adolescents out the elementary school doors. Just as Bryson was boarding the school bus, he noticed his mother's SUV parked among the yellow-and-black buses in the line. Evelyn honked her horn and beckoned him her way with a hand gesture.

"Ma'am! Ma'am!" hollered a middle-aged woman wearing a yellow vest with silver reflectors lining the front and back as she headed Evelyn's way, arms flailing. "You can't park here, ma'am! It's for buses only," she informed Evelyn when she reached her driver's side window.

Bryson chimed in as he hopped into the back seat. "Mama, I don't think you're allowed to park here."

"Did you have a good day at school?" Evelyn asked, completely ignoring the crossing guard, who remained standing beside her vehicle.

"I had a great day, Mama."

"No bullying, I assume."

"No bullying," he reassured his doting mother. "As a matter of fact, Domonic wasn't even in school today."

"Ma'am, can't you read the signs? You can't park here!" the crossing guard repeated, her short gray pixie cut bobbing with each disapproving nod of her head.

"Oh, I saw your sign, and I read it plainly, in fact. I just don't give a fuck," Evelyn responded in an overly pleasant tone before driving off.

"Mama, I can't believe you said that to her."

Evelyn admired her reflection in the rearview mirror as she mashed her lips together, ensuring gloss covered them in their entirety. "Sometimes you have to let people know exactly where you stand, without mincing words. Mama's got a brand-new bag, baby. It's time to show it off to the world."

"Mama, I'll always love you, no matter what."

"Bryson." She positioned her rearview mirror to see him perched in the second row, his seat belt buckled. "What makes you say that?" Evelyn inquired, her eye twitching, as if she suspected him of something.

Did he know what she had done? *No*, she told herself. *There's no way that's possible.* He'd been in school when she'd drowned Mr. Fuboi, as well as when she'd blown the Danielsons' garage to bits, causing Mr. Danielson's untimely death. And then there was Elise . . . Well, not a single soul even knew she was dead yet. He couldn't possibly know.

"I said it because I never want to be without you. When you were gone, it was the worst. You're not gonna leave again. Right, Mama?"

"I'm never gonna leave you, Bryson. Don't you worry," she reassured him, she alone privy to the fraudulence of her reply.

Sometimes good mothers have to lie, she thought, just in time to ease any possible feelings of guilt.

Chapter 12

The What-Ifs

Back home, a soft rhythm and blues ballad echoed from the sound bar atop the enormous floor-model television in the family room. The aroma of garlic, onions, oregano, shrimp, and scallops sautéing in a buttered skillet spread throughout the house. Erick moved his wooden spoon from the skillet to the separate pan of jasmine rice he was frying. He had made it a point to get home early so that he could start dinner before the kids came home from school. With Evelyn just recently getting back to work, he figured fulfilling the duty of cook would be asking too much of her. A seafood medley he prepared with love was on the menu. Erick glanced up at the time displayed on the stove's clock. Four o'clock . . . The time when their children arrived home from school was fast approaching.

Out of nowhere, footsteps sounded throughout the kitchen.

"Hey, Dad! Um, something smells good." Bryson moved in closer, flinging his anime-decorated book bag to the floor. "What are you cooking?" He leaned over the stove, steam from the sauté almost touching his nose.

"Hey there, bud. Get your nose out of the food and go get yourself cleaned up. I'm preparing a seafood feast for the five of us."

"Five? Well, just so you know, Diana's spending the night at her friend Rachel's tonight. So, looks like it's just the four of us—"

"Mm-mmm, that smells good. Hey, Dad, think I could borrow thirty bucks?" Michael interrupted, having just strolled into the kitchen.

"Sure, son. Provided you repay your debt . . ."

"Don't I always?"

Erick nodded in agreement. "My wallet is on the dresser in my bedroom."

Bryson continued to admire the sautéing seafood. "Can I have extra shrimp in mine, please? They look so good." He rubbed his tummy.

"Too bad I'm having dinner over at Lisa's house. Her mom's cooking blows," Michael complained as he attempted to fork out a single shrimp from the hot skillet.

"Don't say blows, son."

"Blows what?" Bryson inquired.

"Never mind your brother, Bryson. You should go get cleaned up for dinner. As a matter of fact, before you do that, I need you to go out and feed Sheba."

"Why are you going over there for dinner if her cooking blows?" Bryson asked, ignoring his father's instructions.

"One day, Bryson, you'll find out exactly why," Erick interjected. "Until then, just know your brother is doing the right thing."

Bryson furrowed his brow. "Like holding the door open for a girl, even though you don't feel like it?"

"Smart kid. You're learning already," Michael remarked before realizing the shrimp was far too hot for his mouth. "Shit! That's hot." He allowed the piece of shrimp to drop from his mouth to the counter.

"Serves you right. Now, get out of my skillet," Erick playfully scolded his son, popping him on the back of his head with the wooden spoon.

"Dad! Now my hair is gonna be all sticky."

"Let's hope you plan on taking a shower before showing up for dinner. If her mother is anything like yours, she doesn't want anyone sitting at her dining-room table smelling like outside," Erick lectured. He made air quotation marks with his hands on either side of his head when he said the word *outside*.

"I didn't think about that. Maybe I should take a shower." Michael picked up his piece of shrimp and tested its temperature with his teeth before gobbling it down. "I'm counting on there being leftovers," he added before rushing from the kitchen.

The moment Evelyn stepped foot in the mudroom, a welcoming aroma filled her nostrils. "My goodness, something smells delicious. Honey, I didn't know you were making dinner. You didn't have to cook. I could have come up with something."

Erick turned and greeted her near the entryway. "Well, now you don't have to."

Evelyn brushed by him as she made her way to their bedroom. "I guess I should get cleaned up, then."

"Is it okay if I get a kiss first?" Erick stretched out his arms. Since her accident, he'd become accustomed to resisting the urge to feel slighted, by acknowledging that she was still in the learning stages of how they were accustomed to treating one another.

Evelyn turned back to her doting husband and stared intently at him. "You're my husband. You can get anything you want from me."

Erick moved closer. "Hi." His eyes softened as he peered into hers. "How was your day?"

This man really does love me, she assured herself. Evelyn could see the truth of it in his eyes. He looked at her as if she were the only thing on earth that mattered to him.

"My day was productive. Interesting, to say the least. I'll say this. You'll definitely enjoy our dinner conversation more than you did our conversation on the way to work."

"Then I'm in for a treat," Erick mumbled, mouth perched closely to hers. He gave her a smooch on the lips as he embraced her, savoring her essence.

Evelyn leaned into his embrace. While she had no memories of their past together, there was something about Erick that she just couldn't turn a cold shoulder to. It was as if some part of her recollected how deserving he was of her love.

"You go get yourself situated. Daddy will set things up for dinner."

Bryson had snuck up behind them. "Sounds good, Daddy," he blurted, mimicking his father's voice as best he could, before bursting into a fit of laughter so contagious his parents couldn't help but follow suit.

Erick hardened his tone. "You haven't fed Sheba yet. Go feed the dog, Bryson."

Evelyn headed upstairs and retreated to the bathroom. She turned on the sink faucet, cupped her hands together under the running water, and collected enough to rinse the day's dust from her face. The moment her eyes closed and the water splashed her face, she saw his gleaming smile, his chiseled jawline, and strong chin. The way his eyes had softened once he realized who she was as she stood before him in his living room pleased her. Colin was merely a fantasy just a few days ago, but now she knew where he lived. Even better, she had secured a place at his table. Evelyn blotted her face with a towel, then opened her eyes. It was time for dinner. Time to sit down with the family she barely knew, a fact that seemed to matter less as the days passed. Heck, Evelyn barely knew herself.

She went downstairs, and as she neared the kitchen, she caught sight of Erick and her boys as they congregated around the dinner table. They all seemed morose. When she reached the table, a look of compassion came over Erick's face.

"Oh, honey, I'm so sorry."

Evelyn's brows wrinkled. The confused look on her face failed to incite a response from him, so she said, "What happened? Sorry for what?"

Then she realized Michael was on his cell phone. Attempting to hear the person on the other end of the line, he lifted his finger to silence his family before placing it in his ear.

"Are you sure she's dead?" he asked into the phone.

"Oh my God . . . Who's dead?" Evelyn's hands shook as they flew to her gaping mouth.

Erick didn't hesitate to put his arm around her and pull her into a comforting embrace.

"They found her in the basement," Michael repeated after being informed of this by the caller.

That was when Evelyn knew they had to be referring to her old friend Elise. "Found *who* in the basement?" she asked, playing along, as if she were oblivious about what had taken place.

Michael ended the call. "They found Elise, Mom," Michael answered, confirming her suspicions.

"Oh, thank goodness," Evelyn blurted, moving her hands from her mouth to cover her chest. It pleased her that Elise was indeed a goner, but she hadn't intended to express her relief so blatantly.

"What!" Erick released Evelyn from his embrace.

"I didn't mean it like that. I'm just so relieved you weren't talking about Diana. For a moment there, I thought I'd lost . . . ." Evelyn mustered up a few crocodile tears.

Erick pulled her in close. "Oh my God, honey, no. Diana is fine. I promise you. Our family is going to be just fine," he assured his seemingly disheartened wife.

On the sidewalk just across the road from Elise's residence, Lisa, Michael's girlfriend, stood twirling one of her long, skinny braids around her index finger. "I can't believe this is happening," she said to no one in particular. She glared fixedly at the flashing red and blue lights atop the police cruiser. Nearly every neighbor on her block stood nearby, gawking at the tragic scene.

Two paramedics emerged from the backyard, pushing along a gurney that carried Elise's corpse encased in a black body bag.

"Another postal worker dead . . . Sir, I don't know what the hell is going on at the Clarkston post office, but we better find out fast," Officer Jan Fackender announced over the police radio from the driver's seat of her cruiser.

"After you finish up there, head back to the station. Maybe we can put our heads together. Get on top of this thing. Whatever it is." Detective Edward Barnes reclined in the chair behind his desk. He twisted one end of his bushy mustache as he contemplated the string of mysterious deaths. Now there was one more to add to the list.

A whiteboard in the corner of his office had listed in black marker the Clarkston post office's most recent deaths and their suspected causes. He studied each case, one by one. Randy, the rural carrier, death by gunshot to the face; Deborah, the delivery supervisor, death by suicidal overdose; now the latest, Elise, who was found lying in a pool of blood at the bottom of her basement stairs. Evelyn seemed to be the single survivor of all the attempts thus far.

I've got to talk to her, Detective Barnes thought, hoping to get some insight into their dilemma.

Less than an hour later, the petite officer made her way through the station, heading straight for Detective Barnes's office, intent on solving these cases. "I just don't get it, sir," Officer Fackender admitted as she entered the room, then took a seat in a chair opposite his. "We've got several dead civilians, and they all worked together. There has to be a connection somewhere."

"Did the coroner enlighten us as to the cause of death?"

"Injuries indicate she fell down the stairs. Her neck was broken, and her skull had been penetrated by a rusted nail protruding from one of the steps."

"So, let's say this was just an accident. That leaves us with one murder and one attempted murder."

"What about Jessica? The young woman we found in the dumpster behind that apartment building up the road from the post office. That case broke my heart. Seeing that woman's dead body wrapped in a sheet and just thrown in the dumpster like a mound of garbage still eats at me. Regardless of whether or not she was a prostitute, she didn't deserve to die and have her body discarded in such a foul manner."

"Our only solace can be had in finding the killer." Detective Barnes pulled one of the manila folders from the pile on top of his disheveled desk. "I've got a feeling the answers we seek lie with this one here." He chucked the file across his desk, toward the edge closest to Officer Fackender.

She read the name printed on the file's end tab. "Marcus Renegat. The mail clerk who mysteriously disappeared . . . Great. Now all we have to do is find him. I always suspected him of something. The way he looked at us when he noticed us tailing him at the bank was no co-incidence."

"Or we find his kid," Detective Barnes remarked, offering up an alternate option. "The last time I questioned him in his apartment, he told me his son had recently moved out. Find out his son's name. We'll see if he can shed some light on the subject. In the meantime, I believe Randy, the carrier we found dead in the tree stand, is being buried tomorrow. I'm thinking it would be a good idea if we attended the burial. Making our presence known just may bring the unsub out of hiding. At the very least maybe we can get them to slip up and make a mistake."

"Sounds like a plan, Detective," Fackender agreed. "Maybe we can get some answers as to how to find this mysterious kid as well."

"Go home. Get some sleep . . . We've got a full day ahead of us tomorrow, Fackender."

Chapter 13

Suspicions Grow

She carried a pile of folded clothing down the hall past the main-floor bathroom. Bryson could be heard singing the intro to his favorite anime cartoon as Evelyn passed by on her way to putting away his laundered garments. If one wasn't already aware of Bryson's obsession with Japanese character art, it became blatantly obvious upon seeing the décor in his bedroom. The anime-themed bed linens matched the valances above his curtains. A vast array of anime figurines lined the top shelf of the oak bookcase in a corner of his room.

Like his mother, Bryson was neat. Everything in his room had its place, even his video camcorder on the tripod near his window. Curious as to what her son had been watching, Evelyn placed the pile of clothing atop his bed, then headed for the window. As she neared the camcorder, her heart dropped into the pit of her stomach. Its lens pointed directly into their backyard and offered a full view of their swimming pool. Evelyn could still hear Bryson singing from the bathroom. Her eyes toggled from his camcorder to their pool a time or two before she snatched the device from the tripod. Evelyn had to know what it was her son had been filming. She worried that her secret was, in fact, no secret at all.

Without any hesitation, she popped open the viewer, then pressed PLAY. A prompt instructed her to insert a tape. Her paranoia pushed her further. She pressed the EJECT button, only to find an empty compartment. Whatever it was he had recorded was no longer there, if he'd even recorded anything at all. Evelyn made an effort to convince herself of the latter possibility. Still, she scanned his room, looking for the collection of tapes she assumed was there somewhere. Evelyn pulled open the top drawer of his nightstand, then pushed around cartoon-themed socks as well as undergarments, attempting to find what wasn't there. Unwilling to give up so easily, she rushed over to his tall dresser and pulled open each drawer, one by one, searching frantically for his tapes.

"Thank you, Mama," Bryson announced as he stood in the doorway of his bedroom, dressed in his anime pajamas, damp curls atop his head still glistening from the shower.

"What?" Evelyn said with a jolt, caught off guard.

"For wanting to put my clothes away," Bryson clarified, eyes combing the places she had searched.

"Oh, yes, your father and I just finished the laundry. I wasn't sure which drawers to put them in, so I put them here on the bed."

"It's okay, Mama. I can put them away."

"Bryson?" Evelyn took a seat on the edge of his bed. "The camcorder you have in your window . . . Were you recording something?"

"I don't have any more tapes. Dad was supposed to buy me some last week, but he hasn't yet."

"How long have you been out of tapes?"

"For at least a couple of weeks."

His reply eased her worry. Getting rid of her son was an action Evelyn wasn't quite sure she had the gumption to carry out.

"What's the matter, Mama? Is something wrong?" Bryson asked, proceeding to put away his clean laundry.

"Everything is fine, Bryson. I just have a lot on my mind."

"Is it Miss Elise?"

"That, among other things."

"I'm sorry about what happened to your friend. I feel sorry for her kids. I couldn't imagine having to live without you for the rest of my life."

"Don't you worry about that, son. I'm home now." Evelyn stood, placed the pile of clothes on the dresser, then pulled back the covers, ready to tuck Bryson into bed. "You should get to bed and get some sleep. You have school tomorrow."

Bryson shut one of his drawers, then climbed under the covers. "Good night, Mama. I love you."

"I love you too, Bryson." Evelyn leaned in, kissed him on his forehead, then shut off the lamp at his bedside before leaving the bedroom.

"I'll always protect you, Mama," Bryson whispered as he shut his eyes, ready to drift off to sleep.

Erick loaded the last of the dirty dishes into the dishwasher, unable to shake the news that Elise was dead. He couldn't help but acknowledge the fact that he'd recently told Evelyn of Elise's past transgressions against her, and now she had turned up dead. His memory of the relief Evelyn had displayed after finding out it was Elise who'd died replayed in his head. *Nah. There's no way*, he told himself. His wife was no murderer. It had to be a coincidence. But he was sure that knowing exactly how Elise had died would certainly alleviate his suspicions about Evelyn.

Desperate for answers, he grabbed his cell phone to do a Google search and unearth whatever information he could find about Elise's demise. Erick was in luck. The local news had already begun releasing information that pointed to her death being accidental. At least that was the theory so far, judging by the online article he read.

Authorities have released information regarding what looks to have been an unfortunate freak accident on Bristol Lane. A thirty-nine-year-old mother of two has passed away due to a seemingly tragic misstep. What was originally suspected of being foul play has now been ruled an accident. This tragic news makes this the third death in recent months connected to the Clarkston post office. An attack of another one of its employees occurred just months ago. . . .

Erick clicked the button on the side of his phone to black out the screen when he heard footsteps nearing the kitchen.

"Is something wrong?" Evelyn asked as she approached. She had noticed him fiddling with his phone when she reached the entryway to the kitchen.

"Elise's death has been ruled a tragic accident."

"How do they know it was an accident? What if the person who attacked me attacked Elise too?"

"Honey, you shouldn't think like that. It'll just give you nightmares."

"But what if . . . ?"

"No buts, no what-ifs . . . You're home safe now, and that's all that matters." Erick pulled Evelyn into a snug embrace while at the same time denying what his intuition was telling him.

"There's something I need to tell you." Evelyn figured there was no better time than the present to tell her husband about her new part-time job.

"What is it, honey?" He released his hold on her.

"Promise me you're not going to worry."

"I can't promise I'm not going to worry if I don't even know what you intend on telling me. How about you just tell me?"

"I got a part-time job," she revealed.

"What? Why?"

"It's just for a little while. I'll be working in a green-house. I figure working with plants would be therapeutic for me. To be quite honest with you, I don't know if I'm ready to go back to work at the post office full-time. You know they still haven't cleaned the bloodstains from my accident off the pavement? I just can't take it . . . not with Elise gone too. It's just too much for me to handle right now."

"I understand, honey. You don't have to explain any further. Thankfully, you have enough sick leave built up to be off for an entire year if need be."

"I think it's best. I'll go back when I'm ready. I promise."

"Whatever you decide is fine with me. I can take care of us either way," he assured her.

"Thank you for being so understanding."

"You don't have to thank me. I love you. I'll always do what's best for you."

"I love you too, honey."

"So, when do I get to see your new job?"

"Oh . . . it's no big corporation or anything like that. The woman I'll be helping is sick and is finding it hard to keep up with her plants. I'll be getting paid twenty dollars an hour, but the position lasts only a few months. That should give me the time I need to recover mentally from all of this."

"Whatever it takes, right?"

"Whatever it takes . . ." Evelyn nodded in agreement, secretly ecstatic that her plan had gone off without a hitch. Not that she had expected much pushback from Erick. She had him wrapped around her finger, a fact she relished.

Chapter 14

Laid to Rest or Back From the Dead

That next morning most of the full-time carriers had called in late to work, so that they were available to attend the funeral of Randy Alky, Rural Route 8's original mail carrier, who was murdered on the job. He had been fatally wounded in the face with buckshot, and his body had been found weeks after the gruesome killing had taken place. Randy's case took precedence with the police, as it was the most heinous of the violent crimes associated with the post office thus far.

At the church where the graveside funeral service was being held, a wreath adorned in red roses sat atop an easel, and in front of the wreath was a portrait of Randy that his loved ones had provided. They'd settled on his senior picture from high school, as it was the last dignified photo of him that had been taken. Frosted tips decorated the top of his mullet in the photo. And he flashed the peace sign, something that he had done often back in those days and that had made him even more popular among his peers. Randy had ridden that wave of popularity until his dying day.

A pair of binoculars before his eyes, Detective Barnes peered through his driver's side window at the funeral goers, studying their demeanor and body language. Since he was quite aware that many murderers not only knew their victim but also would attend their victim's funeral, he left not a single person unevaluated. Detective Barnes had no plans to make his presence known during the graveside service. He'd wait it out, give himself plenty of time to choose those he felt inclined to interrogate first. Especially since the person he had intended on questioning right away was a no-show.

A brisk autumn breeze carried dead foliage from tree branches, and some of it landed atop the black casket as it was lowered into the ground. *Funny thing, funerals*, Barnes thought. Whether you mourned the loss or celebrated the life of another, you were bound to experience heartfelt sorrow. Yet as Barnes shifted the lens of his binoculars from person to person, it dawned on him that there wasn't a wet eye in sight. Over fifty people had come to pay their respects to the popular mail carrier's family, but not a single tear fell. So not one of those in attendance stood out . . . yet. Barnes would have to observe them more closely.

Daniel was in the crowd of mourners gathered around the grave site. Just as the priest requested that everyone bow their head, Daniel's stomach began to grumble. *A grand slam from the local diner sure would be perfect right about now*, he thought as he surveyed the scene around him. Everyone else, it appeared, was bowing their head in prayer, and it dawned on Daniel that few would notice if he walked away. Besides, he would rather not wait in the traffic jam that would follow the priest's final words at the graveside service. It took only a few seconds of mulling it over before he slowly backed away from the crowd and stealthily made his way to the parking lot.

"Winner, winner, chicken dinner . . . ," Barnes said aloud as he tossed his binoculars under the passenger seat, then hopped out of his cruiser. He made a beeline for the hungry mail clerk headed to the parking lot.

"Good morning, sir. I'm Detective Barnes. Would you mind if I had a word with you for a moment?" Barnes called out when he was about fifteen feet from Daniel. "I hate to bother you at the funeral of your friend or loved one. I know how upsetting death can be. It won't take long," the detective added as he closed the gap between them.

Daniel huffed in anticipation of a long conversation, then looked the detective square in the eyes before accepting his extended hand to shake as a measure of good faith. After all, Daniel was about fairness. If anyone ever made the mistake of making him aware of their intentions yet failing to follow through, he'd make sure everyone knew about it. As far as his shortcomings, they weren't to be mentioned, let alone discussed.

"What is it I can help you with, Detective?"

"I was wondering if you could think of anyone who would be capable of committing cold-blooded murder. Maybe give me a clue as to who Mr. Alky was at odds with."

"Randy was always the life of the party," Daniel answered, continuing a slow stroll toward his vehicle. "I can't imagine anyone even taking Randy seriously enough to kill him. He just wasn't an argumentative kinda guy. Even at work, he did his job, told a few jokes, but mostly kept to himself."

"You guys over at the post office have been hit pretty hard lately. By my count, you've lost more than a few employees just over the past few months."

"I can't say they'll all be missed."

His admission piqued Detective Barnes's interest. "And who would that be, might I ask?"

"Look. I wasn't too fond of our supervisor, Deborah, but that's no secret. Most of the regulars hated her guts. She was a real . . ." He hesitated, having decided it wouldn't be appropriate to say the word that threatened to leap from the tip of his tongue. He replaced that word with something much more befitting a funeral. "Piece of work."

"Your supervisor's case was ruled a suicide."

"Word around the office was that Marcus finally snapped and killed her before he ducked out on us."

Detective Barnes was intrigued by the revelation. "Really? What makes you think Mr. Renegat would be capable of killing someone?"

"The way he flipped out on Elise the last time they worked together showed us a side of him none of us had ever seen before. I mean, it's true Elise could be a backstabbing pain in the rear, but he was a little hard on her. More than I'd say was warranted."

"Can you give me an account of what took place?"

Daniel remembered the incident like it was yesterday, and his mind drifted back to that day.

That day Elise had set out to antagonize Marcus. "What are you all hot under the collar about?" she snapped at him. "The new guy pissed you off, huh? What did he do? Try to steal some of your hours?" She knew all too well how Marcus and the new hire felt about one another.

"Eat shit, Elise. Oh, wait . . . It smells like you already have," Marcus uttered calmly, intent on not breaking the death stare he'd bestowed upon the new hire, Jackson, a recently discharged marine. Jackson hated Marcus just as much as Marcus despised him.

Marcus's clever comeback worked exactly as he had intended. Elise was as mad as a hatter. Blood rushed to her head, and her face turned red. She turned her attention to Daniel, then spouted the first lie that came to mind. "Daniel, Marcus told us you'll finally be going to the dentist to fix your teeth."

"What!" Daniel frowned, embarrassed by the comment. He approached Marcus. "I told you. Don't talk

*shit about me, man. I'll kick your ass," he threatened, his
index finger merely inches from Marcus's face.*

*"What a lying little bitch you are," Marcus shouted,
giving up on the death stare to turn his attention to Elise.*

*"Are you calling me a liar, Marcus?" she growled,
further solidifying the lie.*

*"Damn right! I'm calling you a lying little bitch, in
fact!" He had completely lost his cool and, apparently,
any awareness that he was at work.*

*"Marcus! In my office now!" Postmistress Hilary
demanded. She had overheard the entire argument.*

*A wry grin formed on Elise's face. "Explain that one
away, prick," she mumbled as he took the dreaded walk
to the postmistress's office.*

Detective Barnes cleared his throat, snapping Daniel
out of his brief trip down memory lane. His stomach
growling again, Daniel quickly provided him with all the
details he had just remembered.

At the end of his story, Detective Barnes was left
wondering if Marcus had been the culprit this entire
time. What if he had disappeared, only to carry out an
elaborate murder spree, intent on getting rid of all who'd
wronged him? The notion seemed plausible enough.

Meanwhile, Officer Fackender sat in the postmistress's
office, listening to her version of the same story Daniel
had just recited to Detective Barnes.

After the round of questioning had concluded, the officer rushed to her police cruiser. Mr. Renegat's apartment
building was less than a mile away. She thought it high
time she went back there to do some investigating. She
cranked the ignition, steered the cruiser out of the post
office parking lot, and sped down a side street. She pulled
up in front of the modest three-story apartment building

on Main Street at the same time Detective Barnes parked in the alley behind the building.

"Detective Barnes, are you there?" Fackender shouted into the police radio atop her dashboard.

"Fackender, you caught me just in time. I'm about to head into Renegat's apartment building to see if I can gather any more information that might help us. I believe a key piece to the puzzle just presented itself."

"I think we're sniffing the same trail, sir. I'm parked here as we speak. I guess I'll be seeing you inside. Over and out." Officer Fackender hopped out of the cruiser but waited for Detective Barnes to meet her out front before going inside.

A familiar moldy smell pervaded their nostrils as they entered the building.

"I wonder if anyone has moved into the apartment yet?" Officer Fackender mused.

"I imagine people are lined up on a waiting list to get into this place," Detective Barnes replied sarcastically as he took in the peeling wallpaper with vertical stripes.

A hard cough erupted from the opposite end of the dimly lit hall.

"Ladies first," Detective Barnes proclaimed with his hand outstretched.

"Of course." Officer Fackender was always up for a challenge. The petite woman was the bravest officer on the force. Her male counterparts made it a point to let her strut her stuff, but they always remained in close proximity, in case she ever needed assistance. Fackender, however, never had a problem holding her own.

Her hand slid off the knob as she attempted to enter the main office. "Oh, come on." She wiped the grease from the knob off her hand by sliding her palm down the side of her perfectly starched uniform pants. Her second attempt at opening the door, more forceful than the first, proved successful.

"I already take care of noise complaint, Officers. You can carry on with your day." The office manager, who had a thick Russian accent, waved them away as he continued gnawing on the chicken drumstick he'd packed for lunch from leftovers the night before.

"We're actually here to investigate a murder, sir. Can you put the chicken down and answer a few questions?" Fackender replied.

"Listen here." He pointed the drumstick in their direction but remained seated at his desk. "I don't need to put chicken down to talk. I only get thirty-minute lunch, and I still have to smoke and take dump after this. Pardon my French." He bit into the drumstick once more. "By the way, I am new manager. So, no more funny business with killing. I have everything under control. I am Russian, you know?" He smiled, revealing a brown tooth or two, before lifting his bicep to his greasy lips for a peck. "I work security as well. Would you like to see badge? I have here somewhere." He pushed around the papers atop the disheveled desk, in search of his badge.

Officer Fackender halted his search. "That won't be necessary."

"We just need to know if a certain apartment is occupied. Apartment number nine," Barnes chimed in.

"Well, let me check for you. I have computer here in front of me, right? I can do it." He smiled, then began enthusiastically clicking buttons with his greasy fingertips. "You know, I used to be lowly janitor. Now Vladimir move up. I showed them all. Now I am office manager." He clicked a few more keys before finding the information he was searching for. He squinted at the screen, bringing the numeral into focus. "Apartment nine. It is filled. Mr. Renegat lives there."

"We were under the impression that he moved out," Officer Fackender commented.

"It looks like the apartment is paid up until the end of this month," Vladimir assured the officers.

Barnes needed answers. The sooner, the better. "Do you have the master key?"

Vladimir's eyes lit up. "Do I have master key?" he repeated, elated to answer their query. "Of course, I have master key. I am manager, aye?" He cleaned his hands on his jeans, then got up and rushed over to a lockbox attached to the wall. It contained keys that opened each apartment. "See . . . I told you I had it." He snatched a key from the box. "I will let you in." The manager charged forward, brushing by them, and headed into the hallway.

Barnes took off after Vladimir first. "I guess we're following the guy with the key."

Vladimir rushed to tackle the three sets of creaking stairs they would have to climb to reach Marcus's floor. When he made it to the first landing, he tripped on a raised edge of worn carpeting.

"Whoa, whoa . . . Take your time," Fackender warned.

Vladimir pushed up the rolled sleeves of his white-collared shirt and forged on. When he reached the third floor, he knocked loudly on Marcus's apartment door. When no one answered, he opened the door with the key, then turned to the officers. "Let's go look around."

Detective Barnes shook his head. "We'll take it from here, sir. I'm sure you've got better things to do, like eat, smoke, take a dump, maybe?" Barnes chuckled as he and Fackender headed inside the apartment, then shut the door in Vladimir's face.

Officer Fackender raised an eyebrow. "Where do we start?"

"I'll check this bedroom. You can check the other one," Barnes instructed.

"Sounds like a plan. Holler if you find anything."

Barnes recalled questioning Marcus in this very same apartment, only then he didn't have the opportunity to look around. When he flipped the switch on the wall near the bedroom door, a dim light illuminated the room. He walked over to the bed, which was unmade, and noticed stains on the navy-blue bedsheets. He assumed they were dried male bodily fluids.

"Yuck!" Barnes looked disgusted.

He pressed on. After exploring the items on top of the dresser, he opened a drawer, in search of clues, anything that would reveal Marcus's current location. Barnes pushed around a pile of socks and other undergarments in the drawer for a few seconds before something dawned on him. The officer pulled open another drawer. It was stuffed with clothes.

"That's odd." He pulled open the remaining four dresser drawers and discovered they, too, were filled with clothing. "What did he take with him? There's gotta be something here that will give me the piece to the puzzle I'll need to solve this case," he said aloud to himself. His eyes meandered over the floor, then up one of the walls. Nothing. Barnes's gaze settled on the closet door.

"What do you have hiding in there?"

A feeling of utter failure had already begun to weigh him down. Hours, days, weeks, even months had gone by, yet the department hadn't solved a single crime related to the Clarkston post office. Maybe the answers he needed were inside that closet. Clinging to hope, Barnes pulled open the closet door, and his eyes roamed over the multiple sets of navy-blue T-shirts and shorts.

"What a weirdo."

Just then Fackender peeked her head inside the bedroom. "Found out anything yet?"

"He likes the color blue." Barnes continued searching for the clue he knew was there somewhere. "Wait a minute." He had spied a piece of black cloth hanging over the edge of a box on the top shelf of the closet. He snatched down the box, peered inside, and saw what he believed to be a single bedsheet, but his speculation wasn't confirmed until he lifted it from the box, then held it in the air for Fackender to see. "I think we may have found our missing link." Barnes walked over to the window and peeked out at the alley through an opening in the blinds.

"What is it, Detective? What are you thinking?" Officer Fackender rushed over and stood beside him to do the same.

That was when she came to the same realization he had.

"Remember the young woman that was found in the dumpster?" Barnes asked, knowing full well they were on the same page.

Officer Fackender responded as he'd expected she would. "The dumpster I can see from this window . . ." She recalled how Jessica's corpse had looked as it was pulled from the dumpster. It had been wrapped in a sheet just like the one they'd just found. "How could I forget? She was wrapped in a black sheet."

"That son of a bitch got off on looking out this window, knowing her body was there in the dumpster. He had the pleasure of admiring his handiwork every night. Reliving her last horrifying moments." Barnes turned to the bed and ripped off the top sheet. "I'm almost positive that if we test the bodily fluids that have dried on this sheet, they'll match the fluids we tested from the sheet the victim was covered in."

"What are we waiting for? I think we've found what it is we need. We can have forensics come in and comb the place over."

"Did you find anything in the spare bedroom?" Barnes asked.

"It's a disaster. There's a sea of clothing on the floor. The dresser is toppled over. The mattress is halfway off the bed. If Marcus said his son moved, it must have been due to a great deal of angst between them."

"Or maybe Marcus's son saw what he did to the woman in the dumpster. Let's find a photo of the son. There's got to be one around here somewhere. If not, call the high school. I'm sure they've had one on file at some point. Spread the news. We need an alert put out for Mr. Renegat and his son."

After the officers had formulated their next plan of action, they headed for the door. At the same time, an African American woman in her late forties exited the apartment across the hall, pushing a stroller that housed her toddler. Barnes thought it was the perfect time to ask Jackson some questions. After all, he did live in that very apartment.

"Ma'am," he called. He got her attention as she turned her key to lock the dead bolt. "I was wondering if your husband is home. I'd like to ask him a few questions."

"Is that what's required of us nowadays? A husband? Tell me, Officer, what makes you assume I have one? Just because I have a baby . . . ? Am I not capable of taking care of her on my own?"

Barnes quickly attempted to make amends for his outdated speculation. "I apologize. It's just that I questioned a man that lived here a couple of months back. I assumed—"

The woman quickly interrupted what she thought would be a sorry excuse for a sexist inference. "Your assumptions are incorrect. You should update your records . . . I've been living here for over a month. Now, if you'll excuse me, I have an appointment."

"Good day to you, ma'am." Barnes waved, happy to see the woman go.

Fackender leaned in closer to him. "Don't feel bad, Detective. A failed marriage can do that to most anyone. She's still a bit bitter."

"How do you know she's divorced?"

"You can tell by the color difference of the skin at the base of her ring finger. It's much lighter than the rest of her hand."

"That's why I need you on the case, Fackender. You're always finding answers among the smallest details."

Chapter 15

Clarity Surfaces

Although fall was well under way, putting swimming out of season at Lake Callis, midday fishing remained a favorite among its visitors.

"What's that you got there, Billy?" An old man in an aluminum fishing boat called out to his compadre fishing nearby.

"Whatever it is, it's got a strong hold on my line." The elderly man struggled to pull his fishing line from the murky depths. "Luckily, I've got these heavy-duty gloves. This line would slice right through my skin if I grabbed it." He stood up and pulled his line in hand over hand until something began to bubble to the surface. "A shoe! It's a shoe," he shouted once a black sneaker had floated to the surface of the water. The old man thought nothing of it as he pulled the shoe in to disconnect it from his line. It wasn't until an entire corpse floated to the surface that he lost his balance and toppled over and into Lake Callis. "Ahhh!"

"Billy! What are you doing?" Billy's partner quickly started the small motor on the back of his fishing boat and headed that way.

Billy flailed his arms wildly, slapping at the water, attempting to swim his way back to his boat and away from the corpse.

"Whoa, Billy! Looks like you've caught a big one." A look of disbelief washed over his partner's face.

"Fackender, I'd like you to stop at the local post office to see if Mr. Renegat left a forwarding address," Barnes told Fackender as the officers stood in the alley behind the apartment building, a stone's throw from Barnes's cruiser. "In fact, while you're at it, see if you can get a forwarding address for Jackson Pierce as well. I'll get this sheet over to the precinct for testing."

"Detective Barnes? Detective Barnes? Are you there?" a voice called out from the CB radio on the detective's dashboard.

Detective Barnes hurried over to his cruiser and answered the call. "This is Detective Barnes. What's the word?"

"Detective, we've been alerted by Davison police. Two male corpses have been found in Lake Callis. They're sending photos over to the station to verify the identities of the men. According to identification found on the bodies, Marcus Renegat and Principal Sobieski have finally surfaced."

Barnes shuddered. "My God." *This changes everything*, he thought. "Fackender and I are on our way out to the site. Over and out."

The bodies of Marcus and Principal Sobieski were splayed across the sand, atop black body bags, by the time Officer Fackender and Detective Barnes arrived on scene to correspond with Davison authorities. A purple hue radiated under their water-logged skin. The foggy eyes of both corpses remained wide open, a telltale sign of sudden death. The damage done told of a violent fate.

A forensics technician kneeled nearby, accessing the bodies. With gloved hands, he pulled an embedded shard of glass from the cheek of one of the corpses.

"What do we have here? Glass?" Officer Fackender said, gazing at the shard.

"That's Marcus Renegat. He's even wearing a navy-blue T-shirt and shorts like the ones in his closet," Barnes commented.

"It looks like Marcus was brutally beaten before being stabbed in the face. The fingers on his right hand are twisted backward, and the bones inside the appendages are likely shattered. You can tell from the swelling. There must have been a scuffle. But ultimately, it was a bullet to the cranium that ended his life," the forensics technician told them.

"Looks like from point-blank range." Barnes leaned in close.

Fackender added her take on it, helping them both to paint a vivid picture of how things went down. "Looks like a crime of rage."

Mr. Sobieski had also suffered lacerations to his face, cheek, and left eye socket. "Someone was definitely looking to get revenge," Barnes mused.

Fackender shook her head in dismay. "They certainly got it."

A Davison area detective stepped away from the crowd of agents searching the grounds for additional clues to greet them both. "I'm Detective Green. I've been assigned to the case. I hear you may have some background information for me." He stretched his hand toward Barnes for a proper greeting. "I'd love it if you two wouldn't mind heading over to the department so that we could put our heads together and identify these bodies."

Barnes accepted his hand, and the two men shook. "Detective Barnes. Pleased to meet you."

Detective Barnes glanced over at Fackender, then confirmed what they had already surmised. "It looks like Principal Sobieski didn't run off with some bimbo, like his daughter told us he did." He shook his head in despair as he glanced down at the bodies.

"That's them, all right, Detective. Mr. Renegat is even wearing his favorite color," Fackender said, alluding to one of the dead men's navy-blue shorts and T-shirt, as she gazed at his stiffened corpse.

Detective Green frowned. "Someone had to be strong enough to get rid of two healthy, able-bodied men. That takes skill, not to mention training."

Jackson Pierce's military training made him an excellent candidate. Unfortunately, there was no evidence against him. Regardless, Barnes was intent on finding him. The mere fact that he was Marcus's neighbor made him, at the very least, a possible witness to the goings-on across the hall.

Chapter 16

Planting Seeds of Doubt

Evelyn parked her truck in front of the Ravishes' residence, having decided to travel to the greenhouse on foot. She'd rummaged through her closet and found the tightest spandex she could in her vast wardrobe, so that her curves were complemented in a way that would seem irresistible to almost anyone of the opposite sex with a pair of eyes. The sly seductress had made it a point to remain modest as far as bearing skin, only leaving her arms and shoulders exposed. Antagonizing the woman of the house so soon would be far too risky. Her intention was to win Jocelyn over. She believed in keeping her enemies close. Although Colin's wife hadn't done a thing to be considered Evelyn's enemy, she'd at the very least earned the title of competitor.

A wide path had been cleared through thick brush, and oak trees abound, making it easier to navigate the rear of the property. The five-minute hike brought her to the entrance of the greenhouse. With how she would go about exacting her plan at the forefront of her thoughts, Evelyn peered in at Jocelyn through the windows of the structure and watched as she trudged from aisle to aisle, sweeping up loose vegetation to be discarded.

Look at her dragging herself along. How tired and weak she is, Evelyn thought. *This will be like taking candy from a baby. There is no way she can perform like I can.* "It's showtime," she uttered in a low voice before entering the glasshouse with supreme confidence.

"Hi there," Evelyn called, garnering Jocelyn's attention. "Remember me?"

"Well, hello." Jocelyn moved toward the entrance, closing the gap between them. "Colin told me you were coming. I apologize for the other day. My condition is more of a hindrance some days than others. Unfortunately, it affects my vision as well, so this is my first time seeing your face clearly. It's very nice to meet you. Evelyn, right?" She set her broom aside, removed one of her gardening gloves, then extended her bare hand to their new employee.

Evelyn accepted the proffered hand, and the two women shared a handshake. "That's me. I'm glad to see you're feeling better."

"Well, as good as can be expected."

"If you don't mind me asking, what is it that's ailing you?"

"I struggle with MS."

"I see. I'm so sorry."

"Don't be. It's not as if you wished this on me. Besides, you coming to help will assist me tremendously. You just don't know the sigh of relief I breathed when my husband told me he'd hired someone. I'm looking forward to your presence here making my life much easier, I assure you. That being said, allow me to show you what we'll be doing today."

Evelyn followed, not taking her eyes off Jocelyn as she moved about.

"You can start here on this row of plants. The buckets, gloves, and scissors are in the cabinet near the entrance. When you're done trimming one plant, you can just move on to the next. It doesn't have to be perfect. We'll be going over them a second time, anyway. If you need something to drink, there's a bucket full of bottled waters up there as well. I was going to go to the store later to pick up more supplies. Do you think you'll be okay if I leave you here alone?"

"I'm sure I can manage."

"Well, the two ATVs outside both have the keys in the ignition, so if you need to use the bathroom you can just drive up to the main house."

"Sounds like a plan. Let me just grab my bucket, scissors, and gloves, and then I'll pick a plant to work on."

"I'll be right here, if you have any questions." Jocelyn took a seat on the upturned bucket beside a plant she'd previously worked on.

"I've never clipped marijuana plants before. Do you mind if I sit by you while I work?"

"Please. I recommend it, in fact. The last thing we want is for you to cut off too much." Jocelyn set up a bucket near hers. "Here's the perfect spot."

"I appreciate it." Evelyn raced back to the entrance, grabbed a pair of gloves and scissors from the cabinet, then walked back over and took a seat beside Jocelyn.

"So, tell me a little bit about yourself. Do you have any children? I don't mean to pry. It's just a welcomed change to have someone to talk to out here," Jocelyn said.

"It's fine. I don't mind the prying. I have three wonderful children and one of the most compassionate husbands a woman could ever ask for."

Evelyn counted on her admission to give Jocelyn the comfort she needed. Being married meant she wasn't a threat. That alone would ensure Jocelyn dropped her guard, if indeed her walls were up.

"Wonderful. I'm hoping Colin and I will have children someday. He's not too eager, because of my condition. Sometimes I think my husband worries about me too much."

"You're his wife and, quite frankly, his world, if it's just the two of you."

"I guess you're right. I should probably stop being so pushy. I just feel like my biological clock is ticking faster."

"You should enjoy your time together while you can." Evelyn clipped away at the leaves of her assigned plant.

Jocelyn was inclined to take offense but figured making assumptions would be a bit too presumptuous. "What do you mean?"

"Once you have children, there will be little alone time for the two of you," Evelyn explained, masking the true meaning of her statement.

Evelyn's perspective made Jocelyn worry. Not because she wanted her alone time with her husband, but because the revelation brought into question Colin's true motives. She had to ask herself if her husband was actually holding off on having children because he valued his freedom much more than the family they'd planned to have together before saying their vows. As the relationship stood now, they could go anywhere, do pretty much anything they pleased. A baby would be a drastic change for them. A change she wasn't sure Colin could handle . . .

"I hadn't really thought about that," she said.

"It's a good time to start."

The beginnings of Evelyn's plan had taken shape: creating doubt where there was once certainty.

Across town, Erick pulled into the driveway, having picked Bryson up from school that day.

"Are we still going to toss around the ball, like you promised? I need to get some practice in if I'm going to be in the major leagues when I grow up."

"We can toss the ball around for a few. But only for a little while. I'd like to have dinner cooking when your mom gets home from work. She started her other job today."

"Okay. I'll go get my ball and glove." Bryson darted from his father's pickup truck before Erick had the opportunity to change his mind.

"I'll meet you out back," he replied, the door slamming in the middle of his response.

Erick got out of his truck, then headed toward the backyard. He hadn't been back there since Mr. Fuboi's death. His puppy's toy bone still floated there in the center of the pool. *It's about time I tidied this up*, Erick told himself. As he leaned in to put things back the way they were, he caught sight of the cord attached to one corner of the tarp. He moved closer to that corner, kneeled down, and frowned as he studied the condition of the cord. He had thought that at the very least some wear and tear would be visible, given that Mr. Fuboi had weighed the tarp down before it had come loose. *That's odd*, he thought as he rose to his feet to take a gander at the cord on the opposite end of the tarp. No signs of wear and tear there, either, caused him concern. *How is it that the cords did not snap?* he asked himself. He was sure he had tied them to the bolts in the cement as tight as possible.

"You ready?" Bryson called out as he darted from the sliding glass door in the kitchen to meet his father, as planned.

Erick quickly turned to address his eager boy. "I'm ready. Let's get some practice in."

Out of nowhere, Bryson whipped the ball Erick's way, trying to catch his father off guard.

Erick caught the ball barehanded. "You've got to be much quicker than that."

Bryson's eyes lit up with wonder. "Can you teach me how to do that?"

"All in due time, my son. All in due time." He tossed the baseball back across the yard to Bryson. "So, are you excited about going to the zoo tomorrow?"

"I can't wait."

"Your mom should be pretty excited too. She always did love animals."

"I'm not sure if she still does. She's not really the same mama she was before the accident," Bryson revealed before he threw the ball.

"What makes you say that? Are you two doing okay?" Erick caught the ball and held it, eager to hear what his son had to say.

"We're doing great. I'm so glad she's back home. I hope she never has to be away from us again."

"Well, what do you think is so different about her?"

"She doesn't take anyone's crap anymore. You should have seen how she took up for me the other day against Domonic and his dad."

"What do you mean? Is someone picking on you at school?"

"Don't worry. He was, but Mama took care of it. Thanks to her, I haven't had to deal with him messing with me every day. As a matter of fact, I haven't had to look at him for days."

"Did he change classes?"

Bryson shrugged. "No. I haven't seen him at all. I think he got suspended."

"Serves him right." Erick threw the ball, and Bryson caught it with the tip of his glove. "Why didn't you tell me someone was picking on you?"

"I didn't want you to think I was a wimp." Bryson tossed the ball with all the strength he could muster.

"Next time I'd appreciate you having the same confidence in me that you had in your mom."

"I'm sorry, Dad. I didn't mean to keep secrets from you. Mom made me confess. She can be pretty convincing with her big eyeballs."

Erick chuckled. "I know what you mean, son. They are rather piercing."

"Hey, Dad, I thought you said you were going to get me more tapes for my camcorder. I don't have any more."

Erick looked up at the camcorder in Bryson's bedroom window. "What exactly have you been taping, Bryson? You know those tapes are expensive. You shouldn't be wasting them by filming any little thing."

"Mrs. Jones said it's unlikely we have deer that cross over our property. I intend to prove her wrong."

"I see," Erick replied, his mind fixed on recent events. If the camcorder had been pointing out the window at the time of Mr. Fuboi's drowning, he could see exactly what had transpired when he wasn't peering from the attic window that day. It was all he could think about until their rottweiler, Sheba, came barreling toward them, a limp rodent hanging from her mouth.

Sheba roamed the perimeter, bound by her electric collar, keeping the grounds safe from coyotes and free of pests.

"What cha got there, girl?" Erick knelt to see what the dog had in her mouth. "Those moles are no match for you, old girl." His gentle caress of her head told the faithful pooch she'd done a good job. "Come on." Erick stood to his feet, then proceeded to lead Sheba over to a five-foot-deep hole in the ground. A tarp covered the five-foot-by-five-foot rodent grave. It was where they buried them all, until the hole was full. Then, of course, they would cover it with dirt and grass seed before digging another. Sheba had filled over a half dozen holes since the Todds took up residence on their property.

Erick uncovered the hole, then allowed Sheba to drop in the dead mole. "Good girl!"

"Come on, Dad! Are we going to play or not?"

Erick trotted back toward his boy, Sheba alongside him. "Let's go school this kid, Sheba."

Chapter 17

Gathering Intel

Back at the Ravishes', Jocelyn had just climbed into her silver Audi and was about to head off to town to purchase more supplies. She gave the center of the steering wheel two quick taps, honking her horn, before pulling away from the house. Although Colin wasn't home, honking had become a habit of hers. The couple would always honk the horn before leaving as their final "See you later" and upon returning as their initial hello.

Jocelyn had been at the greenhouse earlier and had told Evelyn that she had errands to run and would be gone for a little while. Evelyn couldn't wait to make her way up to the house and search it once the coast was clear. The more info she could find out about their marriage, the better. Dividing the couple would be a delicate operation, but in order to dismantle the bond Jocelyn and Colin shared, Evelyn had to learn what cemented it. She wanted to know their likes and dislikes. Then she could use this information against them.

Fifteen minutes after Jocelyn's departure from the greenhouse, Evelyn rushed to one of the ATVs and sped to the big house. Once she made it to the front door, she crept inside. "Hello! Jocelyn? Colin? Is anyone home?" She had to be sure the coast was clear prior to beginning her search. Other than the sound of the water streaming from that waterfall in their living room, the house was silent. Evelyn walked down the hallway where Colin had previously carried his ailing wife. *Bedrooms are always full of secrets*, the deceitful woman assured herself as she made her way to Colin and Jocelyn's.

Bedroom furniture made of glass and chrome decorated their love den. Evelyn peered up at the vaulted ceiling, questioning how it was the couple managed to afford such luxury. Photos displayed on the shelves of their entertainment center spoke of Jocelyn's affluent lineage. On the left, the images depicted her worldwide travel with her parents, from birth to adulthood, which told Evelyn that her competition was a woman with vast knowledge of the world around her. On the right were photos of her and Colin during their adventures to those very same parts of the globe. The couple looked rather happy in the memories showcased. Judging by the time stamps on some of their photos, they had been together since they were in high school. Evelyn worried whether she would be able to break such a bond. This thought lasted only for a moment before she concluded that Colin had to be growing tired of the feeble woman.

She moved on to the large walk-in closet, stocked with clothes, shoes, and other accessories. It seemed Jocelyn had taken a particular liking to the designer Ferragamo, as had Colin. Belts, shoes, timepieces, and even purses by the Italian designer filled the shelves. Evelyn perused Colin's side of the closet, which occupied more square footage than Jocelyn's. As she let her hand run across Colin's dress suits, her foot grazed a cardboard box stuffed halfway underneath his hanging slacks. The new discovery looked interesting enough to delve into.

She retrieved the box, then pulled back the folded flaps, revealing a stockpile of birthday, anniversary, and holiday greeting cards all addressed to Colin. Evelyn removed one of the cards from its unsealed envelope, then read its message. *Happy twenty-fifth birthday, son. You'll always be the center of our universe, Cutty.* Cutty was his nickname from childhood, she guessed. When Evelyn closed the card and placed it back into the envelope, she noticed an address printed on the left top corner. It was a Clarkston address. Her eyes then moved to the postmarked date in the top right corner. "His birthday is coming up," she said aloud to herself.

Just then, the disarmed security alarm chimed as Jocelyn entered the house. "I swear, you'd forget your head if it weren't attached to your body, Jocelyn," she scolded herself as she rushed through the foyer, then down the dark hallway to get to her bedroom as quickly as possible. The Ferragamo tote bag that sat atop the nightstand housed just what she was looking for.

Leaning against the wall, Evelyn displayed nerves of steel as she hid behind the closet door, clutching a Louisville Slugger. Jocelyn snatched her wallet from the tote bag, then turned back to leave her bedroom. That was when she noticed something strange. The closet light was on, and the door was ajar. She frowned, unable to recall leaving the light on. She tiptoed, moving cautiously, toward the walk-in closet, ready for what was to come next. "Evelyn! Is that you?"

Silence.

She peeked inside after receiving no response. The coast was clear. Not a person in sight. Just to be sure, she scanned the far corners of the closet. Nothing. There was still the space behind the opened door. It was the last place she thought to check. Her heart raced. She worried that someone was hiding behind it. Leaving the front door unlocked was risky, especially since they grew marijuana on the property; however, the only other option would have been to give Evelyn a key, and that, in Jocelyn's opinion, was absolutely out of the question. She inched closer to the door. Little by little she mustered the courage to snatch the knob, pull the door toward her, and peek around it. No one was there. There was nothing other than the bat Evelyn had previously held as she'd contemplated bashing Jocelyn's head in.

"You're overreacting again, Jocelyn," she whispered, her panic, which had ramped up mere seconds ago, dissipating. She pushed the closet door back, then shut off the light before leaving the bedroom and pulling the door shut.

Once Evelyn heard the bedroom door close, she felt it was safe to emerge from behind the hanging garments. She could have easily gotten rid of Jocelyn then, but the risk of being caught was far too great. Besides, Colin's wife had done nothing to deserve death. Not yet, anyway . . .

It wasn't until Jocelyn had hopped back in her vehicle that she noticed the ATV parked out front. "What the hell?" She adjusted her rearview mirror to see it better, thinking something was just not right. Evelyn must be inside the house. But how could I have missed her? she thought, stepping back out of her car to reenter the home. Jocelyn tore up the porch stairs, then pushed open the front door, coming face-to-face with Evelyn.

"Oh my gosh," both women blurted in unison as they placed their hands on their chest.

"You scared me," Evelyn said.

"I scared you? You scared me," Jocelyn replied, looking her over. "It was you in my closet. Why are you wearing my sweater?" At that moment, the tension between the women was palpable.

"I'm so sorry. I don't mean to seem too presumptuous by borrowing it. It's just that when I was watering some of the plants, my shirt got all wet. My lady parts were showing through, and I felt it would be inappropriate to walk around like that, being that your husband will be home soon. I can take it off when I get ready to leave, or now if it makes you uncomfortable letting me wearing it."

Jocelyn appreciated the fact that she would go to such lengths to cover herself, but she felt uneasy about Evelyn going into her bedroom without permission. "Why didn't you say anything when I called out to you?"

Evelyn took no time coming up with a plausible excuse. "I didn't hear a thing. I must have been in the bathroom by the mudroom, changing."

"Well, I appreciate you being considerate and covering up, but that sweater is one I don't work in. You see it's cashmere, and I would hate to ruin it. Let me get you one of Colin's hoodies. He won't mind it reeking of marijuana."

"I completely understand." Evelyn removed the purple sweater, revealing her protruding nipples.

Jocelyn's eyes widened. "Wow . . . I see what you mean."

Evelyn covered them bashfully. "The things us women have to worry about."

"Let me get the hoodie for you." Jocelyn headed off to the back of the house.

Erick made certain he'd given Bryson a task that would keep him busy while he searched for the tapes. He hoped that if he found footage of Mr. Fuboi in the backyard that fateful day, his conscience would be cleared. The possibility that it was Evelyn who had murdered Mr. Fuboi had haunted him every day since his neighbor's death.

First, he checked the camcorder by popping open the tape slot. Of course, it was empty. The suspicious husband placed the camcorder back on the tripod, then searched his brain to figure out the easiest place for Bryson to store the tapes. Bryson wasn't tall, by any means. So the tapes had to be somewhere he could easily reach, Erick surmised. That was when his gaze settled on the full-sized bed at the center of the spacious room. It seemed the most plausible place to look. He had purchased over thirty tapes for Bryson over the years, so the box he was looking for had to be large enough to house them all. Erick dropped to his knees alongside the bed and lifted the bed skirt to peek underneath. That was when he saw it. The shoebox sat there, all by its lonesome. The anxious father reached into the dark space and pulled the box toward him. It was as if he already knew what he would find. It was a fact that shook him to his very core.

"She's your wife, Erick. You, of all people, should have faith in her," he said aloud, trying to convince himself of Evelyn's innocence—an effort that was futile at best. Regardless, Erick had to know the truth once and for all. He pulled the lid from the shoebox, revealing a mass of tapes, each one labeled with the date of its recording. Unfortunately, not one of the dates matched the date of Mr. Fuboi's death. In fact, the recordings stopped well before the incident took place. Erick's discovery failed to provide the peace of mind he so desperately needed, yet the false sense of relief that came over him once he saw there was no tape of that *event* would carry him throughout the remainder of his day. Besides, they had a great day at the zoo planned for tomorrow, just he, Evelyn, and Bryson. The time to let sleeping dogs lie had come, with not an ounce of closure as to what had really happened that fateful day.

"Dad, what are you doing?" Bryson had crept up behind his father without him noticing.

"You said you needed tapes. There wasn't one in the camcorder, and I forgot what kind you needed. Luckily, I found the box." He covered the tapes with the lid, then slid the shoebox back to where he had found it, maintaining a nonchalant demeanor. The last thing he wanted to do was cause Bryson to mistrust his mother.

"Thanks, Dad. I'll be happy to finally be able to record again."

Erick stood. "No problem, son. How about you get cleaned up, so that you can help me get dinner ready? That is, unless you have homework."

"Nope. No homework. I don't even have school tomorrow, remember?"

"That's right. I forgot. It is the weekend. Okay. Well, go on and get cleaned up. I'll see you in the kitchen."

Evelyn peered down at her wristwatch, having been in the glasshouse for hours. Just her alone, pruning one plant after another. *Where the hell is she?* Evelyn thought for sure Jocelyn would be back by now, but neither she nor Colin had shown up to help.

Even though the time for her to head home had come, she hesitated leaving, knowing the main house was unlocked. That was when she heard a fit of laughter erupt just outside. Evelyn turned to see Colin holding his wife captive as he tickled her side. Jocelyn tried to break free from his clutches, but with little effort, allowing him to pull her in close for a warm embrace. As the pair locked lips, a small part of Evelyn died inside. She hated seeing them staring into one another's eyes, so close, so intimate. How desperately Evelyn wanted to be his partner. *All in due time*, she told herself, trying to keep her optimistic outlook intact. Still, she couldn't help feeling slighted. They had left her there alone for hours. The fact that she hadn't had the opportunity to spend time with Colin left her seething inside. "Spoiled little bitch," she mumbled behind clenched teeth.

"How's everything going so far?" Colin inquired as he and Jocelyn entered the greenhouse, huge smiles plastered on their faces.

"It's going pretty good. I think I'm done for today. I should probably be getting home to get dinner prepared." Evelyn faked a smile, as if she were just as happy as they were.

"Of course. I'll give you a ride back up to the house." Colin turned to Jocelyn. "Honey, we can finish hanging the rest of the plants ourselves tonight."

"I'm sure we can handle it. The last thing we want to do is overwork you. We really appreciate the help, Evelyn."

"I appreciate the job. My other one is a bit too much for me to handle at the current time."

"Looks like it worked out perfectly for us all," Jocelyn noted. "I hope you enjoy the rest of your night, Evelyn. I'm going to get started hanging these plants. Work off some of the dinner we just had before it ruins my figure . . ."

Her revelation angered Evelyn even further. *They left me working here alone to have dinner together. How rude*, she thought, feeling it was best she got out of there before her agitation began to surface. "Well, I'm ready when you are."

"Off we go, then." Colin furnished his wife with a peck on the lips. "I'll be right back, honey."

Jocelyn nodded. "I'll be here waiting."

Colin and Evelyn headed out, and Colin gave her a ride up to the main house, where her truck was parked. Once they had pulled up alongside her SUV, Evelyn climbed off the ATV, then proceeded to remove the oversized blue hoodie draped over her torso.

Colin's eyes widened as he peered at her protruding nipples. "Ahem," he said, pretending he was clearing his throat, a bit embarrassed at having noticed she'd taken notice of his interest.

"I got all wet down at the greenhouse. I hope you don't mind." She handed the hoodie over to him.

"Of course not. We wouldn't want you to get sick." He played it off as if the startling moment hadn't happened.

"Bye, Colin. I guess I'll see you later," Evelyn uttered seductively as she climbed into her SUV under his watchful eyes.

Chapter 18

To the Surface

A mass of people had lined up that morning to see the animals. A light breeze rustled the leaves of the maple trees around them as three members of the Todd family headed into the Detroit Zoo. Excited to begin his zoo experience, Bryson rushed ahead to be first in line at the ice cream vendor's stand. With nearly 125 acres of land to peruse, they planned to make a day of it, visiting some of the boy's favorite attractions, among them the National Amphibian Conservation Center and the Great Apes of Harambee.

Erick looked past the zoo visitors in front of him to keep an eye on Bryson. "Slow down, Bryson! We have all day, son! There's no need to rush!" he called out.

Evelyn smiled softly. "He's really excited, huh?"

"He is . . . This is actually your and Bryson's favorite place to visit. Me, I'm more of a movie buff, but you and Bryson, on the other hand, have always been partial to animals."

The excited boy waved his parents over. "Come on, slowpokes!"

"We're coming . . . We're coming." Evelyn picked up speed.

Erick maintained his pace, choosing to lag behind so that he could snap pictures of his wife and son with the

Nikon camera hanging around his neck. For the first time since she had been back home, he witnessed love between the mother and son. When she reached Bryson, Evelyn ran her hand through the short brown curls atop Bryson's head as he picked out his favorite ice cream flavor. The young woman working the stand handed over his waffle cone with two huge scoops of Superman ice cream packed inside it, and then off they went.

"Hey, wait up!" Erick broke into a jog, closing the gap between them. "So where to first?"

"Can we go see the monkeys first?"

"If that's what you want to see, Bryson, that's where we'll head," his mother told him.

They followed the path, passing by a plethora of attractions—the Holden Reptile Conservation Center, the Butterfly Garden, and the American Grasslands—to get to the African Forest. As they neared the habitat, they could hear lots of monkeying around taking place. Barks, screams, squeaks, wails, even grunts filled the air as a group of chimpanzees lounged about on the gigantic rocks, basking in the sun. Some chewed on plants; others flashed wide smiles to signal their aggression toward other chimpanzees.

"Look, Mama, they're gonna fight," Bryson exclaimed before he ran ahead to witness the commotion. Just as the eager boy went to stand at the railing, a woman rushed in and pushed him aside to take his spot, causing Bryson's butt to hit the ground.

He peered up at her from the ground. "Hey! That was my spot."

"Finders keepers, losers weepers," she whispered, assuming he was with the group of boy scouts lined up at the railing.

An instant wave of anger surged through Evelyn's core. Before Erick could even respond, she grabbed the woman by her mane of blond hair and pulled her down to the ground.

"Ah! Ow! What the hell is your deal?!" the woman screamed.

Oohs and ohs erupted from the crowd of onlookers. All eyes had moved from the monkeys to the quarreling women.

Evelyn leaned in closer, so that the blonde could hear her without her raising her voice. "Word of advice. Next time I'd advise you to be more mindful of whose kid you put your greasy palms on." Not satisfied yet with her retaliation, she stepped on the woman's corn dog, which lay on the cement beside her.

Although the woman was inclined to respond angrily, the foreboding look in Evelyn's eyes warned her against it. "I didn't see him there," she said meekly, trying to spin her way out of this situation.

"That's an easy fix. Open your fucking eyes next time."

The woman stood and dusted off her stonewashed jeans. "I'm sorry," she apologized.

"That I can see." Evelyn walked away to join her husband and son at the railing.

Erick stood in awe of his wife's courage. "Wow . . . I've never seen you react so aggressively."

"Nobody touches my kid. Period."

Bryson nudged his father, then whispered, "I told you she was different."

"Come on, Bryson." Evelyn held out her arm for her son to stand beside her. "Let's look at the chimpanzees. Erick, honey, can you take a photo of us?"

"Say cheese."

After the gruesome discovery of Mr. Renegat and Mr. Sobieski's bodies, the Oakland County Sheriff's Office decided to release a statement, hoping to flush out their perp. Detective Barnes stepped out of the station and went before the camera, ready to give an official statement to the gathering crowd of reporters. He cleared his throat, then straightened his tie, prepared to brief them on recent findings.

"Yesterday the bodies of two Clarkston residents were found in Davison, Michigan. The corpses of two middle-aged males, who were thought to have been relocated, were dredged up from the bottom of Lake Callis. It is with great sorrow that I announce that Marcus Renegat, a Clarkston postal worker, and Richard Sobieski, Clarkston High School's beloved former principal, have been officially pronounced dead. We're asking that anyone with information that might lead to the discovery of the person or people responsible for these heinous crimes come forward now to assist in the efforts to get this maniac off the streets. A ten-thousand-dollar reward is being offered for their successful capture. Police are looking into several suspects in connection with the murders."

Barnes removed an eight-by-eleven-inch photograph from the manila folder in his hand, then held it up for all to see. Cameras flashed, snapping shots of the photo of the teenager with medium-length brown hair tucked behind his ears. "This is Andre Renegat, son of Marcus Renegat. If you have any information as to the whereabouts of the teen, please contact the Oakland County Sheriff's Office. As of right now, he is wanted for questioning and is not being accused of any crime. Because the bodies were found outside of our jurisdiction, we are working with Davison police to bring our perp to justice. Over the course of the past few months, our small town has been rocked with murder. We must bring this killer to justice and restore peace to Clarkston and its residents. I'll now take a few questions, but only a few. Then I'll have to get back to work on the case."

One of the female reporters blurted her question, speaking over the rest of the crowd. "Do you suspect these murders are linked to other recent attacks revolving around the Clarkston post office?"

"We are definitely looking into the possibility. Nothing can be ruled out at this point."

"What about the woman who survived an attack just months ago? Has she been able to identify her attacker?" the same reporter quizzed.

"We are planning to bring her in for questioning as well. Hopefully, she can shed some light on the subject. Even the smallest detail can yield great results." Barnes peered out into the crowd. "Anyone else?"

"How do you plan on stopping this killer if you don't even have a clue where they will strike next?" shouted a reporter from his spot deep in the crowd, his hand held high.

"We're going to put all the manpower we can on the streets. Officers will be doing regular patrols to make our presence felt. We will take back our town, and this murderer will answer for the horrific crimes they've committed."

That was when the mass of reporters began shouting their questions all at once.

"Please, one at a time!" Barnes yelled, trying his best to control the crowd.

Back at the zoo, the trio entered the Arctic Ring of Life, an interactive facility that housed seals, polar bears, and even arctic foxes. Bryson was in awe of the water dome that surrounded them. He didn't take his eyes off a pair of seals as they played with one another whirling round in circles above his head.

"Wow . . . This is so cool. It's like we're right in the water with them. I can't believe it," he said, his voice echoing throughout the glass corridor.

"They must have paid quite a bit to build this wing. It's pretty impressive. If only I could land a contract like this," Erick mused.

Evelyn didn't respond, still stewing in her thoughts.

"Are you okay, my love?"

"I'm okay. Just taking it all in. I can't believe I almost missed this."

"Don't think about that honey. You're safe now."

"You're right. I should focus more on the present. There's nothing for me to remember about the past, anyway, right?"

"You'll remember when you're ready. All in due time."

"I need to use the restroom. Can you and Bryson wait here for me? I won't be long. I'm sure there is a restroom nearby."

"Of course, my love. We'll be right here waiting for you."

Evelyn made her way through the small crowd of on-lookers to exit the glass corridor. She recalled seeing a restroom outside, not too far from the Arctic habitat. Piercing pains shot up her spine and radiated through-out her cranium. Evelyn sat down on a nearby bench, closed her eyes, wincing from the discomfort. Memories of that dreadful morning at the post office flashed before her. She recalled the way the masked assailant smelled when he forced her to the ground, just before the mail truck ended their encounter. The scent of his cologne was strong, as was the grip he had on the back of her neck and the joint between her neck and left shoulder.

Evelyn attempted to push the memory back into the depths of her psyche, so that it joined the memories that had yet to surface. "What the hell is wrong with me?" she mumbled as she slowly made her way to the ladies' restroom. She pinched the bridge of her nose as she pushed her way into the restroom, eager to get to the sink. Evelyn made her way over to one of the porcelain sinks, leaned in, then turned on the water as she cupped her hands underneath the faucet. She splashed cold water all over her face, then peered at her reflection in the mirror.

It's time to remember, Evelyn. Evelyn, you have to remember. Don't let him get away with it. He took everything from us. Everything. Everything is ruined now. Are you just going to let him get away with it? Do something, the voice in her head instructed. She closed her eyes, trying to drown out the penetrating sound. It wasn't until someone emerged from a restroom stall that she opened her eyes and tried to regain her composure. Unfortunately, composure would have to wait. Evelyn rubbed her damp hands across her khaki shorts to dry them off. The voice commanded her again to do something. *Don't just stand there. Do something.* She peered at the unsuspecting woman several sinks down from where she stood seething. It was the woman from the chimpanzee exhibit, the one who had pushed her son to the ground.

The woman hummed a tune blaring from her earbuds as she lathered up her hands for a good rinsing, completely oblivious to Evelyn's fast approach. After clutching the back of her head, Evelyn slammed the woman's face against the mirror above the sink, shattering the glass. When she yanked her back from the glass, blood oozed from the woman's head, painting her bosom and pink wife beater crimson. She then slammed the woman's face against the porcelain sink, knocking her unconscious. Evelyn released her grip, allowing the woman to drop to the cold cement floor.

See, that wasn't so bad, was it? the voice in her head inquired as Evelyn exited the restroom, feeling much better than she had when she'd entered.

Fackender and Barnes had finally retreated into the station, out from under the watchful gaze of the gathered crowd.

"Well, that went well," Fackender remarked.

"Let's just hope this little press conference yields some results. We need to subpoena the bank and phone records of both gentlemen. I'd also like to question Mrs. Todd. Maybe she can remember something that will put us on the right trail." Detective Barnes headed back to his office, with Fackender trailing closely.

"I'll get right on it, sir. Would you like me to contact Mrs. Todd?"

His mind exhausted from the day's events, Barnes plopped down in the chair behind his desk. "I'll get Evelyn Todd's statement. You focus on getting that subpoena for the bank records."

Fackender halted her steps at his office door. "Sounds like a plan. Call me if you stumble upon any new developments, and I'll do the same."

Chapter 19

Word Travels Fast

After hearing the news briefing on Michigan broadband radio, the tall, bald, caramel-complected, thirtysomething African American ex-marine had made plans to return to the small town of Clarkston to wrap up unfinished business. With a festering paranoia imploring him to take precautions, Jackson Pierce cruised north on Interstate 75, his white Ford Bronco nearing its destination. There was no way he would allow suspicion to be cast upon him. It was only a matter of time before Evelyn would come face-to-face with the masked assailant who had caused her memory to be washed away. Jackson pressed his boot to the gas pedal as he crossed over the border from Ohio into Michigan with one thing in mind. He had to silence the woman he had once thought was dead.

On their way home from the zoo, Erick battled the urge to question his wife's state of mind. He worried that her retaliation against the woman at the zoo had gone a bit too far. Had he known what she'd done to her within the confines of that restroom, Erick would have had her committed on the spot. He glanced back at Bryson, who remained focused on the movie playing in the headrest of his father's seat. It was then that he decided he couldn't wait any longer. Assuming the oversized headphones covering his son's ears drowned out all other sounds in the vehicle, Erick began his line of questioning.

"How are you feeling, my love?"

Evelyn turned to him, having peered silently out the passenger window since they'd started back home. "I feel great, honey. Why do you ask me that? Do I not seem okay?"

Erick treaded lightly, well aware of Evelyn's fragile state of mind. "Not at all. It's just that you had a pretty . . ." He paused, trying to think of the words befitting their experience at the zoo, before proceeding. "Active day today."

"If you're asking if I'm upset about the dispute I had with the woman who so rudely put her hands on my son, the answer is no. I'm not. She got what she deserved, so . . ." Evelyn shrugged her shoulders.

"I'm not saying you were wrong. I just think you should be a little more mindful of how you handle situations like that. Not everyone takes things lying down like she did."

All emotion drained from Evelyn's face. She couldn't help but feel miffed by her husband's comment. "Do I look scared to you?"

"Honey, that's not what I meant."

"Then please, by all means, clarify what it is you meant. I want to understand, Erick."

"You don't have to get all defensive. I'm not her."

"In a sense, you sure seem to be taking up for her."

"I'm not taking up for her. She put her hands on our son. I'm simply saying not everyone takes physical retaliation lying down. What if she had pressed charges against you?"

"What if *I* had pressed charges against her?"

"Everyone saw what you did to her. Not everyone saw what she did to Bryson."

"Quite frankly, I don't care who saw what. I witnessed her hurt my child, and if you hurt my child, you get hurt. Period. End of story."

Erick let out an exhausted sigh. He hated that his comment had caused strife between him and Evelyn. His intentions were merely to make her aware of what could have transpired. "I'm not trying to argue with you."

"No. What you're doing is trying to talk me out of defending my child when the situation warrants."

"I would never be against you protecting our son," he retorted, emphasizing the *our* in his statement. "I just want you to be mindful of protecting yourself as well. I love you. You are my wife. We've already almost lost you once. If you were to end up in jail or worse, then what? What will we do? How do you think that would affect our kids? Please, I just want you to think before you react."

Or maybe you should leave the thinking up to him, since he stood there and did nothing, like a coward, the voice in her head reasoned. *Is that what you want to be? A coward like your husband?*

"Next time, I'll be more careful," Evelyn assured him, relenting, telling Erick exactly what he wanted to hear.

Bryson spotted a squad car parked in their driveway as the SUV bent the corner near their house. "Why are the police at our house?"

Evelyn's heart pounded; she was fearful of the police's intentions.

Uh-oh . . . I think you've been found out. You'd better get rid of them too, the voice in her head teased. Evelyn pinched the bridge of her nose, attempting to ignore the minor aggravation.

"I don't know why they're here, son. But I guess we're about to find out." Erick turned into the driveway.

"Bryson will do no such thing." Evelyn turned to their son. "I want you to go straight inside once we come to a stop."

Bryson didn't put up a fight. "Okay, Mama."

Even Erick was nervous. He hoped the police weren't there to cart his wife away for the murder of her longtime friend Elise.

The worry they harbored was evident to both of them as the couple locked eyes. Erick brought the SUV to a halt and shifted the gear into park.

"Go inside, Bryson." Evelyn removed her seat belt, then hopped out of the truck. She didn't want her son to see her being hauled off in cuffs.

Bryson climbed down out of the vehicle and did just as his mother had instructed.

Erick turned off the ignition, then stepped out of the vehicle to greet Detective Barnes. "Is there something we can help you with, Officer?"

"Please, call me Detective Barnes. I hate to bother you folks on this beautiful Saturday afternoon, but I need to ask your wife a few questions."

Erick raised an eyebrow. "In regard to?"

"The incident that happened at the Clarkston post office. Like I said, I hate to bother you, but we could really use your wife's help."

In unison Evelyn and Erick both breathed a sigh of relief. Detective Barnes wasn't there to make an arrest, after all.

"My wife is willing to help however she can." Erick stood next to Evelyn, caressing her back with his hand. "Right, my love?"

"I sure will try."

"Come on, honey." Erick extended his hand, directing Evelyn to take the lead up the walkway, then turned to Barnes. "Why don't you come inside, Detective?"

They entered the house, and from his spot in the foyer, Barnes admired his surroundings. Wow . . . You have a beautiful home."

"Thank you. That's all my wife's doing. Please, come this way and have a seat. Can we get you something to drink?" Erick stepped into the living room.

Detective Barnes refused the latter but took Erick up on his initial offer, making himself comfortable on the love seat in the living room once Evelyn had taken a seat in the armchair opposite. "No, thank you. I won't be long." His gaze fell on Evelyn. "Mrs. Todd . . ."

"Please, call me Evelyn."

"Evelyn. I understand you haven't had an easy road to recovery, but it's good to see you've finally been released from the hospital."

"It's been a challenge, but I'm managing."

"Well, there's no easy way to say this, so I'll just come right out with it. We have reason to believe the person who attacked you may have a connection to the recent murders committed here in Clarkston. It's not my intention to frighten you folks, but I'd like to make myself perfectly clear when I say you should definitely be taking precautions to keep yourself safe."

Erick sat down next to Evelyn and gently ran his hand across her back to comfort her. It was comfort he seemed to need just as much, if not more, than she did. "Are you saying my wife is in danger?"

Evelyn dropped her head in despair. *What am I going to do?* she thought. *What if he comes back for me?*

"I'm saying if the person that attacked her is indeed our perpetrator, she should be very cautious of her surroundings at all times." Barnes turned his focus to Evelyn, who was sitting there silently. "Evelyn . . . if there is anything you can tell us about that night, even the smallest thing, please I'd like to hear it. We have people that are trained to decipher even the smallest of details."

Evelyn remained silent, a captive of her thoughts. *Don't tell him a thing*, the voice warned. *We can handle this ourselves.*

"Evelyn, are you okay, my love?"

Her husband's words snatched her back to reality. "I'm okay, Erick." She looked up to address Detective Barnes. "I'm sorry, Detective. Unfortunately, my memory was damaged that night. I can't remember anything. Not even my family."

Her admission dashed nearly all Barnes's hopes of their finding the unsub. Their most promising lead had become a dead end. Barnes feared more deaths would soon befall their quaint little town. "I'm sorry to hear that, Evelyn. It looks like I've wasted your time here." He stood to leave.

Erick followed suit. "I'm sorry we couldn't be of more assistance, Detective. I'll show you out."

"Enjoy the rest of your day, Evelyn," Barnes said.

"You too, Officer." She nodded as he stepped away from the love seat.

"I'll be right back, my love. I'm going to see the detective out."

The moment she heard them walk out the front door, flashes of that terrifying early morning began to play in her head. What she had previously recalled unspooled like a movie. It all felt so real. Even the agony she felt that morning became ever more present in that moment. Evelyn squeezed her eyes shut, pinching the bridge of her nose, trying to keep herself from allowing the memory to drift away. If she could endure the dreaded feeling long enough, maybe a clue would reveal itself. She recalled the way he forced her to the ground, the way he loomed over her in that threatening stance, yet Evelyn couldn't see his face or the color of his skin. But somehow, she could smell his cologne, as if it were permeating her nostrils now. Her assailant reeked of it. Even as she ran out into the open, his stench lingered. Suddenly the truck's lights blinded her, forcing the recollection to vanish from her mind. Evelyn's eyes opened, and she saw Erick standing in front of her.

"Are you okay, honey?"

"It's just a headache. I'll be fine," she lied, refusing to admit to her husband that she'd recalled the fateful incident.

Don't tell him. If he knows, it'll ruin everything, the voice in her head demanded.

But maybe he can help, Evelyn thought, reasoning silently with the voice.

Help? How can he help? What's he going to do? Talk it out? We have to protect ourselves. It's the only way. We'll buy a gun. That's it . . . a gun, the voice demanded.

"Maybe you should lie down. You don't look so good." The crazed look in her eyes caused him concern.

"I think I should. Just for a little while." Evelyn stood, then proceeded to head back to their bedroom.

Erick ran his hands over his face from the frustration of it all. What if his wife's attacker returned to finish the job? How would he go about protecting his family? He pulled the card with Detective Barnes's number from the pocket of his jeans and looked it over. *Let's just hope I never have to use it*, he thought, shoving the card back down in his pocket.

Back at the station Officer Fackender and Detective Barnes met up to discuss their findings. Neither of them looked very happy.

"The lead was a complete waste of time. Mrs. Todd couldn't tell me a damn thing. She can't even remember the night she was attacked." Barnes flopped down in his chair, feeling the weight of his defeat. "She was our single solid lead." He loosened his tie in an attempt to calm his anxiety. "Please tell me you had better luck."

"Well, the news I've got isn't much better. It could take up to ten days to get the subpoena for the bank records." Fackender stood idly at his office door.

"We don't have ten days! Our perp is going to strike again. I can feel it in my bones, Fackender. Something is coming. If we sit by, waiting for paperwork to be filed, someone is going to die. I don't care if I have to go down there first thing in the morning and get the information myself. Something's gotta be done, and fast. I have a friend down at the branch who owes me a favor. Let's hope he sees the severity of our situation."

"Let's hope so."

Chapter 20

Temptation

The next morning Evelyn took it upon herself to drop Bryson off at school. "Hey, buddy, wait up." She stopped her little boy as he pulled at the door handle to hop out. "I got you something. I hope you like it." She turned, then handed him a miniature box.

"Wow. Thanks, Mama." He rushed to pop open the top to the box, revealing an anime-themed wristwatch. "I love it!"

"Do you know how to read an analog clock?"

Bryson eagerly strapped the watch onto his wrist. "You taught me how when I was six years old. I remember."

"Don't lose it, okay?" she said, with a foreboding look.

"I won't lose it. I'm a big boy. Are you going to pick me up from school?"

"Your dad and I haven't worked that out yet, but one of us will be here. I promise."

"Okay. I love you, Mama."

"Catch you later, alligator."

Bryson chuckled. "You're supposed to say, 'See you later, alligator.' And then I say, 'After a while, crocodile.'"

"Then I'll see you later, crocodile," she teased, secretly aware of the right words.

"It's alligator, Mama!"

She smiled, cluing him in that she was goofing around. "Have a good day at school, son."

"Have a good day at work, Mama." Bryson hopped out of the SUV.

Evelyn watched her son until he was safely inside the building before pulling off to commence her day. The fact that her attacker was still on the loose had begun to agitate her, and so had the nagging voice in her head. She was agitated enough to keep guessing what his next move would be. Be that as it may, her anxiety wasn't as high as Erick's. The fact that she was the one who'd murdered Mr. Fuboi, Mr. Daniels, and Elise was enough to plant seeds of doubt about her attacker's return. As she cruised down Main Street now, completely oblivious to her surroundings, Evelyn allowed her paranoia to fade into the background and brought Colin back to the forefront of her thoughts.

Jackson popped open the medicine bottle he'd retrieved from the dash, then spilled out his dose of Prozac for the day in his hand. He was to take it as prescribed to combat his anxiety as well as his violent mood swings. One pill every morning was what the doctor at Veteran Affairs had ordered. Jackson watched patiently from the driver's seat of his parked Bronco until Evelyn had passed by, then began to pursue his target. He didn't know what she remembered of the morning he assaulted her, and the last thing he wanted to do was alert her of his presence, so for now, he would watch and wait for the perfect time to execute his plan.

At the same time, Evelyn was busy working on her own plan. She figured stopping to pick up a couple of frappes for herself and Jocelyn would be a great way to start the day. Evelyn walked into the bustling café and considered the many choices at her disposal.

"Who's up next?" a young, red-headed barista called, and then she motioned for Evelyn to step forward.

"I haven't done this in a long time," Evelyn confessed.

"Hey, medium mocha frappe, no chocolate drizzle, heavy whip. It's been a long time." She smiled softly. "We all wondered how you were doing." She raised her hand to usher over one of her fellow employees at the opposite end of the counter. "Hey, Josh, look who it is!"

Josh rushed over, catching a glimpse of Evelyn on his way down the counter. "Oh my gosh! We thought you were dead!" the flamboyant young man shouted when he saw it was her.

The red-headed barista reprimanded him by giving him a backhanded tap on the chest. "He didn't mean it like that. We had just heard you were hurt pretty bad."

"I'm sorry, but I don't recall your faces," Evelyn told them.

"Can you remember anything?" a wide-eyed Josh asked, leaning over the counter.

"I can't say I do." That was when she began to smell something familiar. A scent reminiscent of her worst recollections. The scent became so strong that she completely tuned out the two at the counter, then turned her head to see the person wearing it. Right behind stood a man. Evelyn's gaze traveled up his torso, beyond his muscular pecs, until she and Jackson were face-to-face.

"Do I know you?" she asked frankly. Evelyn had no recollection of her former coworker.

Although Jackson saw her disconnect plainly, he couldn't be sure whether his identity would suddenly dawn on her. "I don't know. Do you?" he replied, testing the waters.

"It's just that you're standing awfully close. I wouldn't want someone to get the wrong idea."

The slight was a blow to his ego. Jackson had always had a thing for Evelyn. Yet no matter how much he hated her, it didn't diminish his desire for her. Playing it cool, he stepped back, leaving an arm's length of distance between them. "I apologize. I must be really excited about the coffee." He smiled, further masking his insecurities.

Evelyn quickly turned back to the counter. "I'll have that thing you mentioned before. Two actually, please."

"Chile," Josh remarked, making it apparent he'd noticed the shadiness in Evelyn's interaction with Jackson.

"Two medium mocha frappes, no drizzle, heavy whip, coming right up." The barista flung her long red ponytail behind her back, then got to work filling the order.

Evelyn stepped to the side and scanned the contents of the glass case before her. There were doughnuts, croissants, tarts, Danish, scones, and slices of pie, along with a plethora of other pastries, all showcased under a shimmering light. Regardless of how enticing that assortment looked, the only thing Evelyn could think about was the scent of that damn cologne. *It's him. It has to be. You can't deny it. I won't let you*, the voice in her head insisted. *There's got to be hundreds of men in the area who wear that same cologne*, she thought, silently reasoning with the irrational part of her brain.

Figuring the only way to reach a solid conclusion about the man's identity would be to find out more, she turned to him and said, "Your cologne is very intoxicating. What brand is it?"

"It's Light Blue, by Dolce & Gabbana," he revealed, eager to share the name of his choice fragrance.

"I've never heard of it."

"It's certainly not cheap."

"I bet." Evelyn gave him a fleeting smile before grabbing the cup holder containing her frappes from the to-go counter. "Enjoy your day."

She exited the café, then quickly climbed into her truck and placed the cup holder with the frappes on the middle console. Instead of driving off, she waited. Curious, she wanted to see which vehicle the stranger drove and, more importantly, whether or not he'd follow her. After watching him hop into his Bronco, coffee in hand, she started up her SUV. Evelyn cruised by Jackson, as if completely oblivious to his presence.

The coast was clear. Jackson had surmised as much, anyway. He followed Evelyn down major streets for several minutes, until she veered off onto one of the back roads. *It'll only be a matter of time before she notices me*, he thought, worried, as the landscape had become more rural, with nothing but trees in their vicinity. Finally, a narrow dirt road on the right side presented him with a way out. Jackson turned off the back road onto the narrow one, leaving Evelyn to continue her journey alone.

"Going so soon?" She glanced at each of her mirrors, one after the other, trying to spot him. There was no sign of the stranger with the familiar cologne as she peered out into the densely wooded area.

He'll be back, the voice in her head warned. *He'll be back, and we'll be ready*. Her alter ego was already plotting.

After traveling the back road for a few miles, she came upon the graveled road leading to the Ravishes' home. Evelyn's focus quickly shifted to the object of her desire, Colin. *I hope he's home early*, she thought as she pulled to a stop in front of the main house. She climbed down out of her Yukon and then retrieved the frappes. As she was closing the driver's side door, Evelyn could see a cloud of dust rising into the air. Seconds later an ATV came up over the hill, heading in her direction. To her delight, Colin was driving. He smiled when he caught sight of her. Oh, how she loved that smile. . . . His gleaming white teeth and perfectly chiseled chin made her lustful heart flutter.

He pulled up alongside her. "Want a ride?"

She stared into his eyes, wanting to straddle him right then and there, but reined in her urge, worried she might seem too hasty. "I'd love one."

"I see you brought coffee. I'll try my best not to make you spill it, but as you know, the road gets a little bumpy."

"They're frappes," Evelyn remarked, lifting the cup holder as she climbed onto the four-wheeler and sat behind him. "And I have perfect balance, by the way."

"Hang on. Just in case." Colin pulled off, then cautiously made a U-turn to head back down the path toward the greenhouse.

Once they made it there, he hopped off first, then grabbed the cup holder from Evelyn so that she could climb off with minimal effort.

"Where is Jocelyn?" Once she was back on her feet, she looked around, casing the scene to judge just how far she could go.

"She had a doctor's appointment. She shouldn't be too long."

"I guess the second frappe is for you, then." Evelyn reached for one of the frappes, leaving little distance between them. "I love that smell," she said as she handed him the cup.

Colin assumed Evelyn's compliment referred to his cologne. "Thank you," he hastily remarked, his chest puffed out under his V-neck white tee.

Evelyn noticed how her words seemed to stroke his ego. "I was referring to the coffee. But I have to admit, you do smell delightful as well."

Colin chuckled lightly. "What an interesting choice of words."

"Well, if I had said *sexy*, it would've made you uncomfortable." She removed her coffee from the holder, which was still in his grasp.

"It would take much more than that to make me uncomfortable. I doubt if anyone could accomplish that."

"You're very sure of yourself."

"It comes naturally."

"Does it?" she murmured before taking a sip of her coffee. Somehow his words came off as a challenge. A challenge Evelyn gladly accepted . . . .

She headed toward the greenhouse, and Colin trailed behind her. He tried not to look down at her rear as she walked ahead of him. A futile effort at best. *Look, but don't touch*, he reminded himself. Over the years Colin had built up a mass of self-control. Being married for so long, he had turned down his share of women. Weak moments he'd had in the past were behind him now. They had been for quite some time. *Hurry up and get home, Jocelyn*, Colin silently urged his wife as he peered down at his wristwatch.

"Do you mind if I sit next to you?" Evelyn asked as they stepped inside the greenhouse. "I'd like to check out your technique. I really could use some tips on working faster."

"Sure, I'm right here." He took a seat on his bucket, then placed his frappe on the ground nearby.

Evelyn sat her frappe on the stool near the cabinet. "You know, I have to admit, I am a little nervous."

"Don't be nervous. I won't let you mess up." Colin proceeded to trim his plant.

"It's not that. It's just that I've never been around a man that had this kind of effect on me before."

"I don't understand what you mean." He continued clipping, completely oblivious to the proposition she was about to spring on him.

Evelyn approached as slowly as a lioness stalking her prey. Once she was upon him, she let her hand glide gently across his bicep, paused behind him for a second, then ran her hands down his muscular pecs. She quite enjoyed the feel of his perfectly sculpted body.

Colin spun around to face her; then he fixed his eyes on hers. "What are you doing?" he calmly inquired, already having an inkling of what it was she intended to do.

"You can touch me if you want to," she said in a soft, quiet voice.

Colin stood, attempting to shake off the lustful urge overtaking him. "I don't think that's a good idea, Evelyn."

"What's wrong? You don't want to?" She frowned at the notion.

"It's not that. You are very beautiful." His eyes studied her frame. "But I love my wife. I can't do this to her. She trusts me. I just can't. I won't betray her trust. It's not right." He refused to do this, yet not as adamantly as he could.

"How would she find out? I'm certainly not going to tell her." Evelyn proceeded to unzip her jacket, revealing a sheer teal bra with leopard-print lace trimming. "It'll be our little secret."

Out among the brush, there stood a stranger clawing at the back of his neck. Jackson's agitation neared its peak as he peered down at the immodest adulterers from the tree line on the Ravishes' property, eyes filled with hatred.

Meanwhile, Colin couldn't deny the fact that Evelyn's confidence had turned him all the way on. The more he looked at her, the more it became apparent he was fighting a losing battle. His blood was pumping. It was like he had taken a shot of adrenaline. Colin hadn't felt like that in years. That was all it took to weaken his defenses. He pushed his strong hand down inside the front of her leggings, then across her bare privates until his fingers were able to glide underneath. Evelyn trembled under the influence of his touch and the feel of his member standing at attention. Her hand massaged the bulge through his sweatpants. On Colin's face emerged a sly closed-mouth grin, as he was undoubtedly flattered by the dampness between her thighs.

He leaned into her. "You must really like me."

"Let me show you how much," Evelyn whispered, just before allowing her tongue to taste his.

Only her second day on the job and she'd already nearly fulfilled her aspirations. Colin clutched her round rump with both hands and lifted Evelyn until her legs were wrapped around his waist. Her hands held either side of his face as their tongues intertwined. Their lips remained locked as Colin made his way to the cabinet full of supplies, and once there, he allowed her back to rest against it.

"How do you want me?" she inquired.

He looked deep into her eyes with a seriousness she had not observed before. "I have choices?"

"You, Mr. Ravish, can, without question, have me however you'd like." Evelyn brandished a look to match her lover's.

The admission roused his desires even more. "That's how I like it," Colin whispered, wrapping his hand around her neck to lightly grip her throat.

That was when they heard the car horn as Jocelyn pulled into the driveway.

"Looks like I'm going to need a rain check," he uttered softly before allowing her feet to touch the soil. Colin furnished her one last soft peck on the lips, causing Evelyn to blush. The encounter would be enough to satisfy her for the moment, as it gave her more than enough to fantasize about until their next salacious tryst.

Colin headed out of the glasshouse, then hopped onto the ATV to head up to the main house. He forced out a long breath, sighing, as he shook his head in disbelief of what had transpired. *You can't have sex with her, man. Don't do it*, he warned himself. *Your birthday is coming up. You and your gorgeous wife are going to Bali to celebrate. Your life is perfect. Don't go fucking it up over a piece of ass. You've got to find a reason to fire her. It's the only way.* Colin made up in his mind that second that he'd figure out a way to get rid of Evelyn without Jocelyn getting suspicious. He had no idea the storm his treachery would rain down on him.

"Thou shalt not covet thy neighbor's wife," Jackson seethed, gawking at them from the tree line, as their transgressions had caused him to recall his ex-wife's against him just months ago. Discovering her riding the stiffened cock of that young marine in that cheap motel had been enough to scar him for life. His wounds remained fresh. Not to mention the fact that Evelyn had brushed him off in the past . . . Those were his recollections of the events, anyway. Either way, Jackson would make them pay for what they'd done. It was just a matter of how. . . .

Chapter 21

Search for Truth

Across town, Detective Barnes walked through the doors of Credit Union Bank, gnawing on a toothpick that hung from the side of his mouth. The manila folder in his grasp he kept close to his person. The authorities were hungry for a solid lead. Considering they'd previously witnessed Marcus Renegat making transactions at the bank, he hoped this lead would pan out. Prior to Marcus's disappearance, he was a suspect in the murders that had begun plaguing the city of Clarkston months ago. Detective Barnes was hell-bent on finding out what transactions Marcus had made at this bank, if indeed he had made any. Maybe his financial records would lead to some sort of clue. They needed something to go on.

The fact that so far things were looking as bleak as they had when the crisis began was disparaging, to say the least. Detective Barnes was at his wits' end. Someone at this bank was going to help him regardless of how he had to acquire the intel. Barnes looked around, carefully observing his surroundings. There was one person in particular he sought. Once his eyes had settled on the man he needed to see, the detective headed straight for him. It was a normal day. Busy as usual. Many of the townspeople, especially state and government workers, banked at this credit union. At least ten people were waiting in line to see a teller, yet only two windows were open. Fortunately, the person he needed to see was the manager. The head guy got to leave his cubicle every so often and stand around in the lobby, asking customers if he could lend a hand.

"Is anyone here to open an account?" asked the rather short middle-aged African American man with the clean-shaven face and waves as deep as the ocean. He buttoned the jacket of his blue suit before flashing a smile as he greeted customers nearing the counter.

Barnes spoke up. "I sure could use some help."

The bank manager's eyes lit up when he saw his old friend. "Detective Barnes."

"How's it been, Gregory?"

Both extended a hand for a firm handshake.

"I've been pretty good. How about yourself, Detective?"

"I can't complain," Barnes replied.

"What can I help you with? Are you ready to switch over to Credit Union Bank? Do business where it's better?" the other man said with open arms.

"Let's talk." Detective Barnes didn't want to give away his reason for being there. He wanted to get Gregory back into his office so that their conversation would be private.

"Let's step into my office."

The bank manager led the way back to his spacious corner office. It was evident the job paid well. Gregory got comfortable in the plush black reclining office chair behind his neatly organized desk. "So, what is it you need, Detective?"

Detective Barnes closed the door behind them. "I need some account information on a Marcus Renegat and possibly a Richard Sobieski."

"Aw, man, you know I can't give you that without a subpoena, a warrant, or something. Where's the court order? I assume you have something, right?" He had a stern look on his face as he spoke.

Barnes didn't have what Gregory wanted, but he'd certainly come prepared. "A case came across my desk recently. Check it out." He tossed the manila folder down onto the desk in front of him.

Gregory's eyebrows wrinkled; he was curious about what the officer wished to reveal. He flipped open the folder and perused its contents. Soon the stern look on his face waned as embarrassment set in. He shifted around in his chair, trying to somehow regain his dignity or, at the very least, appear that he was. "Hey, man, that was a, uh . . ."

"Hey, I'm not here to judge you. Besides, solicitation is a minor issue, and we have bigger fish to fry. If you help me, maybe I can help you make this go away." Barnes paused, giving the other man a second to think it over before proceeding. "Do we have a deal?"

The detective's proposition was one Gregory couldn't turn down. "You've got yourself a deal, Detective." Gregory sat up in the chair to begin his search. "What are the names you're looking for? I can look them up in the database."

"Marcus Renegat and Richard Sobieski."

"How about you write the names down here and we'll go from there? If you have their Social Security numbers, that would help." The bank manager slid a pad and pen across the glass desktop, toward Barnes.

Before the detective knew it, he was back at the station, excited to go over his findings with Officer Fackender. Finally, he'd gotten a lead that hadn't turned out to be a dead end.

Barnes met up with Fackender near the front door. "I've got more pieces to the puzzle. We've just got to put them together," Barnes announced as he tore through the station on the way to his office.

Fackender followed closely behind, eager to hear what he'd discovered. "Let's put our heads together and see what we can figure out."

Barnes took a seat behind his desk, then began rummaging through a bottom drawer filled with files. He pulled out a manila folder containing the file they'd started on Marcus Renegat. "Bank records show that Mr. Renegat made a large withdrawal from his account a couple of months ago. At the same time, there was a large withdrawal from Mr. Sobieski's account. I don't think this is a coincidence. Did we get specifics back from forensics yet? I'm curious as to how long the bodies had been there in the lake."

"Not yet, sir. But I'll put in a call to the Davison Police Department to gather any new developments. I did call the high school. Seems Mr. Sobieski hadn't been to work in almost two months."

"Why was he not reported missing?"

"Apparently, he told his secretary he was going to be out and to take care of things while he was gone. That's what she told me, anyway."

"So, we're left wondering how Mr. Renegat and Mr. Sobieski are connected. Was someone bribing them both? And what happened to the money they withdrew? We need to find out where Mr. Renegat's son is. Let's see what information the high school has on him. Check to see if he has a juvenile record. Also, we need to find the mother. The last time I questioned Mr. Renegat, he mentioned his son had just moved out. The next thing you know, Mr. Renegat is dead, and his son's room is destroyed."

"Destroyed, as if someone was looking for something. Maybe they were looking for the money," Fackender remarked.

"What the hell am I missing?" Detective Barnes leaned back in his chair, pondering plausible scenarios. "Maybe he tore up his son's room while looking for the money, found it, then kicked him out. That alone could make the kid want to kill him and disappear."

Fackender saw the plausibility in his speculations. "A father murdered by his son. It wouldn't be the first time we've seen a case such as that."

That following afternoon a lawyer said his goodbyes and waved from Elise's porch steps after informing her children about the contents of their mother's last will and testament. Turned out the deceased woman had been rather resourceful, to say the least. Every two weeks she had funneled as much of her check as possible into a retirement fund, which had been matched. This, along with other financial arrangements Elise had put in place, assured her children would be well taken care of. Indeed, it turned out she was worth more dead than alive.

Elise's propensity to be prepared hadn't stopped there. In fact, the day she'd initially hypnotized her good friend Evelyn, she'd recorded the entire session. The tape was to be delivered to a particular person in the event of her demise. Remaining oblivious as to the tape's contents, her lawyer would do just as he had been instructed and would mail the tape to the named recipient, Erick Todd, thereby fulfilling her final request. The sharply dressed novice attorney climbed back into the driver's seat of his classic Mercedes-Benz, looked over the address printed in the center of the envelope, and concluded it couldn't be far from his current location.

I should just drive it over and put it in the mailbox, he thought and found that alternative much more favorable than waiting in line at the post office. Besides, the most difficult part of his job was over. The process of going over the estate with the family always did leave him feeling drained. But after he downed a few coffees, coupled with reviewing one of the cases in the mounting pile atop his desk, Elise's death and her surviving brood would soon become a distant memory.

After a little over a month of the house being on the market, an agent finally removed the leasing sign from Mr. Fuboi's lawn.

Jackson sat in his Bronco, stewing over the encounter he had witnessed at the Ravish property. There was no way he could turn a blind eye to the things that had transpired. Yet he remained conflicted as to how he would proceed. Would he take her life or cast the eye of suspicion upon Evelyn? There was also the question of how he'd deal with Colin. Whatever he decided to do, it had to be done with caution. It was only a matter of time before the police would piece things together. He pondered taking Bryson to lure her into a trap, but as he watched a sharply suited young African American man stick a manila envelope into the Todds' mailbox, he began to consider alternatives.

"What do we have here?" he said aloud, his curiosity piqued.

He waited patiently as the gentleman got back into his vehicle and drove off. That was when he drove up alongside the mailbox to retrieve what the man had deposited. The snatch was swift. Not a single soul that lived on the block was outside to witness the crime. Most adults were picking up their children from school or were at work, so it was the perfect time to go unnoticed. Even so, Jackson knew better than to peruse the envelope's contents at the scene. Someone would be home soon, and then his cover might be blown. Evelyn hadn't recognized him in the café, yet he was certain that if she caught him out in front of her residence, something would click in her mind. Then everything would be ruined. Jackson shifted his car into drive, then pulled away from the mailbox as he tossed the envelope onto the passenger seat. The AM stations were the best way for him to gather information when he wasn't in front of a television, so Jackson turned the radio on, then flipped through the stations until he found one broadcasting the local news.

"The identities of two deceased Clarkston residents have been discovered through the swift combined efforts of the Clarkston and Davison police departments. Two male bodies were recovered from the bottom of Lake Callis by a local fisherman just days ago. Tune in to the evening news for the latest updates and news coverage regarding this gruesome crime," announced the radio disc jockey.

Jackson hastily switched off the radio, fearing the walls were closing in on him. The authorities had found the bodies. It was only a matter of time before they'd come looking his way. The jilted husband turned killer was sure of it.

"Damn it!" Jackson slapped the steering wheel with one of his palms as he drove faster.

As Jackson's fear of capture grew stronger, Detective Barnes inched closer to finding his perp. A seasoned detective knew the best way to find a killer was to learn about the victim. That was what brought him to the Clarkston post office that day. He needed to find out why the killer had chosen these postal workers to target.

"Thank you for agreeing to see me, Mrs. Osborne."

"Please, Officer, just call me Hilary."

"Hilary, I'd like to ask you a few questions about your recently deceased employees. It's important that we find the person or people responsible for these murders, as we believe that more of your staff could be in danger."

"You really think so?" Her face flushed from dread.

"I don't mean to make you fearful, but yes. If I were you, I'd be very mindful of my surroundings, especially if you are out and about alone."

"My God." Hilary's hands lifted to cover her gaped mouth.

"That's why it's so important that you answer my questions to the best of your ability. So that we find this maniac and restore peace to the city of Clarkston."

Hilary's hands fell into her lap. "I'll answer as best as I can."

"I need to see the employee files for Randy Alky and Marcus Renegat."

Hilary sprang into action, hopping up from her chair to flip through the second drawer of the tall gray file cabinet. She pulled files from the drawer, then handed them over to the detective.

"How did Randy seem the last days before his death?" the detective asked.

"That would be hard to say. He had been suspended before the time of his death. So he hadn't run his route in days."

"Who worked closest with him?"

"He worked alone except for the days he trained his sub, Jackson."

"Jackson?" Barnes thought it strange that Jackson's name had come up again.

"Yes, Jackson Pierce. He took over the route when Randy was caught drinking on the job."

"Randy must have been pretty upset."

"I wouldn't know. Deborah, one of my head supervisors, implemented the action before she committed suicide. There seems to be a dark cloud looming over this office." Hilary trembled, as if she'd caught a case of the chills.

"Let's hope we can get back to sunny days. Would you mind if I took the files of every deceased employee whether his or her death has been ruled accidental or not? Just the ones from the past year."

"Whatever you need, Detective."

With his box of files in hand, Detective Barnes walked out of the post office, breezing right by Jocelyn, who had entered bearing a platter of brownies for the staff. She waved at him, a pleasant smile plastered on her face, like a good, law-abiding citizen.

It was people like Jocelyn who restored his faith in humanity. The humanity Barnes had sworn an oath to protect.

Chapter 22

Turning Up the Heat

Over at the Ravishes, Colin was busy with his own dilemma. His heart felt as if it would beat out of his chest. The sweat that had beaded along his hairline had already begun to run down his face. It could be attributed to the hard work Colin was putting in that day, but it was most likely due to the fact that he found himself alone with Evelyn yet again. *Please keep clipping*, he silently willed her as she sat directly across from him, every so often stealing glances at the object of her desire. Colin noticed but tried to focus his gaze on the plant before him, so as not to award Evelyn with any eye contact.

"It won't be long before we'll be doing the last pruning," Colin lied, attempting to speed up the conclusion of her services there.

"Oh really? Jocelyn said we'd be hanging them after this."

"I wasn't aware she was keeping you on for the entire process."

"Is that really what's going on, or are you trying to get rid of me, because I make you uncomfortable?"

"I told you, it takes a lot to make me uncomfortable." Colin finally gave her eye contact.

"Ouch." Evelyn squealed, snatching her hand away from the pair of scissors with which she'd cut her finger.

Blood leaked from the wound, and when she raised her hand, it traveled up her arm, then settled in the crease of her elbow.

"That looks pretty bad." Colin sprang up from his bucket seat to help. He stood at Evelyn's side, examining the wound, then decided on a course of action that his better judgment warned against. "I have some bandages and antiseptic up at the house. We should get those gloves off and clean the wound."

"Whatever you say." Evelyn gazed up at him, eyes granting him permission to take her right then and there.

Colin broke eye contact, disregarding her silent advances. "I guess I'm driving." He headed for one of two four-wheelers just outside the glasshouse.

The wounded woman kept her hand elevated as she followed closely behind him, a sinister grin on her face. Evelyn could tell Colin had started to have second thoughts about their previous encounter. Fearing he wouldn't fulfill her fantasy, she had to act fast. That was why she'd sliced into her skin in the first place. A small price to pay in order to get close to the man of her dreams, she reckoned. Evelyn climbed onto the bike behind him and wrapped her good arm around his abdomen. As they traveled along the trail, her hand ran up his sculpted pecs underneath his white V-neck T-shirt. Officially caught off guard, he hesitated to put a stop to it. Until her hand crept down to the semi-erect member inside his sweatpants.

"Whoa!" Colin swerved, kicking up a cloud of dust and gravel, but they'd made it to the front of the property, to his relief. "We should really concentrate on getting you cleaned up." He abruptly pressed the brake.

"Sounds like a good idea. I am leaking."

He couldn't help but find the hidden meaning in Evelyn's remark, yet this time Colin was hell-bent on not feeding into her salacious taunts. "We have an infirmary room in the basement. I'll get you patched up down there." He helped her off the four-wheeler, and the two proceeded to head inside the house. In order to get to the basement, they had to travel through the immaculately clean kitchen. Evelyn could see their reflections in the stainless-steel appliances as they passed by.

"Be careful going down the stairs. The last thing we need is for you to trip and fall." Colin opened the door to the stairwell, then pulled at a hanging chain above his head to shed light on the steps.

During their descent, Evelyn repeatedly squeezed the forearm of her injured arm, forcing more blood to spill from the slice in her finger. "I'm not feeling too good." She fell against Colin just as they reached the bottom of the stairs. He caught her, lifted her up, and placed her on the leather sofa, then sank to his knees beside her, Evelyn kept her eyes closed. She enjoyed the way his hand explored her neck to check her pulse and temperature. Assuming she'd fainted, he had time to admire how firm Evelyn's breasts looked in her spaghetti-string spandex top. Colin was tempted to run his hands between them. Instead, being a Good Samaritan, he got up to complete the task at hand. He opened a double-doored wooden cabinet full of medical supplies and grabbed the rubbing alcohol, an antiseptic, bandages, gauze, and ointment so that he could fix her up.

"This isn't the first time I've had to clean you up." Colin cleaned her wound, then patched it. "I must admit, you are beautiful." He admired her further, his gaze studying her frame. When his eyes settled on her face, her eyes were open.

"How do we keep meeting like this?" she said in a hushed tone.

"I'm not sure. You seem to be pretty accident prone."

Evelyn smiled softly. "I'm starting to think you're my hero."

"I'm no hero. I am just doing the right thing."

"Do you always do the right thing?" She sat up, leaving her legs open, with Colin between them.

He didn't shy away. "I try to."

That was when she took her chance, lifting his arms to rest on her thighs. "Are you trying to right now?"

Colin swallowed hard. His heart pounded, and the marijuana he'd smoked earlier just so happened to be weighing heavily on his decision making. "I'm not doing anything wrong yet."

Her brow lifted when the meaning of his declaration sank in. "You said 'yet.' Does that mean you want—"

Colin's lips met hers, halting her inquiry before she could finish. He'd finally given in to the fire in his loins. Evelyn's spaghetti straps fell down off her shoulders with a brush from his fingertips.

Their bodies burned with desire. Colin's desired to taste her nectar, and she to conquer his heart. He gripped the bottom of her chin and lifted her head, then let his opposite hand run down her neck and travel between her breasts. "I'm tempted to taste you," he whispered, finally breaking his silence.

"Let's not waste time thinking it over." She moved his hand from her face to a place more fitting. "Touch it." She let his hand free to explore her warmth.

"Look at me." Colin pulled her attention from her crotch to his eyes. "Take these off," he said as he tugged at the elastic belt on her pants.

"With pleasure. What else can I do for you?" She took off everything standing between his member and the moisture between her thighs.

At the same time, Colin removed his shirt, then dropped it.

Their tongues became intertwined as he massaged her slippery lips below her waist, nearly gliding into her center. Evelyn's legs were trembling; her breaths were shallow. She threw her head back, bracing herself for his entrance. But Colin didn't want it that way. If he was going to sleep with Evelyn, he wanted to get every possible bit of satisfaction out of it.

"I want you to look at me," he demanded, pulling her chin back down to make eye contact with her. "I want to see how good my dick feels inside you."

She granted him her full attention as he pulled her toward him, hands pressed firmly to the sides of her rump. It stimulated him even further to see her mouth open as her eyes rolled up beneath their lids.

"You want all of it?" he whispered.

Evelyn moaned, lifting her bottom to assist with the ride he furnished. "I want it all," she cried out in ecstasy.

They'd enjoyed four climaxes within their brazen forty-five-minute sexual encounter before Colin bent Evelyn over his wife's sewing table in one corner of the basement. A flicker of light reflecting off a photograph that hung on the wall alerted Colin as to Jocelyn's arrival home. "My wife is home." He turned and saw her vehicle's fog lights through a basement window. Both panting, sweating naked adulterers sprang into action. By the time, Jocelyn stepped into the kitchen and noticed the basement door was ajar, they were fully clothed and re-enacting the patching of her wounded finger.

Footsteps creaked on the wooden stairs. "Is someone down there?" Jocelyn called.

"It's just Evelyn and me, honey. Come on down."

Upon hearing her husband's reply, Jocelyn continued her descent into the basement. She gasped when she saw that Colin was applying antiseptic to one of Evelyn's fingers. "Oh, my goodness. What happened? Are you okay, Evelyn?" Concerned, she hurried over and peered at the flesh wound.

"I'll be fine. It's just a cut. Besides, your husband is fixing me up pretty good."

"I think it's best she head home, though." Colin's gaze met Evelyn's. "You can't clip any more today with your finger like that. Besides, you'll be of no use to us if you further injure yourself."

"I guess you're right. I should be heading home, any-way."

"We'll walk you out." Colin motioned with his hand for them all to head up the stairs. "Shall we?"

"I'm gonna grab a few things down here and clean up these bandages," Jocelyn told him. "Feel better, Evelyn."

"Thanks. I will." Evelyn waved goodbye and mounted the stairs.

"I'll meet you upstairs, honey." Colin kissed his wife on the forehead, then headed up the stairs after Evelyn.

Jocelyn felt something was amiss but couldn't really pinpoint what it was. Even if she did, she'd never admit she thought Colin would be unfaithful to her. Not after all those years. She looked around the room, studying her surroundings. Nothing looked out of the ordinary. The sewing machine was a bit crooked. Still, that was nothing Jocelyn couldn't fix with a nudge of her hand. So, she did just that, then proceeded to clean up the mess Colin had made.

Out front, Colin saw Evelyn on her way. He opened the car door and watched as she climb inside the Yukon.

"Thanks. I guess I'll see you tomorrow?" she said as she placed her key in the ignition.

"Like I was saying, the pruning is nearly over, and with your hand like that, you should probably stay away from sharp objects for a while."

"Okay." Evelyn dropped her head, hiding a frown.

"I was thinking you should come over to my office building and assist with the business side of our operation. We have an audit coming up soon and could use some help going over files. What do you say?"

When she heard his offer, her smile returned and so did her quickly diminishing confidence. "Does it come with any perks?" She started the engine.

Colin chuckled lightly at the notion, then turned to walk away, calling out his last request. "Tomorrow, ten a.m. I'll text you the address." He waved while continuing his departure.

An all too delighted Evelyn accepted his offer. "Whatever you say, Mr. Ravish."

Now I'll have Evelyn far enough away from Jocelyn for her not to become suspicious, he thought. His altered plan would work out nicely for him. At least Colin assumed as much.

Chapter 23

Groundwork

Intent on making Colin hers, the lust-stricken adulteress drove off, her mind filled with an idea she had to achieve that very aim. *What better way*, she thought, *than to befriend the woman who loves him most?* Evelyn had actually concocted the half-baked plan after rummaging around in the Ravishes' bedroom closet. Her findings now led her to a massive log cabin home on Rattalee Lake Road.

"How nice," she said aloud when she rolled to a stop in front of the home. She let her eyes take in the lush landscaping around the property—landscaping that made it look more like a botanical garden than a home. *What a lovely place for a wedding*, she mused. She fantasized that she herself was standing, adorned in full wedding attire, beneath the rose-covered arbor in the courtyard. Of course, Colin graced her fantasy: he lifted her veil to fulfill his role as her new husband. Just before they were about to kiss, her daydream was cut short by the appearance of a petite woman. She exited the house and climbed into her Jaguar.

"That has to be her," Evelyn declared, assuming this was the woman who had birthed her beau. When the Jaguar pulled of the driveway, Evelyn waited for about thirty seconds, then drove slowly behind it. She tailed the unsuspecting mother through town, waiting for her to make her first stop. After she patiently followed the Jaguar for nearly twenty minutes, her person of interest pulled into a shopping mall in a neighboring town. Evelyn waited for her to park, then did the same—parking nearby, but far enough away not to be noticed. All she had to do was wait for the perfect opportunity to spark up a conversation with this woman.

Macy's was Colin's mother's favorite place to shop. Practically everything she was wearing she'd purchased from the popular retailer. Color coordinated from top to bottom, she wore her salt-and-pepper hair in a pixie cut, and her neat tresses matched her stone-gray eyes and the pantsuit she'd put on that day. You could tell she was a serious woman. One about her business. She climbed out of the Jaguar and headed into the store. Evelyn quickly got out of the Yukon and walked twenty paces behind her. After twenty minutes of browsing, Evelyn finally made eye contact with her in the men's department and flashed her a pleasant smile. The tightly wound woman neglected to smile back and instead riffled through the men's garments, searching for something in particular. Evelyn had an idea what the woman could be shopping for, since she'd seen the date postmarked on one of Colin's old birthday cards. His birthday was drawing near, so she surmised that his mother was selecting a gift. No better time than the present to initiate her plan . . .

"So, which do you think a man would prefer?" Evelyn inquired as she held up two shirts for the woman to compare. With no one else in the vicinity, it didn't seem obvious that she'd targeted Colin's mother.

Her head tilted forward, chin tucked, she peered over the top of her thin rectangular specs. "Depends on whom you're buying for."

"It's for my boss. His birthday is coming up, and I wanted to show my appreciation by getting him a little something."

"Is he an older gentleman? Because both of those shirts seem more for an older, more seasoned man."

"He's only in his thirties." Evelyn closed in on the woman.

"I'm actually here picking out a gift for my son. His birthday is coming up. Maybe you can find something better suited in this section."

"The shirt you're holding looks nice," Evelyn said, attempting to flatter the unenthused woman.

"I'm sure my son will like it. He has a taste for anything designer."

Her admission made Colin sound like something of a gold digger. But given that his family obviously had money, Evelyn quickly dismissed the notion.

"Sounds like your son has good taste."

Colin's mother countered, "In clothing at least . . ."

Her comment led Evelyn to believe his mother was displeased about the woman her son had chosen to marry. The prospect of getting rid of Jocelyn looked more promising than ever before. The ladies continued to chat as they perused the men's department, sharing their common interests. All the while, Evelyn never mentioned the person who connected them.

Over at the Oakland County Sheriff's Office, Barnes and Fackender stood in Barnes's office, their attention focused on the whiteboard that listed the deaths thought to be connected to the Clarkston Post office and its employees. The list had gotten longer and now included Jessica, Marcus, Elise, Mr. Sobieski, Randy, and Deborah, whose death they had begun to suspect wasn't a suicide at all.

"What is it, Fackender? What is it that connects these victims?"

"We're onto something, Detective. I can feel it," Fackender replied just as the telephone rang.

Barnes answered the call. "This is Detective Barnes." After a few seconds, his brows lifted, and his eyes beamed with optimism. Fackender knew then and there they'd been blessed with a break in the case.

Barnes mashed his head against his shoulder, pinning the phone there, to free up his hands to search through files atop his desk. "Are you sure it's a match?" His clenched fist lifted and shook in celebration of the break-through. "Thank you." Detective Barnes slammed the receiver against the phone's base. "Hot damn it! We've got a break."

"I'd love to hear it."

"The DNA from the skin fibers found on the sheet in Mr. Renegat's closet matches the DNA found on Jessica, as well as the sheet she was wrapped in."

"So, Marcus Renegat killed Jessica. But why?"

"Looks like we've come upon our next quest. How about you tackle this one and I'll follow up on the Randy Alky murder?"

"I'm on it." Fackender made a hasty exit.

Jacksonville, Florida, was where Fackender finally caught up with the former Mrs. Renegat, who now went by Mrs. Meek. Sitting poolside, sipping a margarita, the frail brunette dug around within the confines of her bikini top, feeling for her dose of calm for the day. If you had asked Marcus when he was alive, he would have said it was the fault of her new husband that she'd developed a drug habit. But in reality, Mrs. Meek had been intro-duced to hydrocodone during one of her hospital stays, courtesy of Marcus himself. The life the two of them had shared had eventually driven her into a state of constant dread and severe depression.

After years of tears, bruises, threats, and abuse, she'd married the doctor with whom she'd worked for over a decade. At the start of their relationship, he had felt sorry for her, but as time went on, his affection for her had grown, and so had his desire to save her from the PTSD she suffered due to all the abuse she'd endured at the hands of Marcus. Unfortunately, by then the doctor's new bride was already knee-deep in her pill habit. Being a physician meant Dr. Meek worked much of the time, making it easier for him to turn a blind eye to her demons. He worked while she relaxed, a fact that didn't bother Dr. Meek in the slightest. In his eyes, his wife deserved to live like a queen. After all, for more than a decade of her life she had been treated as if she were subhuman.

Mrs. Meek's cell phone vibrated on the other side of the glass patio table, and she popped the pill she'd retrieved into her mouth while deciding whether or not she would take the call. Mrs. Meek swallowed the pill dry, not even taking a sip of her afternoon cocktail. When she finally did pick up the phone, she sat there, staring blankly at the caller display window, having realized that the area code for the incoming call belonged to the place from which she had escaped. The number wasn't one she recognized, making her even more hesitant to answer the call.

"He holds no power over you," the mentally battered woman declared aloud, giving herself a short pep talk, before mustering up the courage to flip open her phone.

"Hello."

"Hi. I'm looking for Mrs. Meek, formerly Mrs. Renegat."

"And who may I ask are you?" Her face contorted, as she was displeased from hearing her ex-husband's last name uttered in her ear.

"I'm Officer Fackender, with the Oakland County Sheriff's Office. Is this Mrs. Meek?"

She couldn't deny the answer to her question roused her curiosity enough to entertain a conversation with the caller. "This is Mrs. Meek. How can I help you?"

"I don't know how to say this delicately over the phone, so I'll just be completely forthright. Your ex-husband has been found dead. I'm sorry. My condolences to you and your family, of course."

A dead silence came over the line as the officer's words sank in.

"Mrs. Meek, are you okay?"

Marcus's ex-wife breathed a long sigh of relief. Even though it had been over a decade since she left that man, the abuse he had put her through remained fresh in her mind. "A reckoning finally came." She grinned as the words slipped effortlessly from her lips.

"A reckoning? What a strange thing to say upon hearing about the death of your former husband."

"You know something even more strange? The fact that someone could profess to love another yet in the same breath wish them dead. It's what he used to tell me on a regular basis. That I was so useless and would be better off dead. His favorite line before he would strike," she replied. "I remember the last time. Andre had to have been about five then. I was getting dinner ready when he grabbed me by the throat and forced me up against the wall in the kitchen. Slowly my feet lifted from the floor. He had to ensure I couldn't make a run for it. So that he could wail on me without resistance."

She paused, forcing out a deep sigh, before continuing to relate the torture she'd suffered at the hands of Marcus. "The blows came one after another. Over the years his demeanor became more aggressive. The strikes were harder than ever before . . . Anything would set him off. One day in particular he felt I was dressed inappropriately. And, of course, the slut had to be punished. By the time he finally dropped me to the floor, I vomited all over myself. He grabbed a fistful of my hair, then dragged me across the puke, giving it a once-over with my beautiful dress. I screamed. Screamed at the top of my lungs . . . Still, he didn't care. I think my begging excited him.

"When he finally let go, his boot came crashing down on my ribs. All I could do was curl up in a ball and cry. Cry as my children stood by, gripped with fear . . . Even as his face contorted to express the displeasure he harbored for me, I saw contentment in his eyes. It fulfilled him to drag me down to my lowest point. It was the only way he felt worthy. The moment I accepted my reality was the moment I was ready to do something about it. So, before you judge me for describing his death as a reckoning, consider what I've been through. Me and every other woman unlucky enough to cross his path."

"I apologize, Mrs. Meek. I didn't mean to minimize the trauma you've experienced at the hands of your ex-husband. I just wanted to make you aware of our findings and ask you a few questions, if that's okay."

"What is it you want to know?"

"When was the last time you spoke with your ex-husband?"

"The day I left him."

"What about your son? It's my understanding that he stayed with his father. When was the last time you spoke with him?"

"The day I left," she repeated, only this time her voice was lower. A fleeting feeling of shame washed over her.

"Not at all?" Officer Fackender couldn't believe what she was hearing. What kind of woman leaves her five-year-old kid with an abusive man just to save her own hide?

"You have no right to judge me. Who do you people think you are!" The volume of her voice became increasingly elevated. "You never helped me! That man could beat me because his slacks weren't ironed to his liking. And still you guys never lifted a finger to help me, or my children, for that matter! You can take your opinion and your notification call and shove them up your lazy, bureaucratic, doughnut-eating asses!" Mrs. Meek slammed her cell phone shut, tossed it onto the table, then sat back and took a long sip of her drink. She quickly wiped away the tear that had fallen from the corner of her eye, and with it went any feelings of guilt Officer Fackender had caused to boil to the surface.

"It was better off that way," she whispered, to further convince herself that leaving her son was indeed the best option she had at the time.

One more pill . . . That should make it all better. She went digging into her bikini top.

Chapter 24

Digging Deep

Detective Barnes had decided to follow up on the Randy Alky angle, and so the afternoon found him at the edge of the murdered man's backyard. Barnes ducked under the restrictive yellow tape wrapped around oak trees at the perimeter of the yard to search within its confines. Going at it alone, he combed the site for clues. With all the new evidence coming to light, he assumed there had to be something they had overlooked here. Something that would blow Randy's case wide open.

Staring at the tree stand—this one an enclosed platform about twelve feet off the ground and secured to a large tree, to give hunters a better vantage point—where the ill-fated mail carrier had met his demise, Barnes imagined the look of terror in Randy's eyes as he stared into the barrel of that shotgun. Although fragmented pieces of what once was his head had been picked up and carted off with the rest of the evidence by authorities, blood spatter remained. Barnes recalled the way Randy's body had landed, wedged into a corner of the tree stand. He stood at the base of the tree, nodding his head in despair. If he wanted to truly connect with the scene of the crime, he needed to go up onto the tree stand. No pussyfooting around, so to speak.

Having made up his mind, he climbed wooden planks secured to the tree to reach the tree stand, and once there, he allowed his eyes to roam over the crimson-stained wood. Then Barnes stood in the very place Randy had been perched when the buckshot hit him. Nothing resonated with him as he peered down at the ground. "What could you have done to provoke a crime so heinous?" he asked aloud, eyes searching off into the distance. The property, a vast tract of land covered in trees, a winding shallow stream running through it, attracted a variety of the region's wildlife. Sixty yards or so into the brush, a fawn moved its nose back and forth over something stuck to the ground beneath the leaves. Whatever it was refused to budge, and so did the fawn. Not until a white-tailed doe came up along beside it and nudged it did the fawn scamper along.

Over the years Barnes had learned to trust his intuition. *Maybe, it's a sign. It can't hurt to check,* he thought. Before climbing down out of the tree stand, he looked for something to mark his destination and decided on the large boulder just feet from where the animals had been standing. His boots pushed through dead foliage, and he hoped that something would reveal itself along the way. Loud buzzing from singing cicadas drowned out most of the other sounds as the detective moved past protruding branches and decaying logs. Barnes even jumped the shallow ravine to make it to that spot near the big gray boulder. The moment his foot hit metal buried under leaves, he knew he'd stumbled upon something significant.

He brushed aside the leaves and uncovered a metal latch. "What do we have here?" He pulled hard on the latch, and an edge of what appeared to be a wooden hatch broke through a layer of soil. As he yanked harder, the entire hatch emerged in its entirety. A final tug opened the hatch, revealing a set of stairs leading down into the darkness. Bomb shelters weren't uncommon on properties as large as Randy's. Barnes removed his flashlight from his belt and used it to light his way as he descended the stairs. An underground room with concrete walls, nearly fifteen feet long and just as wide, housed a cot, refrigerator, generator, and shelves stocked with canned goods. Things seemed perfectly normal until the flashlight illuminated a sex swing hanging in the center of the room. The red cage behind it held an array of toys of the sadomasochistic variety. Restraints, dildos, vibrators, violet wands, a Wartenberg wheel, even an erotic electro-stimulator. The list went on.

"What kinda weird shit was going on down here?" Barnes's light moved slowly across the photos pasted on the back wall. The photos were of women who, Barnes presumed, had participated, willingly or not, in a sexual experience here, and they were arranged in what was a mural of sorts. Women of different ethnicities, all depicted in ecstasy.

"Is this what landed you in the grave?" he mumbled, noticing some of the women in the pictures wore a wedding ring. "Was it a jealous husband who did this? Or maybe even a jealous woman?" he asked himself as his flashlight beam hovered on one of the photos. He had no idea about the clue he'd stumbled upon.

It was another lead. Nothing solid, but a lead nonetheless, and so Barnes clung to hope.

The next morning at the office, Evelyn, wearing a pair of stilettos and a silver V-neck button-up blouse, lay spread eagle on Colin's mahogany desk. She guided him over her, her hand gripping his black tie, the only thing covering his chiseled torso.

"How am I doing on my first day at the office?" she inquired seductively. Colin undid her top three buttons to reveal heaving breasts. They invited his lips, and so he kissed her bosom softly, glancing up at her between pecks to see how she reacted to his touch.

He teased her, letting his hand run casually up the inside of her thigh until it reached the warmth between her legs. "So far, so good."

Evelyn took in a deep breath, his touch causing her body to tremble. Her back arched as her head fell to the side, hiding her hungry expression.

"I love the way you react to the feel of my fingers. I have something else for you." His dress slacks and boxers fell down around his knees, unleashing his elongated appendage.

Evelyn moaned in ecstasy as Colin eased his way inside her. After grabbing her by the waist, he slid her down closer to him, every inch of his rod gliding into her narrow space. When she threw her arms up over her head, his morning coffee slid off the desk, and the mug shattered when it hit the floor.

Everything about what they were doing in that office was wrong, yet it felt right in every way. Colin loved the way she felt. It was much different than the intercourse he had with his wife. Although he loved Jocelyn, their sex life wasn't exactly without its challenges. Much of the time her multiple sclerosis made it difficult for her to moisten for him. Evelyn, on the other hand, was drenched before he had even laid a hand on her. That fact fed his monstrous ego.

Down on the ground level, in the lobby of the Renaissance Center, Mrs. Ravish's three-inch heels clicked across the gleaming graphite floor. Heads pivoted in her direction, the petite woman's mighty presence demanding attention. She had donned a champagne-colored three-piece pantsuit with a lengthy jacket. The gift bag she carried in her right hand had a helium balloon attached, and the little tag read HAPPY BIRTHDAY. The proud mother pressed the button for the sixty-first floor, stepped in the elevator when it arrived, and headed up to see her boy. She had funded the office space for her son, the money spent mere pocket change for her. Anything to see him happy. Regardless of how generous his parents were with their finances, Colin wanted his very own empire, and he planned to build it through the production of marijuana and cannabis-based oils.

On the sixty-first floor, the secretary's eyes sprang open when the elevator doors parted and Mrs. Ravish appeared. "Mrs. Ravish, good morning! I wasn't expecting to see you here!" He stood from his seat, clutching a handful of official-looking documents. The pressure to make yourself seem essential was intense whenever Colin's mother showed up at the office. Devin, a beefy twenty-year-old college sophomore, had frequented the same fitness center as Colin. One day they had struck up a conversation, and they'd realized they had quite a bit in common as far as their interests were concerned. That was how Devin had landed the position of secretary.

Although fewer than five staff members worked in the office, every one of Colin's staff was someone he'd met while carrying out his everyday activities. The office had a down-to-earth feel to it, yet Mrs. Ravish insisted everyone dress in business casual, because of the swanky downtown location. Today Devin wore an olive-green fitted, short-sleeve button-up, khakis, and a pair of brown loafers. Mrs. Ravish didn't tolerate nonsense, but she wasn't without a pair of eyes. Any woman with a pair of eyes could see that Devin was a specimen to be admired.

"Good morning, Devin." She lowered her designer frames, then managed to muster up a smile. "Staying productive, I see."

She'd taken notice of the fact that his words had come out much louder than necessary, which didn't surprise her in the least. He had merely sounded the "boss is in the building" alarm. The fact that her presence evoked such a response from him stroked Mrs. Ravish's ego. When it came to her and her son, the apple really hadn't fallen far from the tree.

"Indeed, I am. We'll certainly be ready for the audit. I assure you of that. Is there something I can do for you?" He came out from behind his desk and partially blocked Colin's office door.

"I'm not here for business. Just dropping off Colin's birthday gift early. I'll be out of state when my Cutty celebrates his birthday."

"I'm sure he'll appreciate that, Mrs. Ravish!" Devin hoped Colin could hear their conversation.

"Devin, step aside please," she demanded, maintaining her calm demeanor.

He extended his hand, stepping to the side. "Yes, of course. I apologize. It was good to see you."

When she opened the door, Colin was seated at his desk, flipping through paperwork. Evelyn busied herself with cleaning up pieces of the shattered mug. Both had managed to get fully clothed. But the fact that Evelyn's Ferragamo heels were off her feet made his mother suspicious. Lucky for Colin, it wasn't his mother he had to worry about. She would never turn her back on her only son.

"Cutty."

"Mama." Colin's face lit up at the sight of her, and he was thanking God it wasn't Jocelyn. He didn't waste a second getting up to greet her at the door with a peck on the cheek.

"I don't get hugs anymore?" she asked, displeased by his fickle greeting. Mrs. Ravish often found things not up to her standard.

He was so immersed in his relief that she wasn't Jocelyn, he'd forgotten how to properly greet his mother. Nothing Colin couldn't smooth over, though . . .

"Oh, don't act like that, Mama." His strong arms wrapped her in a snug embrace. "You know I love you more than any woman on God's green earth."

Evelyn let out a low huff, then played it off as a cough after realizing she wasn't the only one who'd heard it.

"Who might this be? And why are you so sweaty, Cutty?" Mrs. Ravish backed away, keeping a keen eye on Evelyn.

"That's why I didn't want to hug you. I was moving some office furniture around. It gave me a workout," he explained nonchalantly.

"Can't you pay someone to do that?"

"I'm quite capable, Mama."

"What about her?" She stepped toward Evelyn.

"Oh, hello," Evelyn remarked, finally having turned around. "My name is—"

"I know you," Mrs. Ravish interrupted. "My shopping buddy." She smiled.

Evelyn returned the smile. "Well, what are the odds? It's so good to see you again."

"I wasn't aware you worked for my son." She turned to address Colin. "Oh, Cutty, you've got a good worker here. And she cares." Mrs. Ravish gave Evelyn a wink.

Colin was perplexed. "So, how do you two know each other?"

"I told you she's my shopping buddy, son. Oh, you have a bit of Chapstick on your cheek." The doting mother moved toward him, then wiped away the smudge with her thumb.

"Thank you, Mama. So, to what do we owe the pleasure of your visit?"

"Well, since I'm going out of town and won't be here for your birthday, I thought I'd bring by your gift. Is that okay?"

"Of course it is. Gift or no gift." Colin leaned in to embrace his mother once more in appreciation of her generosity. When they stepped apart, she handed her son the gift bag, which he set on his desk.

"Don't keep us in suspense. Let's see what you got, Cutty." Evelyn smiled seductively.

"Yeah, Cutty . . . let's see what you got," a voice called out from the doorway.

Jocelyn strolled in, unannounced. Devin gave an aloof shrug as he stood in the doorway behind her.

"Honey, what are you doing here?" Colin asked her.

"Is that the greeting I get?" Jocelyn frowned, livid at having heard Evelyn call her husband by his childhood nickname.

"I'm sorry, baby." He rushed over to close the distance between them, then pulled her in for a hug and a kiss.

Her eyes studied Evelyn's face as she ran her hands down Colin's back. *Oh, this bitch is bothered,* Jocelyn surmised, maintaining a pleasant smile on her face. She knew the look of envy well. Jocelyn also noticed the change in Evelyn's attire. When did she start wearing Ferragamo? she wondered, though she had a pretty good idea as to the time frame. The fact that Evelyn's stilettos were not on her feet gave Jocelyn more cause to fret that yet again she had found herself in the midst of a competition. Competing for her own husband was where she put her foot down, however. That was something Jocelyn refused to do ever again.

"Hi, Mom. It's good to see you." Jocelyn did her daughterly duty by sharing an embrace with her mother-in-law.

"You look a little tired, Jocelyn. How have you been feeling?" Colin's mother frequently shined a light on Jocelyn's flaws. The slights were due to her insecurity over the fact that Jocelyn was just as high class as she was.

"I'm doing as good as can be expected. You, on the other hand, look great. You look so vibrant and healthy. Did you gain weight?" Jocelyn knew the comeback would work on her mother-in-law's last nerve. While Colin's mother took the direct route with her criticism, Jocelyn had to operate with a little more subtlety. Out of respect for Colin.

"Nonsense, dear. I've been the same weight since high school," Mrs. Ravish remarked, rebuffing her daughter-in-law.

Colin took the chance to clean up the dent his wife's comment had made. "Mama's been slim and trim since birth."

"That's right, son." Mrs. Ravish smiled. "Now, enough about me. Open your gift."

"It's not even my birthday yet," he protested bashfully.

Colin's mother wasn't having it. "Don't you deny me seeing a smile on my baby's face."

"Since you put it like that, I'll oblige." He walked over to his desk and dug around in the gift bag. After searching through the tissue paper, he pulled out a small box and then told the three women that there was jewelry inside it, since he'd guessed what his mother had gotten him. "Oh, Mama. You're the best," Colin praised her before even opening the box. Then he lifted the lid on the box to reveal a chrome Movado watch with a black face.

"Oh, how nice," Evelyn and Jocelyn sang in unison.

"Thank you." Colin kissed his mother on the cheek before removing the watch Jocelyn had purchased for him and putting on his new Movado.

In the past that would have bothered Jocelyn but not anymore. Colin had a watch for every day of the month.

"Looks good on you," Evelyn chimed in.

Jocelyn had heard enough of Evelyn's cute remarks. Quite frankly, the vibes she was giving off weren't meshing well with Jocelyn's. "It does. And now you get a chance to show it off at lunch."

"Lunch?" Colin asked.

"Yes, lunch. That thing you eat in the afternoon to nourish you." Jocelyn playfully poked his rock-hard tummy.

"You're here to take me to lunch?"

"Not only am I going to take you to lunch, but I'm also going to take the best mother-in-law in the world to lunch." Jocelyn's declaration earned her some brownie points in Colin's mother's eyes. "Who better to have lunch with than the most important women in your life?" she inquired, all the while stealing glances at Evelyn. Jocelyn played chess well. Evelyn had underestimated her.

"Well, let's get out of here. I could go for some lunch. I know the perfect place." Mrs. Ravish headed out, leading the way.

The trio left Evelyn standing there alone, with only the documents to keep her company. Once the door closed behind them, she dropped the papers on the floor. "Stupid bitch."

She can't be too stupid, the voice in her head teased. *You're the one still standing here.*

Her alter ego was right. Evelyn shut her eyes, struggling to control the storm brewing inside her.

After their impromptu lunch, Jocelyn and Colin pulled up to their home in their respective vehicles. Colin got out, expecting to head inside, maybe enjoy some alone time with his wife. Unfortunately, Jocelyn had other plans. She'd been fuming about Evelyn ever since their encounter at the office. There wasn't a thing you could say to convince Jocelyn that Evelyn hadn't been trying to push up on her husband. The way she looked at it, though, Colin was either turning a blind eye or being manipulated. Either way, she wanted Evelyn gone.

The second the couple made it through the front door, Jocelyn unleashed her insecurities. "Why did she call you Cutty?"

"Who?"

"Evelyn. She called you Cutty. How would she even know that name?"

Colin shut the front door, then walked toward his wife. Well aware that the situation at his feet was a delicate one, the adulterous husband spoke softly, so as not to rouse his wife's anger. "My mother addressed me as Cutty when she first arrived. I'm assuming Evelyn thought the nickname was funny."

"What about her heels? Why were her shoes off?"

"Beats me. Maybe her feet hurt. I told her to dress business casual. She could have worn flats."

"I just don't trust it. I think she likes you."

"That woman is married and has three children. And if you haven't noticed, her husband is of a slightly different variety."

"Oh please. Eating vanilla doesn't exclude you from liking chocolate."

"Is that why you're always watching movies with Brad Pitt?" Colin joked, trying to lighten the mood.

"I'm serious, Colin. I want you to fire her," she demanded, her facial expression conveying, "Or else." "I don't feel comfortable with her working at the office with you."

Colin knew better than to argue. Besides, Evelyn meant nothing to him. Given that they had had more than one salacious encounter, he suspected she would soon become clingy. "No problem, honey. I'll call her tonight and let her know her services are no longer required."

"No worries. *I'll* call her. That way she can't make you feel bad. I know you have a weakness for the wounded."

"If you'd feel more comfortable calling her, go right ahead." Colin let the words leave his lips, yet on the inside he was as nervous as a salmon swimming up a stream of bathing bears. The cheating husband prayed that Evelyn wouldn't expose their little secret out of anger. "I'm gonna go get out of these work clothes. You have her number, right?"

"I have it." Jocelyn watched her husband as he headed back to their bedroom, wondering how he really felt about firing Evelyn. His take on it didn't really matter. Evelyn's time with the Ravishes was over, and Jocelyn couldn't wait to deliver the disappointing news.

Chapter 25

Teed Off

As the sun began making its descent, Erick and his oldest son, Michael, carried a bucket of golf balls to the back of the family's property and teed off.

Evelyn busied herself with washing dishes, all the while gazing up at an infomercial on the television nearby. Sure, her eyes were glued to the tube, yet if you asked her a question about what had intrigued her so, Evelyn wouldn't be able to form a viable response. Unless, of course, it involved Colin. He was all the lust-crazed woman could think about—the man of her dreams. Evelyn had even gone as far as to title him her hero. Those erotic fantasies of her and him were enough to steam the kitchen windows if the heat coming off the running water in the sink wasn't enough.

Elsewhere in the house, Diana stood, perplexed, staring at the many choices of attire hanging in her bedroom closet. She'd already rejected seven outfits. Picking out something to wear was a crucial matter for the high school senior with ample popularity. The last thing she wanted to do was to choose the wrong clothes. Diana would search through that closet all night if she had to; instead she used the ace in her proverbial pocket, a best friend. Diana grabbed her cell phone from the mahogany dresser and dialed, calling for reinforcements she could count on.

Across the hall, Bryson leaned back against his headboard, gaze glued to one of the home movies on his camcorder. Judging by the awestruck look on his face, the film that demanded his attention wasn't lacking in shock value. The young boy wouldn't take his eyes away from the screen. Several minutes in, Evelyn burst into the room unexpectedly.

"Bryson, what are you watching?"

He sat there frozen, as if caught in the act of something wicked. Words refused to be uttered. Suspecting the boy was hiding something, Evelyn bolted toward him. Just as she reached the end of his bed, her phone rang, demanding her attention. "You wait right here. I want to see what that is that's got you so interested." Evelyn wagged her forefinger at Bryson before turning to rush from his room.

She'd left her phone on the kitchen counter, next to the sink. Right before Jocelyn was about to hang up, Evelyn answered the call. "Hey there," she uttered softly, assuming it was Colin.

"Good evening, Evelyn. This is Mrs. Ravish."

"Jocelyn. What can I do for you?" she asked, her tone now back to normal.

"Nothing. That's actually why I was calling. I wanted to inform you that your services would no longer be needed. We've got everything under control, so we don't need the help. You can pick up your last payment, or I can mail it to you tomorrow. Whichever is easiest."

Jocelyn's words were like a punch to the gut. Devastated, Evelyn slowly lowered herself into one of the chairs at the kitchen table. "I can pick it up," she replied calmly.

"Perfect, I'll actually be at the post office in town tomorrow afternoon. Let's plan on meeting up. I'll give you a ring before I head into town."

"Sounds like a plan," Evelyn replied under staggered breaths. Her heart had been broken. The fantasy was over. She couldn't believe Colin had allowed his wife to discard her so easily.

"Enjoy your night." Jocelyn disconnected her call with a smile.

It's all her fault, you know. She wanted you out of the way because she could see how much Colin loves you, the voice in Evelyn's head told her.

Heart thumping, Evelyn felt as if she were about to explode. Her lip twitched, a side effect of the embarrassment Jocelyn had caused her.

You're just gonna sit there and look stupid, huh? The voice simply wouldn't let up.

"Shut up. Just shut up." A watery-eyed Evelyn sprang up from her seat and paced the floor. "I've got to see him. I have to know why he did this." Evelyn snatched her car keys from a small hook near their mudroom door, then headed out of the house to see Colin.

A mass of emotions took their turn surfacing as she sped down the dual-lane highway. She swerved around slower drivers at every opportunity, anger, lust, obsession, betrayal, heartbreak, even envy taking their toll on her.

She thinks she can erase you. Make it as if you were never even there. What do they call it? A non-factor? the voice in her head said.

Evelyn ran her jacket sleeve across her nose, wiping the mucus from her upper lip. Her face was a mess of wet and dry tears. The desperate woman thought about what she would say once she saw him, how she would profess her love. . . . Evelyn worried whether it would be enough for Colin. She feared Jocelyn's ill health would pull at his heartstrings, guilt him into keeping her off the staff.

What are you gonna do if he refuses? her alter ego inquired.

"He won't." Evelyn stopped along the road to the Ravishes' home and threw the gear into park.

Tossing and turning, Colin couldn't seem to get even fifteen minutes of solid sleep that night. Each time he drifted off to dreamland, Evelyn was waiting there for him. The first time he'd shut his eyes, he'd seen her in a bubble bath littered with rose petals. The second time, Evelyn had been lying naked atop crimson silk sheets. In his bed, of all places . . . Each time, he envisioned her beckoning him. Colin woke up after each episode, trying his best to shake the enticing fantasy from his thoughts. After all, there was no need for him to torture himself. As far as the adulterous husband knew, Jocelyn had made sure he would never see Evelyn again.

Now he got up from the bed, leaving his wife sleeping peacefully in their bed. Colin headed for the living room, figuring he'd lie on the couch, pick a show to binge-watch, and tune in until he conked out. Out of nowhere, a car alarm sounded, prompting Colin to spring into action. Navigating through the dark, with only the fluorescent lights from the waterfall illuminating his way, he darted to the front door.

Within seconds, he grabbed his key from a hook by their door and rushed out to the porch. As he stood there, he pressed a button on his key fob, disarming his car alarm. "Who's out there?" he called out, not wanting to step off the porch, as he was wearing only his boxer briefs.

Nothing but crickets could be heard. Colin squinted, sharpening his vision, to study the perimeter around his SUV. "This can't be real," he said aloud to himself upon catching a glimpse of what appeared to be Evelyn's silhouette. He closed the front door behind him, then stepped barefoot out onto the leafy lawn. "Hello. Is there someone out here?" He stepped closer to his SUV.

That was when she emerged from behind his vehicle, wearing nothing but the skin in which she'd been born.

"What are you doing here?" His eyes bucked wide.

"You . . ." Evelyn rushed toward Colin, then pounced on him the moment he was within reach. She wrapped her legs around the object of her desire, straddling his waist. "I came all the way over here to finish what we started. Don't disappoint me, Mr. Ravish."

They locked lips, and their passion erupted as Colin had his way with Evelyn just outside his front door. He'd never experienced an adrenaline rush like the one his daring mistress provoked in him. Colin was clueless as to how he'd stop this freight train of an affair from derailing and consequently destroying his marriage. Even worse, he didn't know if he truly wanted to. At least not while he was in the act. Wrong had never felt so right. If he planned to resist her seductive ways, Colin needed to stay far away from Evelyn. Until then, he'd enjoy her nectar one last time.

Erick rang his wife's cell phone for the eighteenth time since realizing she wasn't home. He'd come inside after a few rounds of golf, and when he hadn't found Evelyn in the kitchen, he'd assumed she was in a different part of the house. Lo and behold, once he'd emerged from the shower, his wife had still been nowhere to be found. Blood boiling, Erick tried to keep calm as he dialed her number one more time, but to no avail.

Upon hearing her voicemail greeting yet again, he growled, "Why the fuck isn't she answering her phone?" Frustrated, he tore off his towel, slipped into the boxer briefs and pajama pants he'd spread across the bed. He covered his strong, damp torso with a white V-neck T-shirt, then slipped on his house shoes, all the while his gut twisting. Something wasn't quite right. As opposed to guessing, Erick intended on finding his wife to clear up any misconceptions.

After their scandalous romp, Colin sat in Evelyn's truck, reflecting on the choice they'd made. Evelyn pulled her shirt down over her head, covering her breasts, then smiled softly, biting her bottom lip. She couldn't remember ever having felt so heavenly. Colin, on the other hand, had since allowed his lustful feelings to fade and had come to the harsh realization that what he and Evelyn were doing had to stop.

She ignored the reluctance she saw in his eyes. "Can I see you tomorrow?"

"We can't do this anymore, Evelyn."

"You don't mean that. What we have is meant to be. I can feel it. You can't possibly not want me anymore." She leaned over the center console to kiss him.

Colin allowed the gesture of passion, but only for a moment, before he rejected her advances altogether. "I said no, Evelyn. I can't." He remained adamant, forcing her away from him, his hands gripping her biceps. "I'm sorry. Please, just stay away. This is over." Colin abruptly exited the SUV and headed back toward his house.

A tear ran down her trembling cheek. "You don't mean that," Evelyn murmured in despair.

Meanwhile, a dark figure loomed in the shadows, watching Colin as he made the trek back to his front door.

Colin, completely oblivious to the stranger's presence, pressed on until he heard the sound of a twig snapping under the Peeping Tom's boot.

"Is somebody there? You should know this is private property." Colin squinted as he gazed into the bushes along the path. Colin wasn't too worried; he was used to his property attracting riffraff because of their ingenious side hustle. "I suggest you get out of here, and don't come back," he proclaimed as his final warning before mounting the porch steps. When he opened the front door, Colin was stunned to see his wife, Jocelyn, standing there.

"Honey, what are you doing up?" he asked her.

"I was just going to ask you the same thing. You're nearly naked," Jocelyn answered, suspicious of her husband's actions.

"My car alarm went off. I think I saw someone wandering around on our property. Hopefully, I scared them off."

Jocelyn took her husband's words as gospel. "I'm sure you did. Let's go back to bed."

Colin closed the front door, then secured the dead bolt as he peeked out the peephole. "Yes, I'm exhausted."

"Did you get in a good workout today?"

"Better than I've had in a long time," Colin responded, his rendezvous with Evelyn fresh in his mind.

Meanwhile, Evelyn traveled along Dixie Highway, struggling to come to terms with the decision Colin had laid down moments ago. What he'd said to her sent her reeling through a whirlwind of emotions.

Under the illumination of the full moon, cheap motels, gas stations, and topless bars became ever more present along the winding road. Distraught, Evelyn drove aimlessly, in a daze, hoping to find clarity as to how to become the victor of Colin's heart. Unfortunately, nothing she could come up with brought her more satisfaction than getting rid of Jocelyn permanently. Something inside her, though, told Evelyn that this action wouldn't sit well with Colin. And she had to consider his feelings too. He'd been with Jocelyn since they were younger. The last thing he would want was for harm to come to his already ailing wife. Evelyn pulled off the main road onto a smaller one near a gas station in the neighboring town of Waterford.

Look at you now. Gave up all your goodies, and he tossed you out like trash. It's Jocelyn's fault, you know? She's too weak. I told you. You're not wounded enough for him. The voice in her head refused to let up.

"But I've recovered." Evelyn gazed at her reflection in the rearview mirror as she came to a stop at the light.

No one wants a woman who doesn't need a man, the voice advised her further. *You'll have to get rid of her . . . It's the only way.*

Just then, Evelyn heard shouting coming from the gas station. She turned her head to the right and watched, aghast, as a pimp slapped his whore's cheek. She lowered her right window to make out what was being said.

"I said, you're working all night if I say so! Now, hurry up, so we can make this money," the pimp yelled as he yanked his trick toward the gas station doors.

The wobbling prostitute maintained her balance on her four-inch heels as she proceeded inside to pay for their gas, pulling at the hem of her fitted black body dress as she went. "Whatever you say, Daddy," she said just before the door shut behind her.

"You damn right." He flicked his cigarette across the concrete, then pulled a miniature comb from the pocket of his Adidas jacket, figuring his gelled black comb-over could use some maintenance.

"I'll never be a victim again," Evelyn vowed before exiting her vehicle. The hunting knife she'd pulled from under her seat fit narrowly in her side purse.

On his way around to the side of the building, the pimp noticed her in the darkness. She wasn't his type. Her purposeful eyes told him so. The pimp sucked at his teeth.

Evelyn hurried into the gas station and quickly took note of the trick attempting to settle a dispute with the gas station attendant.

"You gave me a ten, ma'am. Not a twenty," the attendant asserted.

"You a damn liar. I know what I gave you. Y'all always trying to cheat somebody up here. That's why I hate coming up in this muthafucka."

Evelyn headed straight toward the restrooms, but instead of going inside the ladies' room, she exited the building through a different door, one that brought her to the back side of the gas station. By wedging a rock against the open door with her foot, Evelyn made sure it would remain cracked open until her return. A smile appeared on her face when she heard the stream of urine hitting concrete just beyond where she stood.

The pimp had his head thrown back as he relieved himself, penis partially poking through the fence separating him and Evelyn. That was when she took her chance. After retrieving her knife, she dashed over to him, quickly grasped the tip of his member, then chopped off three inches of the squishy appendage.

"Ahhh!" he hollered, in agony, as he dropped to the ground, clutching the spot he had once revered.

Evelyn hurried back inside to wash the blood from her hunting knife in the restroom sink. A flickering fluorescent bulb above the dingy sink was her only guide. The restroom reeked of urine and whatever substance was floating around in the clogged toilet, amid a mound of tissue. Evelyn hurried as she rinsed off the pimp's blood, the stench nearly causing her to lose the contents of her stomach.

As she left the restroom, she heard the pimp yelling and watched as his trick raced through the gas station doors. Evelyn was right behind her to survey the commotion. Of course, she soon surmised there was nothing further she could contribute to the situation, so Evelyn headed on her way, leaving the trick to save her pimp. If she so pleased . . .

Sure, emasculating him had satisfied her momentary desire for justice. Yet the nagging voice in her head persisted. *So, how are you gonna get rid of her?*

Evelyn climbed behind the wheel and drove away. A quarter mile down the road, she stopped at the flashing yellow traffic light, pondering her next move. Killing Jocelyn was a concept that was becoming more probable, though it was barely plausible. Colin's affection being ripped from her the way it had been felt like a fate worse than death, and this fueled her motivation to get rid of Jocelyn. *There's no way she can cope without him,* Evelyn thought.

You may as well put her out of her misery, the voice conceded.

Bright headlights hitting her rearview mirror blinded Evelyn, pulling her from her deep reverie. The driver behind her laid into the car horn, pressuring her to hit the gas. She pushed her foot down on the gas pedal and left the bright lights in the distance, but only for a second. The menacing lights grew large in her rearview, and the horn sounded again as the front bumper behind her nearly slammed into the rear of the Yukon.

Looks like someone else needs to be taught a lesson, her alter ego announced.

"What if it's someone from the gas station?" Evelyn blurted, paranoia taking hold.

Does that make them indispensable?

"I'm just going to pull over." Evelyn grabbed her purse, the knife inside it, from the passenger seat as she eased the Yukon onto the shoulder.

The vehicle followed her to the side of the road and rolled to a stop. Its occupant got out and tentatively approached her window.

"Evelyn, what the hell are you doing out here!" Erick yelled, tapping his knuckles on her driver's side window.

Upon hearing his voice, Evelyn thought she was imagining things, but when she looked up, she saw Erick standing there, and reality set in.

"Honey." She rolled down her window, eyes bucked with surprise. "What are you doing here?"

"You first," he insisted, an infuriated look contorting his face.

"I just—"

Erick cut her off before she could give her explanation. "Save it. Let's just get home. You can explain there." Frustrated, he turned, then headed back to his pickup.

Chapter 26

Trouble Next Door

Erick paced the floor of their bedroom, attempting to extinguish his fury before unjustifiably unleashing it on his wife. He wondered what she had been out there doing. The logical part of his brain found it hard to come up with a viable scenario. Why would she possibly leave after dark without telling him, or anyone else in the house, for that matter?

"So, are you gonna tell me why you were wandering around in the middle of the night?"

Cue the crocodile tears. If one thing rang true, it had to be the fact that Evelyn was a champion at manipulating her husband's emotions. She had found gullibility one of Erick's greatest weaknesses. "Promise me you won't be upset. I tried as best as I could." She sulked, taking a seat on the edge of the bed.

"What are you talking about, my love?"

"My boss called while you were out playing golf. I was fired. They said my services are no longer required. I guess I'm just broken. I can't do any job right."

"Why didn't you call me inside and tell me?"

"I needed some space. Some time to think . . . It's not easy telling your husband you're a failure. For the second time."

"Oh, my love. You'll never be a failure in my eyes." He had bought her excuse, deep down inside wanting to have one. After all, what reality would he have to confront if he got to the truth? A truth Erick wasn't willing to face . . .

Evelyn smiled, her gaze settling on her purse with the knife tucked inside it, as she and Erick shared an embrace.

Evelyn's eyes popped open at the crack of dawn, and there was one thing on her mind, Jocelyn.

Down the hall, Bryson stared from a window in his room that gave him a view of their front yard. His shoulders slumped as he watched his new neighbors pull up to the house next door. To his dismay, his not so friendly classmate Domonic got out of the car and carried two suitcases to the door. "You've gotta be kidding me!"

Domonic saw Bryson peering at him from the window and flashed him a sly smile before Bryson closed the blinds, obstructing his view.

"I can't believe we can afford this house," Domonic admitted in awe as he and his mother waddled into the foyer of their new abode.

"And we got it fully furnished! What a deal!" Mrs. Danielson exclaimed.

Mr. Danielson's tragic death had paid off well. With life insurance, retirement savings, and a 401k, he had left his family well taken care of. For Mrs. Danielson, never again having to be a victim of her husband's abusive rants was a dream come true.

"Well, go pick out a bedroom. There's four of them. But I've got dibs on the biggest one, the one with the en suite bathroom," she told her son.

Domonic tore through the Victorian-style abode, his worn sneakers staining the cream carpet.

"Take your shoes off, boy. You're ruining the carpet. We've got money now. Act like you've got some class," she demanded on her way to the kitchen to see if the previous owners had been nice enough to leave a bottle of whiskey.

"Mama, Mama! You're not gonna believe this." Bryson knocked frantically at his parents' bathroom door.

"What is it, Bryson? I'm in the shower."

Erick entered the room, apron tied around his waist, having prepared breakfast for the family. He hoped to cheer Evelyn up, since she'd been canned the night prior.

"Bryson, your mom is in the shower. Can't it wait? Why don't you come and have breakfast? Your mom will join us at the table."

Although Erick's suggestion left Bryson dissatisfied, the amped-up boy had no other choice but to take his father's advice. "Fine." He reluctantly left his parent's room.

Ten agonizing minutes went by before Evelyn finally joined her family at the kitchen table to partake in their morning meal. "Smells good." She inhaled the aroma of bacon and maple syrup.

A steaming pile of fluffy scrambled eggs filled the bowl at the center of the table. Even with the plethora of tasty vittles available for consumption, Michael grabbed a bagel, kissed his mother on the cheek as she entered the room, then headed out the door.

"Enjoy your day, everybody. I've got practice, so you'll have to enjoy breakfast without my witty conversation."

Erick spoke up. "Enjoy your day, kid. We love you."

Diana was already well into her stack of blueberry pancakes when her mother walked in. "Mom. Thank God you're out of the bathroom. Bryson is driving me insane."

She stuffed her earbuds into her ears, drowning out further communication with Destiny's Child's new single "Bootylicious."

"What is it, Bryson? What's got you so amped up?" Evelyn asked.

"We have a new neighbor," the boy said.

"Well, that's nice. Hopefully, they'll cut the grass."

Erick nodded his head enthusiastically, partially because of her comment, and partially in response to the taste of the hickory-smoked bacon he had bitten into.

"That's the thing. It's not nice at all," Bryson countered. "It's one big disaster is what it is."

"Bryson, you act like our neighbor is the grim reaper." Evelyn sat down beside him. Even though she had more pressing issues on her mind, she felt it was important that she heard her son out.

"Worse. It's Domonic."

"Domonic, the bully from school?" Evelyn exclaimed, in shock.

"I saw him and his mother moving bags in this morning."

Erick chimed in, feeling the need to put a positive spin on their situation. "Bryson, I thought you said yourself things were settled between you two? Is he still picking on you?"

"No. Everything is fine, but that doesn't mean I want to live next door to him."

"Maybe you should give him a chance. Most people become bullies after being bullied themselves. Sometimes you just need to start fresh," Erick advised.

Evelyn didn't agree, but she wasn't going to contest what her husband had said, especially in front of Bryson. She allowed him to take this softer stance, deciding it was best for her son to view his father as entirely reasonable.

"I think your father may have a point. It's okay to give some people a second chance." After all, look what she'd gotten away with so far.

Once he finished breakfast, Bryson kept himself busy with his ball and mitt in the backyard. He could see Domonic on the other side of the row of pine trees separating their properties. Bryson tossed the baseball high into the air, then caught it as it descended in front of him. Domonic watched, clutching his mitt tight to his belly. He wanted desperately to play with Bryson, so that he blended into the affluent neighborhood and was accepted by the other residents. But he had been so mean to Bryson, Domonic feared he'd never find a friend there.

"What position do you play?" Bryson yelled out to him, pushing away all apprehension.

Domonic brandished a wide smile as he squeezed by long tree limbs to close the distance between himself and Bryson.

Chapter 27

Never Giving Up

Late that morning, Evelyn strolled into the postal store just across the road from the annex building. She'd received a text from Jocelyn informing her she would be there with her wages. Evelyn had yet to decide how she would get rid of Jocelyn. Deep down she held on to hope that she could convince Colin to abandon his wife. If this happened, Evelyn wouldn't have to get her hands dirty. She wanted this not for Jocelyn's sake, but out of fear she'd risk losing him altogether. Killing his wife could very well be a deal breaker.

"Evelyn, oh my gosh! It's so good to see you. Are you coming back to work soon?" Christian inquired from behind the front counter as she handed over a customer's change.

Evelyn came closer, not wanting to draw attention to herself. She was a little embarrassed she had bowed out of work under the assumption she couldn't handle it. "Hi, Christian. I'm actually here to meet Mrs. Ravish."

"Ooh, the cookie lady. She left this envelope for you." Christian pulled an envelope from her apron, then handed it over to Evelyn.

"She's gone?"

"I couldn't say. The last time I saw her, she was headed around the corner there to check her post office box."

"Thanks, Christian. Well, it was good seeing you."
Evelyn waved goodbye.

"You know, Mercury must be in retrograde or something. There's been lots of people from my past popping
up," Christian replied, trying to keep Evelyn there and
talking. The Clarkston postal store was often quiet. It
didn't take long for boredom to set in during a shift.
Christian's only opportunity to brighten her workday
was a lengthy conversation with Evelyn, one chock-full
of juicy tidbits from her personal life. Whatever information she could gather would certainly make for good
office gossip. Idle minds, you know . . .

A voice sounded from behind the greeting cards, dash-
ing Christian's hopes. "Ma'am, do you have some tape
I can borrow?" inquired a customer, attempting to seal
the care package she intended to ship off. The feeble old
woman stretched her back upright and was still barely
able to see over the five-foot greeting-card display.

Seeing Evelyn duck out of their conversation to allow
her to tend to the customer, Christian rolled her eyes
in frustration. "Yes, ma'am. It's right behind you. Four
bucks a roll."

"Four dollars! That's just preposterous," the old woman
complained.

Evelyn darted around a corner and headed to the side
of the building where the post office boxes were. She
couldn't wait to look Jocelyn in the eye and tell her what
she thought about being fired so tactlessly. As Evelyn had
learned already a time or two, some things didn't go as
planned.

She passed by a man checking his post office box
and frowned when she smelled his cologne. There was
something familiar yet unknown about the man, but it
was his scent that caused her footsteps to slow. She had
smelled that same scent in the café that day. *Is it him*

again? she questioned. Then her thoughts were taken over by a memory of the early morning she was attacked. She had smelled this very scent that morning. Evelyn remembered the bright headlamps of the oncoming mail truck, the way they had blinded her. Her recollection startled her so much that she turned to face the man. Alas, her big brown eyes fell upon an empty hallway. The stranger had gone, taking with him the haunting scent.

When Evelyn arrived back home, she could see Bryson tossing a ball with the little fat kid she'd made fatherless not long ago. That was how she thought of it, anyway. Glaring at the pair over the top of her sunglasses, she pulled into the driveway. Evelyn hadn't thought Bryson would actually be friends with Domonic. His actions told Evelyn her son had a heart much more forgiving than her own.

"Hey, give me a second. Wait here. I'll be right back," Bryson instructed Domonic, handing the baseball over to him.

"Sure." Domonic did as his new friend asked, busying himself by tossing the ball high into the air, then catching it as it descended.

Preferring not to be embarrassed by his mother, Bryson darted to her vehicle and hopped into the passenger seat to talk in private. "Hey, Mama. Before you ask, just let me explain."

"I'm waiting." Evelyn removed her sunglasses to see him without any obstruction.

"Remember what you said about second chances?"

"I do."

"Well, Domonic is going through a tough time. His father had an accident, and now it's just him and his mom. I know how hard it was for me when you were gone. Having a friend like me around would have helped. So, I've decided I'm going to start playing with Domonic."

He is *a pussy. I knew it.* The voice erupted out of nowhere. Of course, no one except Evelyn heard it.

She swallowed, resisting the urge to respond in a negative way. To her son, she spoke kindly. She wanted him to live as he saw fit, as long as he wasn't being pushed around.

"It sounds like you've really thought this over, Bryson. If that's the conclusion you've come to, then I respect your decision."

"Thank you for not giving me a hard time about it." Bryson grinned, looking at his mother in admiration.

"I'll always support you, Bryson. Always. You'd do the same for me, right?"

"Of course I would. I love you, Mama."

I've got such a wonderful kid, Evelyn silently acknowledged. "I love you too. Now run along and play with your new friend. Looks like he could use the exercise."

"You should see his mom." Bryson hopped out of the SUV.

Yes. Run along, you wonderful little asshole, the voice remarked.

Refusing to leave his desk for lunch, Barnes combed through the photos he'd confiscated from Randy Alky's bomb shelter. He hoped to identify some, if not all, of the women photographed, and discover the connections that would solve the murders.

"What cha got there, sir?" Fackender strolled into his office, ready to disclose her findings.

Barnes leaned back in his chair. "Check them out." He pointed toward the photos of scantily dressed women spread out on his desk. "During my reevaluation of Mr.

Alky's property, I stumbled upon something I assume he meant to keep secret. After traveling about a football field's length of the way into his yard, I uncovered it. Down in the earth, he had a bomb shelter built. It was more like a sex dungeon of sorts. These photos are of the women who endured his experience."

Fackender began picking up the photos one by one and studying them. "This one I've seen." She had paused at the photograph of a young woman who she was sure was someone named Lydia. "It's one of the students who had trouble with Mr. Sobieski years ago. I have her file in my office. In fact, I have all the women's pictures. Let's just see how many links Mr. Sobieski and Mr. Alky have in common." She rushed from his office to get the files from her desk.

Chapter 28

Common Ground

Jackson Pierce sat in his Bronco at the corner of his old stomping grounds. His favorite street on Rural Route 8. He had so many memories there. Had taught so many lessons . . .

He recalled a time when Mrs. Teresa, the old woman who lived in the house near the opposite corner, hadn't been frightened to death of him. He had wooed her, so to speak, with his good deeds and impeccable manners, but one day, a day he had refused to take his medication, his true colors had begun to surface. By the time she'd realized his intentions were malicious, it had been too late. He'd unearthed her demons and used them against her. To this day, she kept up her tradition of resting on her porch swing as she observed the neighborhood's activity. But each time that mail truck came up the block, she'd rush inside. Mrs. Teresa never wanted to see Jackson's face again, and the former marine seemed to be okay with that. That, and the fact that she'd think twice before trying to drug the truth out of someone.

Next door, Mr. Escobar waxed his gunmetal-gray BMW convertible. Jackson could tell how content the man was with his life, as well as with the worldly possessions he'd amassed all on his own. It made Jackson feel good to see this man, who had once been on the receiving end of betrayal, now happily coupled. He credited himself for running off Mrs. Escobar's mister.

Just then a barefoot and pregnant Mrs. Escobar stepped out onto the front porch, with a glass of lemonade for her husband. Pamela had become a new woman, a faithful and loving wife, thanks to Jackson's warnings.

The small muscular man across the street wouldn't so much as look in the couple's direction. Jackson noticed the way he turned his attention toward his own property after Mrs. Escobar emerged from the house. The beating Jackson had furnished the man in the past was enough to keep his penis in his pants, and it had taught him the valuable lesson that cheaters never prospered. When it came to Mrs. Escobar at least. The bitter man continued blowing dead leaves from his lawn with an electric leaf blower attached to his back.

All seemed well on Jackson's old route. He relished the results his efforts, although extreme, had manifested. He'd managed to foil Mrs. Teresa's plans to drug and extract vital information from him, and, in so doing, her past transgressions had come to light. He'd beaten and threatened the adulterous Mr. Trionfi so that he would stay away from Mrs. Escobar, ending their salacious affair. And Mr. Sobieski, well, he was completely out of the picture. . . .

Barnes and Fackender decided to tackle their next lead together, and so they blew by Jackson's Ford Bronco, failing to notice his presence. Their focus remained on finding more clues to solve the case. Barnes turned into the driveway of Mr. Sobieski's family home. Questioning Sobieski's stepdaughter as to his crude behavior would be a shot in the dark, but they had decided to take their chances. The young woman was the last of his relatives in

Michigan. Something had to come of a talk with her. Any background information into his and Lydia's relationship would help. Lydia and Mr. Sobieski's stepdaughter had attended the same high school several years back. Odds were they had known one another.

Barnes led the investigation, and so he was the one who rang the doorbell after they climbed the steps to the huge wooden wraparound porch. Both of them gazed around as they waited for someone to answer. It wasn't long at all before a skinny young woman with a long blond ponytail opened the door. Her big blue eyes grew wide when she realized that the authorities stood before her. Every time she saw them, a tragedy seemed to befall her. First, her mother had passed away, leaving her with her perverted stepfather. And just months ago, he had disappeared, only to be found dead. At this point, the young woman wasn't expecting good news from the cops.

"Can't I just live a normal life?" she mumbled.

"I'm sorry, sweetheart. I know it's been difficult for you," Barnes replied. "We just want to ask you a few questions about your stepfather. A little insight into his personal life would definitely help."

"Fine," she murmured disapprovingly. Leaving the door open, she made an about-face and headed to the living room, which was right off the foyer.

As a gentleman should, Barnes allowed Fackender to enter first, and then he closed the front door behind him. The house remained decorated just as it had been when her mother was alive. Her grandmother's heirlooms still lined the ledge along the fireplace, and even the side tables that accompanied the flower-patterned living-room furniture were in the same place.

Shelby flopped down on the sofa. "So, what is it about my dear old stepdad you wanna know?"

Fackender took a seat on the love seat across from her, while Barnes remained standing.

"Do you know anything about your father having trouble with any of the students at your school several years back?" Barnes asked, cutting right to the chase.

Her eyes wandered about the room, telling them that she knew more than she was comfortable with sharing. She played with her ponytail, twisting the end of it around her index finger, another indication that she was prevaricating.

"No. But he was the principal. The only people who had problems with him were students that got suspended."

"Can you think of anyone who might have been angry enough to hurt him?" Barnes asked as he removed a small envelope from his pocket. He withdrew five photographs from the envelope.

She shrugged her shoulders nonchalantly. "Not really."

"I want you to look at some of these photos. Tell me if you know any of the women. I've blurred most of their bodies because of the inappropriate nature of the photos," Fackender said, then handed over the photographs. "Take your time. Anything you can tell us would help."

Shelby began perusing the pictures one by one. She paused at one of the photos for a moment, having recognized the young woman as someone she knew from high school. The next photo, Shelby couldn't take her eyes off. It was her old friend Lydia. When the women in the photos had both been girls, Principal Sobieski had expelled them from his school.

"Does she seem familiar to you?" Fackender inquired, noticing that she had paused.

That was when she began feeling the weight of her stepfather's demons. "A few of the women here do," Shelby admitted.

"How do you know them?"

"I went to school with them. This one was my best friend." She frowned, peering down at Lydia's snapshot.

"What happened, if you don't mind me asking?"

"She wasn't a good friend. I always felt like her relationship with my stepfather was a little more personal than it should have been. It seemed like when she'd come over to hang out, it was just to get closer to my stepfather. At first, I thought I was just being paranoid, but then I saw them standing so close, they nearly kissed. At that moment I knew our friendship was all a ploy. That's when I told her I never wanted to be friends with her again. By then she had started running with a bad group of girls, anyway. They were all sexually active. Lydia and I just went down two different paths. I wished her the best. But last I heard, she was selling her body out of one of those cheap motels on Dixie. That's all I know."

"Well, you certainly said a mouthful," Barnes remarked, satisfied with their findings.

That evening Mrs. Danielson prepared lasagna for dinner. It was a special day. They'd moved into their new home, and she wanted to enjoy a home-cooked meal.

"Come on in here, Domonic. Mama made lasagna for you to celebrate our new digs."

Domonic plopped down in the fancy cherry-oak dining-room chair, left behind by Mr. Fuboi's estate. "But it's Stouffer's," the boy complained.

"Listen here, boy. You best be appreciating the meal before you. There are kids out here starving. Wishing they lived in a house like this . . . kids that wish for a mother to cook for them . . . This ain't something you come by normally, so you better appreciate it. Now, get me an oven mitt, so that I can get the biscuits out. I got the Red Lobster kind from the market." The woman was nearly out of breath. Even with her light loose-fitting attire, her weight made it hard for her to keep cool.

"Fine," he huffed.

"I told you about that attitude, boy," she said, having noted his disapproving tone.

Domonic got up, grabbed an oven mitt from the kitchen drawer for his mother, and handed it over to her. *I don't know why she can't get it herself*, he complained, but to himself.

From the kitchen window, he saw that the Todds were out back barbecuing. Dominic wished he had a family like that. They all looked so happy. Mr. Todd was flipping steaks on the grill, while Michael tossed the ball with Bryson. His sister, Diana, relaxed in the hot tub, immersed in a melody blaring from her iPod. Evelyn sat reading a novel that had everything she'd become accustomed to: crime, mystery, betrayal, even murder. . . .

Domonic picked up the pair of binoculars in the bay window. Mr. Fuboi had often spied on the family next door, attempting to find fault where he could. It always had bugged him that Erick made more money than he did. Now he didn't have to worry about that, because he was dead. Even so, he'd be turning over in his grave if he knew who had obtained his beautiful abode.

The little boy peeked through the binoculars for a closer look. He zeroed in on the blood he saw depicted on the cover of the book Evelyn sat reading. The title, he saw, was *Compelled to Murder*, and this made him even fonder of Bryson's mother. *I'm gonna become part of that family*, Domonic vowed. He wanted nothing more than to have a normal family. Attaching himself to the Todds was as close as he would get. Domonic was sure of it.

During dinner he pondered how he'd go about earning the Todds' trust. He knew Evelyn wasn't too happy about the way he'd treated Bryson. If he were going to win them over, he needed to know much more about them than he did now.

"I'm full, Mama. Can I go outside and play for a little while before it gets dark?"

"Sure. Go make you some friends." She blinked lethargically and slurred her words, as she was well into the bottle of Cognac she'd found in the cupboard. "I was just about to come out and sit on the porch. Enjoy our new digs."

Domonic got up from the dinner table without another word, ignoring his mother's rambling. Neglecting to clear his plate from the table, the chubby boy darted through the house, on his way to retrieve what he thought would nurture his and Bryson's blossoming friendship. With gusto, he tackled the crème-colored carpeted staircase as best he could. Domonic burst through a door to his right and entered a room still filled with boxes of his belongings. The stack of cardboard boxes near the closet had all his toys stored inside them. Luckily, the boy knew just the one he was searching for. Domonic placed the top two boxes off to the side so that he could open the third one in the stack.

"There they are." His eyes lit up when he saw the walkie-talkies in the box of toys.

Domonic snatched them up, then headed on over to the Todds'. Out back, Bryson was tidying the yard, collecting his balls, bat, pogo stick, and a plethora of other items that had kept him busy throughout the day. When he caught sight of Domonic, his new friend was making his way through the row of pine trees.

"Hey, Bryson! Wanna play Black Hawk Down?"

"I can't. Not right now, anyway. It's time for me to go inside," Bryson answered, regrettably declining the offer.

"Here. Take this." Domonic handed over one of the walkie-talkies. "So we can talk to each other."

Bryson smiled. He thanked God Domonic was no longer bullying him. Accepting one of the walkie-talkies was a welcomed change, given that he'd become accustomed to Domonic taking from him as opposed to furnishing him with resources. "Cool. Thanks, Domonic."

"No problem. Now we can talk to each other anytime."

"Maybe I'll give you a chirp after I finish cleaning up."

"Okay. I'll talk to you later." Domonic turned and headed on his way.

As Bryson tucked himself into bed that evening, the walkie-talkie, which was lying atop the pillow beside him, chirped. Initially he froze, not wanting to answer for fear of his parents hearing him and realizing he was still awake. Ultimately, the kind-hearted little boy couldn't let his friend down. The walkie-talkie chirped again as he went to reach for it. And then he heard Domonic's voice.

"Hey, you there?"

Bryson rushed to turn down the volume, then answered. "Hey, what's up?"

"What are you doing?"

"It's my bedtime," Bryson admitted, a little embarrassed about having to be in bed so early. The last thing he wanted was for Domonic to think he was a baby. "So, I'm in my room, watching television," he lied, hoping to gain admiration for his supposed act of defiance.

"You won't get in trouble?" Domonic asked.

Feeling pressure to keep up the charade, Bryson replied, "It's worth it."

Domonic harbored doubts as to the truthfulness of Bryson's claim that he was defying his parents. "So, what's the worst thing you've ever done?" he asked, challenge in his voice.

Silence loomed between them as Bryson struggled to come up with a story worthy of honorable mention.

"How about I go first?" Domonic said, relieving his new friend of the pressure.

Bryson played it off as if he hadn't just choked on his first test. The innocent little boy wanted desperately to prove he was cool enough to hang out with Domonic. "Okay, you go first, then."

"One time I was over at my uncle Randy's house with my dad. My dad used to go over there a lot to keep from arguing with my mom. Anyway, after about an hour of sitting in front of the television alone, I figured they weren't coming back in from the woods anytime soon. My uncle always kept a fridge full of beer. Have you ever had beer before?"

"No." Bryson replied, staring fixedly at the walkie-talkie as he ducked under the comforter. Eager to hear more, he added, "What does it taste like?"

"It doesn't really taste that good, but it makes you feel different—"

"Different how?" Bryson interrupted, chomping at the bit to know more.

"So, I went to the fridge and opened it up. My uncle had stocked it with a case of Dirty Thirties ale. At first, I only took four cans. Neither of them would notice they were gone, anyway. After pounding those down, I let out a big ole burp. Beer either makes you burp or gives you the hiccups. That's when I started to feel really relaxed. More like I hadn't a care in the world. I didn't even care if my dad and uncle walked in on me. By the time my uncle and dad made it back up to the house, they found me passed out on the carpet, surrounded by a bunch of empty beer cans."

"Did you get into trouble?"

"No. They laughed at me. My uncle woke me up and made me drink a shot of whiskey to teach me a lesson. Now, that stuff tastes horrible."

"I've never tasted it before."

"Wanna try it?"

Bryson's interest was piqued. "But how would we get some?"

"The people who used to live in this house left some here. I can sneak some out tomorrow if you want me to. Unless you're afraid."

If he can handle it, then I can handle it, Bryson concluded silently. "I'm not afraid. I'll do it."

It was exactly what Domonic wanted to hear. "Hey, do you think your mom will let me trick-or-treat with you guys this year? It's kinda hard for my mom to get around." Halloween was coming up in a couple of days, so Domonic thought now was the perfect time to cement his plans. "Are you guys going trick-or-treating on Halloween?"

"Of course. I wouldn't miss that for the world."

"Do you think it would be okay if I went out with you guys? My mom doesn't get around very well." Domonic made sure to offer up an excuse that would tug at Bryson's heartstrings.

"I usually just walk around the neighborhood to get candy. People are pretty generous around here."

"We can walk together, then. You can show me around."

Bryson agreed. "Sounds good to me."

"Cool. I'll see you tomorrow, Bryson. Tasmanian devil over and out."

Tasmanian devil. What a cool handle, Bryson thought, and then he came up with his very own on the spot. "Alucard, over and out."

"What's an Alucard?"

Happy to educate Domonic, Bryson proceeded to give his take on Alucard, the anime vampire. "He's a good guy. A vampire who is practically invincible. But he feeds on the despair of his enemies, not just their blood." Bryson hoped his explanation validated his choice in Domonic's eyes.

"Well, see you tomorrow, Alucard. Over and out."

"Over and out."

Chapter 29

Mischief

The rising sun's bright rays cut through crème-colored vertical blinds that dressed the Todds' bedroom window. Erick rolled over and wrapped his arms around his sleeping wife, taking in the scent at the nape of her neck. She smelled like coconut. For him, taking her essence into his nostrils felt heavenly. Her curls being bound in a ponytail made it easy for his lips to grace Evelyn's skin. How he wanted her so. His morning wood protruded through his boxer briefs. Days had gone by since they'd had intercourse. Erick didn't want to put too much pressure on his healing wife, yet he could no longer fight the urge to partake of Evelyn's nectar.

The horny husband ground his pelvis against her smooth, firm rump, hoping to wake her for a morning romp. At first, she played possum, lying there wide awake, thinking maybe he'd give up. Minutes went by, but to no avail. Erick knew exactly what he wanted and didn't intend on stopping until he'd gotten it. Under the silver satin sheets, he lifted her negligee and then let his fingertips explore her body. Her soft, dark skin roused his desire even more as he moved from her thighs to the chocolate mounds atop her torso. *If anything is going to work, this is it*, he thought, knowing her breasts were a sensitive area. She'd often referred to them as her spot.

As he caressed her breasts, her juices began to flow. Unable to resist his touch, she began to push back, rolling her hips to grind against him. His already erect penis made his silent plea for affection even more enticing. Erick slid down her yellow lace panties to gain access to his kingdom, anticipating its warmth. That was when Evelyn put her hand behind her and grabbed Erick's member. She stroked it, compounding his excitement.

"Oh, baby," he hummed seductively, pushing closer to her until he dived into her walls.

Evelyn bit into her pillow, her well-endowed husband filling every inch of her space. She couldn't deny he felt heavenly inside her.

Suddenly, they heard tapping at the door. "Mom, Dad?" Bryson called out from the opposite side of their locked bedroom door.

"Damn it," Erick mumbled quietly before saying more. "Bryson, your mother and I are just waking up. We'll be out in a second."

He refused to wait. "I just want to know if I can go over to Domonic's house?"

Erick didn't care; he just wanted to finish what he and Evelyn had started. "Sure, bud. Have fun," he answered, not wavering from the passionate stroking he was awarding his wife.

"Okay. Thanks." The boy darted off to commence the exciting day he had ahead of him.

When the doorbell chimed, Domonic sat up in bed, wondering who could be at their door so early in the morning. He climbed out of bed and rushed down the stairs, knowing all too well the grouchy state this intrusion would put his mother in. Little did he know that she had conked out due to drunkenness and thus was in no way going to wake up anytime soon. Domonic peered through the slim vertical window beside the front door and noticed his eager neighbor standing there.

"You're up early," Domonic greeted Bryson as he opened the door.

"I figured we've got a lot to see. You wanted me to show you around the neighborhood, right? There's no time like the present."

"I'm not exactly dressed. I haven't even had breakfast."

"I didn't think about that. I haven't had breakfast, either." Bryson's shoulders drooped, as he assumed he'd have to go home and wait.

"Hey, do you like Froot Loops?" Domonic asked, rekindling Bryson's hopes.

His eyes lit up with excitement. "I sure do."

"Come on in. We'll have breakfast, and then maybe you can show me that anime character you were telling me about last night."

"Sure." Bryson happily accepted his offer. He had never been inside that house when Mr. Fuboi owned it, so Bryson took his time taking in the scenery around him. It didn't surprise him that Mr. Fuboi had had impeccable taste. Though everything the Danielsons had contributed to the abode seemed to tarnish its luster a bit. He could tell that Domonic and his mother were fish out of water. They'd even started using the wine rack to hold all their beverages; one-liter soda bottles, forty-ounce bottles of malt liquor, even Boone's Farm wine had its place on the rack against a wall in the kitchen.

Domonic proceeded to pull two bowls from the cupboard before handing one over to Bryson. "You'll have to make your own bowl. I'm not your mom."

"Fine with me. I'm a big boy."

The boys filled their bowls to the rim with cereal and milk, then carried them to the family room, opting to eat in front of the television.

Domonic passed Bryson the remote. "Let's see what you like to watch."

"That's easy." Bryson accepted the challenge, turning the station to the first anime-themed cartoon he could find. "This is the good stuff."

"Is this the show with Alucard?"

"Yup. He's the guy with the black hair and the long cape-like coat. Just watch how he gives his opponents chances to kill him before he annihilates them." Bryson gobbled down spoonfuls of cereal while taking in his favorite show.

Domonic studied Bryson as his eyes remained glued to the tube. He wanted desperately to fit in, but even more, he wanted to transform Bryson into a carbon copy of himself. "So where are we going to go first? Do you have anything interesting around here?"

"We've got plenty of cool things around here. Don't worry. I'll show you the fun stuff," Bryson replied, not taking his eyes off the television.

Once he was done with breakfast, Domonic threw on a pair of jean shorts, slid his walkie-talkie onto his belt, then grabbed a clean T-shirt so they could begin their journey.

Moments later, he came tearing down the stairs to meet Bryson, who'd run back to his house to get his walkie-talkie. Just in case the two got separated, they wanted to be able to make it back to one another.

Bryson was ready and waiting when Domonic emerged dressed for their adventure. The pair stood on the porch, looking out at their affluent neighborhood.

"Where to first?" Domonic asked.

"How about we go to the creek?"

"Lead the way, Alucard."

"Okay, Tasmanian devil."

Bryson was elated he had found a new friend in Domonic. Unfortunately, he remained ignorant as to the boy's malevolent intentions.

They walked over a mile down the side of the road, since the neighborhood in which they lived was devoid of sidewalks. Rural Clarkston had more of a country feel to it than a suburban one. It was a town with abundant lush forests around it. Winding creeks ran through them, making the environment even more inviting to those who preferred the more tranquil side of life. Living in a rural place had taught Bryson to be more resourceful. While Mr. Danielson had barely taught his son to tie his shoe, Erick had made sure Bryson was equipped to survive in the wilderness alone. The boy could almost tell the time by the position of the sun. If there ever came a time when he found himself stuck in the wilderness, Bryson could live off berries and other fruits in summer, and in winter, he could fish in the stream to sustain himself. The boy was proficient in making traps, finding the resources to survive, and constructing shelters out of old tree limbs.

"Wanna try to catch some fish?" Bryson asked his friend.

Domonic frowned. "But we don't have any poles. How can we catch them?"

"We can use piles of stones to trap them in the shallow end of the stream. They'll be easy pickin's, then. I'll show you how."

Bryson proceeded to show Dominic a few of his handy tricks. By the time their adventure in the woods came to an end, Domonic had become a more capable human being, thanks to his new friend.

But once Bryson's lesson had been completed, it was Domonic's turn to do some teaching of his own. As the pair made their way back toward their neighborhood, Domonic stopped dead in his tracks and made a suggestion. "Let's go that way." He pointed in the direction of the town.

Apprehensive about wandering around areas he had never explored, Bryson tried to talk his way out of it. "I can't show you anything that way. I've never been more than a mile or two away from the house by myself."

"I thought this was supposed to be an adventure. What the hell did we even bring these for?" Domonic complained, pulling his walkie-talkie from his hip.

Bryson buckled easily under the pressure. "Fine. Lead the way." He sighed, having a feeling he'd made the wrong decision. If his parents found out he'd wandered that far from home, he would be in big trouble.

They trekked another couple of miles before commercial businesses began to appear. Shops, restaurants, even a doctor's office or two lined the road they traveled. Finally, they came to a stop.

"Check it out." Domonic alerted his pal to an empty old house off the side of the road, surrounded by overgrown brush. White paint was chipped all along the outside of the rundown structure.

"Does anyone even live there?" Bryson's face contorted. He'd never seen a home so dilapidated.

Not pausing another moment, Domonic headed toward the property. "Let's find out." Grass so tall it stretched over their heads lined the cracked cement walkway to the old wooden porch.

"Are you sure this is a good idea?" Bryson asked, following on the heels of his curious friend.

"Sure. Why not?"

"We're trespassing."

"Calm down, Bryson. I'm not gonna call the cops. Are you?"

"Of course not. I just—"

"You're just trying to come up with a reason to chicken out," Domonic interrupted, not allowing Bryson a chance to voice his qualms. "It's okay. I understand. You don't have to be ashamed of being scared."

"I'm no chicken, and I'm not scared. In fact, move. I'll go first." He rushed ahead of the chubby, sweat-drenched boy and took the porch stairs two at a time. He came to halt at the front door.

"Go ahead. Open it," Domonic demanded.

"Fine. I'll open it." Bryson swallowed hard, his throat dry from their lengthy journey. He placed his hand on the old circular brass knob, then slowly began twisting it. But he couldn't open the door. Bryson turned to address an already approaching Domonic. "I don't think it's unlocked."

Unexpectedly, Domonic raised his right foot and thrust it at the wooden door. "Ah, shit," he yelped then, having plowed his sneaker through the hollow wood.

Bryson stood stunned at the entire scene. All he could think about was the fact that they'd broken more than a few laws already. The boy worried what his father would think of his behavior.

"Why are you just standing there? Help me get my foot out," Domonic complained, snapping Bryson out of his momentary trance.

Keeping his worries to himself, Bryson sprang into action, grabbing hold of Domonic's leg. "On the count of three, pull your leg back, " he told his mischievous friend. "One, two, three. Pull!" He tugged hard on his friend's pant leg, while Domonic simultaneously pulled his leg back.

With their efforts combined, the boy's leg was ripped from the hole, causing him to fall back onto his buttocks.

"Are you okay?"

"My foot is out of the hole, isn't it?" Domonic smiled.

"So, what do we do now?"

"We go inside."

"But we can't get in the door."

Domonic huffed exasperatingly as he stood to his feet. "If you think I came all this way to give up now, you're sadly mistaken. We're getting inside this house."

Bryson stood beside Domonic and peered through one of the dirt-shrouded windows, attempting to see what was inside. Wiping the dirt away with the bottom of his T-shirt didn't make an ounce of a difference.

"Hey, Tasmanian devil, maybe we should check around back."

"Good idea. Let's go."

In unison, the misfits leaped from the top step of the porch into the long grass below. Forcing back clumps of thick grass mixed with an overabundance of weeds, they forged ahead with their plan.

"There are bugs everywhere." Bryson waved his hand wildly, fending off small swarms of pesky flying insects.

Not exempt from fending them off himself, Domonic cheered Bryson on. "Come on. We're almost there." That was when a long set of stairs leading to a massive deck that stretched around the back of the house came into view. "It's right up ahead. Just a few more feet."

The boys reached the stairs, climbed to the top, then plopped down and stretched out on their backs from exhaustion.

Bryson panted. "That was exhausting."

Domonic sat up, more important issues on his mind. "We should have packed lunch."

Bryson peered up at the odd pentagram-shaped window in the attic of the house. "What do you think is up there?"

"Let's find out." Domonic got up, then charged toward a stone frog sitting atop a rock in a corner of the deck. In a brazen attempt to enter the residence, he tossed the frog to the side, lifted the rock, and carried it in the direction of a sliding glass door with short steps.

"What are you doing?" Bryson started to panic. "No, no, no, no, no." He pleaded with Domonic not to do what he thought he was about to do.

Smash! The rock crashed through the glass door, sending shards everywhere, before landing on the kitchen floor.

"I can't believe you did that!"

"You better believe it, Alucard. I'm the Tasmanian devil, and sometimes the Tasmanian devil gets crazy." Domonic snatched his walkie-talkie from his belt. "Now, get out your radio, partner. We're going exploring. You take the top, and I'll take the bottom. Let me know what you find." He stepped into the dimly lit, seemingly vacant house.

Although all power had been shut off in the residence, light from the rising sun beamed in through the many windows adorning the structure.

Bryson stepped inside slowly, pieces of shattered glass crunching under the soles of his sneakers. "Smells like mothballs." His nose wrinkled in reaction to the stench. Despite that, he continued to move deeper into the home. Playing the role he had been summoned to fill, Bryson, aka Alucard, searched the premises. He tried to stay along the outer perimeter of each room, using the light shining in from outside to navigate his way. He walked around the worn wooden floors of the living room and dining room. Then he left the large open dining room and stepped into the hallway, where he discovered a set of double doors. The house appeared to be empty; Bryson had not stumbled upon a single piece of furniture thus far. Curious, he pushed open the doors and found himself in a room that had to be a study. It was empty as well. Even the shelves along the walls were starved for books.

Meanwhile, Domonic, having set out to survey the basement, discovered the basement door, Unlike Bryson, he had a small flashlight handy, so after yanking the door open, he pulled the flashlight from a pocket of his jeans, clicked it on, and shined it down into the pitch-black space below. You'd think he would have been too scared to death to take the plunge. Domonic, though, had nerves of steel. The narrow beam of light illuminated cobwebs as he started to make his way down the basement stairs. Pulling aside the cobwebs with his hand as he went, he reached the bottom of the staircase and stepped down into soft soil. The sensation of the ground sinking under his feet was unnerving as he peered around the wide-open space.

He ran his flashlight across the area in front of him, mouth agape. He'd never seen a basement like this one before. The walls were made up of damp uneven stone. There were symbols and signs carved into the stones, but Domonic had no idea what they meant. Disregarding his fear, the daring lad stepped closer to examine one of the walls. When he had made it halfway across the dirt floor, squeaking sounded behind him. Domonic turned without hesitation, then aimed his light at a fat rat scurrying between brass table settings to make its way across a long rectangular table covered by a dirty white sheet. Rats didn't freak him out; he was much braver than that. It was the five wrought-iron candleholders placed strategically across the table that made him question the nature of the house they'd entered. The boy stepped closer to the table.

Domonic's heart thumped harder as what was before him became visible. Five massive wooden chairs with burgundy suede cushions had been placed around the table. He pulled a lighter from his pocket, then lit the long black candles in the holders one by one. As the room became illuminated, the boy thought it safe to put his flashlight away.

"What the heck kinda basement is this?" he asked himself out loud.

A humongous pile of old garments nearly touched the ceiling in one corner of the basement. A door leading to another part of the basement had a wooden plank securing it, making it apparent that the area that lay beyond it was off-limits. For Domonic, though, unspoken rules weren't to be followed. Of course, he headed straight for that door. The boy grunted, using all his might as he dug the soles of his shoes into the soil for stability and lifted that one-by-five-foot plank bit by bit. "Almost there," he squealed before finally removing the plank after a few more seconds of struggling to accomplish his feat. The wooden plank hit the soil, and the iron door popped open, at which point a stench pervaded the air. A foul odor so unbearable that Domonic lifted the collar of his T-shirt and used it to cover his nose. "Geez . . . It smells rancid down here."

He pulled the walkie-talkie from his waist, contemplating going inside the basement room he'd discovered. "Hey, Alucard. Do you copy? Have you found anything interesting?" he said into the handheld device.

All the way upstairs, Bryson busied himself with searching the stuffy attic. He fumbled to grab his walkie-talkie, and once he finally had his hand around it, he mashed the button on its side. "This is Alucard. I copy. I'm in the attic right now. Nothing up here but a bunch of cardboard boxes and some mannequins with a bunch of pins stuck in 'em. What do you see down there, Tasmanian devil?"

Domonic had yet to enter the room he'd worked so hard to gain access to. For a second there, he considered the fact that he might be too chicken, and this revelation pushed him forward into the darkness. "Hold on, Alucard. I'm gonna check it out." With his free hand, he took his flashlight back out and illuminated the pitch-black space in front of him. "Ahhh!" He screamed in horror at the sight of a man with pins in his face staring right at him, but then he realized it was one of the mannequins Bryson had spoken of. The fact that he'd screamed so loud infuriated the boy. His fear had leaped to the surface, and with it came a wave of anger.

Domonic clipped his walkie-talkie to his belt, then took out his lighter and set the mannequin ablaze before sending it to the dirt with a swift kick. "Stupid mannequin." The boy turned to check out the rest of the room and saw many mannequins, all of them looking right at him. A few seconds passed before he realized it wasn't his flashlight that made them suddenly so visible, but the blaze behind him. It had quickly gotten out of control. Flames taller than Domonic now licked the ceiling. There was no way he could put out the fire now. Besides, there wasn't a droplet of water in sight. Smoke engulfed the room, forcing the coughing miscreant to flee. Once he emerged safely from the smoke-filled room, Domonic closed the door behind him, hoping to smother the blaze. Either way, he thought it best he and Bryson got out of that vacant house as fast as they possibly could.

He grabbed his walkie-talkie to relay the message. "Alucard! Alucard! Do you copy?"

"Alucard here. I found some old treasure," Bryson answered, referring to a small pouch of jewelry he had discovered.

"I'm gonna come up and check it out. We should probably be leaving soon. Tasmanian devil, over and out."

Domonic tore back up the wooden stairs, but when he'd nearly reached the top of the staircase, soil stuck to the bottoms of his sneakers caused him to slip, and he fell back down a few of the brittle wooden steps. "Owww!" he cried out as wooden splinters tore the skin on his belly. Domonic rolled over and examined the cuts and scratches. Although he was bleeding, none of the cuts were deep enough to require stitches. He forced back the tears threatening to reveal themselves, stood up, then continued up the stairs. By the time he'd made it to the living room, he could see smoke filling the study. "We've got to get out of here."

"Alucard! Alucard!" he yelled into the walkie-talkie. "We have to get out of here."

"What's the big deal?"

"I think the house is on fire."

"What? Fire!"

"We need to go now, Bryson!"

The fact that Domonic had neglected to refer to him by his code name told Bryson the situation was serious. He stuffed the pouch of jewelry into his pocket as he turned to leave the attic. "I'm coming down now." Just then the floor beneath him gave way. "Ahhh!" he screamed as the bottom half of his body was swallowed up by the rotting floor. "Help! Help me! I'm stuck!" he hollered frantically, fearing he would be trapped in the blaze, which, unbeknownst to him, had been set by his mischievous friend.

Domonic bolted toward Bryson's location as the fire burned through the floor of the study. Panting, nearly out of breath, he made it to the spot where Bryson sat helpless.

"Hold on, Bryson. I'm gonna pull you out." The boy reached out his hands, looking intently into Bryson's eyes. "Grab hold and don't let go, okay?"

Bryson began to let his fear get the best of him. "Oh my God. I can smell the smoke, Domonic. Pull me out. Hurry!"

"I'm gonna pull you out. Just trust me. You have to calm down."

Domonic pulled as hard as he possibly could, attempting to free Bryson, but to no avail. Sweat poured from his brow, drenching his face, while blood did the same to his belly.

"You're bleeding." Bryson was in shock over the entire ordeal.

"I'll be okay. It's just a few scratches. We have to get you out of here. I'll be right back. I promise."

"Please, don't leave me like this." Bryson started to cry as his friend bolted from the attic.

Domonic thought about leaving Bryson there, but he couldn't abandon the only friend he had. There was only one thing he could think of doing, and the chances of it working were slim. Regardless, Domonic felt he had to at least try. After all, it was he who had gotten them into the disastrous situation in the first place. Using the top of his shirt as a shield from the smoke, he searched the floor below, trying to find the room in which Bryson's legs had broken through the ceiling. With all that had gone wrong that day, the boy prayed for something to go right. "Please. Please. Please. Don't let my friend die," he murmured. Finally, he pushed open a bedroom door and found Bryson dangling there.

Domonic lifted his chin and shouted at the ceiling. "Bryson! Bryson! Can you hear me? I'm right under you."

"I can hear you," Bryson replied, wiping the tears from his face.

"Don't worry. I'm gonna get you out of here."

An old toy chest sat in a corner of the room, collecting dust. *Nope, I can't use that*, Domonic concluded.

Domonic's eyes combed the nearly empty room, but he found nothing that could be of assistance. Stopping his search was out of the question, however, so he headed for the closet. Upon opening the door to the small closet, his last hope became his greatest. Domonic's eyes lit up as they fell upon a cot that had been folded, then tucked away. It was their way out. He dragged the cot across the floor, positioned it just under Bryson's legs, and opened it up.

"Bryson, I have a bed under you. I need you to let go and let yourself fall through. On the count of one, two . . ."

Bryson didn't wait for a three count. He threw up his arms, allowing his small body to plunge through the air. Within seconds, he plopped down on the mattress, prompting the boys to cheer in unison, "Yes! We did it!"

Bryson leaped from the cot. "I'm free! You saved my life, Domonic! Thank you." He grinned in admiration of his friend, having no idea it was he who'd caused the fire.

Still, more pressing issues challenged them.

"We're not out of danger yet. We have to get out of here. The fire is spreading, Bryson."

"Then what are we waiting for? Let's go."

Bryson and Domonic ran for the bedroom door, then bolted down the smoky hallway that led back to the stairs. Unfortunately, the flames had already started scorching the staircase, their only way down. The boys coughed, fanning the smoke away from their nostrils.

"It's over. What are we gonna do now? I don't wanna die like this." Domonic was out of ideas.

"Come on." Bryson grabbed his arm and pulled the devastated boy back to the room from which they'd just escaped. "We're not gonna die. Not today, anyway. We're gonna jump."

Bryson pulled the mattress off the cot. "Domonic, don't just stand there. Open the window."

"What a great idea!" Domonic rushed over to open the window. He lifted the sash as high as it would go to give them the room they needed to squeeze the mattress through the opening and send it down into the grass below.

A nervousness overtook Domonic as he thought about plunging to his death from the dilapidated second story of the house. "You can go first, since it was your idea."

Bryson tossed his walkie-talkie out first. "Okay. Let's make this quick, or we're toast." The eager boy flung one of his legs out the window, then lifted the other and allowed it to hang out as he took in the scenery below him. "My mom always says, 'Ain't nothing to it but to do it,'" Bryson announced before taking the leap. "Look out *below*!" With a plop, his body hit the mattress. He was safe.

"You did it!" Domonic screamed from up above.

"Now it's your turn. Throw down your walkie-talkie."

Domonic tossed it down as Bryson had suggested before climbing through the window. He took a deep breath, preparing himself for the plummet.

"On the count of three," Bryson called up to him. "One, twooo . . ."

"Bombs away!" Domonic hollered before taking his plunge. *Plop!* "Now, that was an adventure," he announced as he rested atop the mattress.

"We've gotta get out of here before the cops come and we get arrested for trespassing and arson," Bryson urged.

The boys, their faces stained with soot and ashes, grabbed their walkie-talkies, then tore through the brush, trying to put distance between themselves and the burning house as quickly as they could.

"I wonder how the fire started, anyway?" Bryson said when they came to a stop to catch their breath.

"I don't know . . . I'm just glad we made it out alive." Domonic had to make sure what had happened at that house remained a secret. Even though Bryson had no idea he'd started the blaze, if adults found out about their so-called adventure, they'd undoubtedly decide that the fault lay with Domonic. For this reason, Domonic wanted his friend to swear he would not say a word about today. "Hey—"

"What's wrong?" Bryson interrupted, more than ready to get going again. "We should keep going."

"I just want to make sure we are on the same page. You can't tell anyone about what happened today. Not even your parents. They'll think we started the fire, and we'll go to jail until we're old men."

"I won't tell anyone. I promise. But how are we going to explain the cuts on your stomach and all that blood?"

"I scratched myself when we were roaming through the forest."

Suddenly, they heard sirens blaring.

"They're onto us. We have to get out of here," Domonic said in a low voice.

The boys took off and ran farther into the overgrown vegetation, unaware they'd just carried on the long, destructive tradition known as Devil's Night.

Bryson and his pal Domonic were exhausted, filthy, and famished by the time they completed the journey back to their neighborhood.

"Remember, not a word of this to anyone. The missions of Alucard and Tasmanian devil are top secret," Domonic remarked as the pair approached Bryson's driveway.

"I definitely don't want to wind up in jail, so you don't have to worry about me spilling the beans."

"Hey . . . I just remembered, we forgot to bring the beer."

"Maybe next time." Bryson waved. "I'm pooped."

"Yeah. Me too. I'm gonna go get cleaned up before my mom sees what I did to my shirt."

"I'll chirp you later, Tasmanian devil." Bryson waved goodbye as he headed up the driveway.

"See ya, Alucard."

Chapter 30

Not So Innocent

The entire family sat around the dinner table that night, partaking in the delicious meal Erick and Evelyn had prepared. Since she'd been fired, Evelyn had more time to spend at home with her husband. With Erick owning the construction company, he had free rein when it came to making decisions. Whether or not he showed up, he was getting paid. Of course, he took advantage of this, taking off the next two days to spend time with his loved ones. Evelyn, on the other hand, was still stewing about being fired, on top of being jilted by her lover. No one would ever know the agony hiding behind her smile as she placed a dinner roll atop each of her children's plates. Evelyn wondered what Colin was doing at that very moment. *Probably having a romantic dinner with his wife*, she decided—a revelation that tore at her gut. Not even the good loving her husband had furnished her that morning could erase her fantasies of Colin.

Erick gazed at his wife, remembering their salacious a.m. romp. A chill ran up his spine when he thought about the way her back had arched as his fingertips moved across her silky chocolate skin. The drastic difference in their skin tones was an aphrodisiac for Erick. Her darkness called out to his loins even at their dinner table.

"Geez, Dad, she's not going to disappear," Diana remarked, noticing her father staring in admiration at her mother. "If I had a dollar for every instance I've seen you guys looking at each other like that, I'd be rich by now."

"Too bad your mom doesn't look at me like that anymore," Erick said, attempting to guilt trip his wife. Though she hadn't spoken about it, he could feel the disconnect between them.

"How would you know? I could be watching you while you sleep," Evelyn said in her defense.

Erick smiled, relishing her response. "Now, that's what I'm talking about!"

"That's actually pretty creepy, Mom," Diana interjected, adding her two cents.

Erick moaned. "Creepy. I like it." He smooched the side of his wife's neck, forcing from her the getty smile he was looking for.

Evelyn squealed as his lips tickled her skin. "Honey," she cooed.

Michael finally took his eyes off his cell phone long enough to chime in. "Hey, Dad. Remember that time you drove into the garage with the kayaks still strapped onto the truck because you were too busy gawking at Mom? You see where that got you, right?"

"At least we got two new kayaks out of the deal," Erick commented.

Evelyn wagged a hand in front of her. "Enough about me. Let's dig in. I hope you guys like it. Your father told me I used to make this all the time. I hope my seafood lasagna tastes as good as it did in the past."

"I'm sure it's delicious, my love."

"Bryson, you've been really quiet. In fact, we've barely seen you all day. Did you have fun with Domonic?" Evelyn said.

Bryson was stuffing his belly, and it took him a minute to answer his mother. "It was a real adventure."

Evelyn narrowed her gaze at him. "What did you two get into?"

Bryson's eyes roamed the table to see if they were all listening. All that attention on him made him uncomfortable. He knew his brother, Michael, could tell when he wasn't being truthful. Bryson may have had his parents snowed but not his older brother. You could say Michael had been there and done that. Not arson, of course, but small mischievous acts of his had gone unnoticed in the past.

"I just showed him around. We went to one of the creeks, and I taught him a little about nature survival. His dad didn't teach him stuff like that."

Busy with his text messages, Michael was none the wiser.

Erick smiled proudly at his son. "You're a good boy, Bryson, and an even better friend."

"What did you show him?" Evelyn asked, making idle conversation in an attempt to keep her mind occupied with something other than Colin.

"I taught him how to navigate the forest so he wouldn't get lost, how to tell time by the sun, how to fish without a fishing pole, how to find berries you can eat, how to tell if a plant is poisonous . . ." Bryson rambled on, comfortable telling his truths.

"Wow, I guess you two were busy. Looks like you worked up an appetite," Evelyn noted as she watched him scarf down his lasagna.

"Holy crap! Check it out!" Diana pointed to the television mounted on the wall in a corner of the room. A breaking news flash was on display. "Turn it up, Dad."

"What's this?" Erick snatched up the remote, which was lying beside his cup, to do as his daughter had requested. The rest of the family gawked in silence at the newscaster standing out in front of a burning house.

"Breaking news. This is Maggie Hatcher on the scene with fire trucks, police officers, as well as first responders, who are attempting to assess and get a handle on the chaotic scene you see before you. This tragic scene kicks off Devil's Night here in Clarkston. I can't be too presumptuous by calling it an act of arson, but we can't ignore the facts. This house has been abandoned for quite some time, and we all know what today represents. Unfortunately, for the first time, we have what appears to be a case of arson rocking this quiet suburban town.

"Firefighters are working diligently to put out the blaze, which has even spread to the overgrown brush beside the property. I, for one, would say this is getting out of hand. Let's hope we can put a stop to this now. Police are asking for volunteers to patrol neighborhoods tonight. If you would like to help, you can contact the Oakland County Sheriff's Office.

"Again, this is Maggie Hatcher, bringing you this breaking news. We'll be back with an update on our nightly news."

Erick turned the volume back down. "I can't believe someone would do such a terrible thing, especially around here. Maybe we should be on the lookout."

Bryson sat in silence, eyes bucked wide, as he stared at the television screen. He couldn't believe the fire had made the news. The boy prayed no one had seen him and Domonic at the scene.

"Bryson, are you okay?" Evelyn leaned over and wiped the sweat from his hairline, snapping him out of his trancelike state. "You don't look so good."

"I'm fine, Mama."

Erick looked over at his youngest son. "Bryson, you don't have to worry about anyone doing anything to our house."

"Maybe we should help with patrolling tonight." Evelyn thought it would be a good idea for them to do their civic duty, as it would be good for her family's image.

"I wouldn't mind helping out," Erick offered.

"Do you think I could see if Domonic wants to come?" Bryson asked.

Erick nodded his head. "I don't see why it would be a problem. Hey, what's Domonic doing for Halloween?"

"Actually, I wanted to talk to you and Mom about that. As you know, Domonic doesn't have many friends, and his mother is too big to walk around the neighborhood with him. I wanted to ask if he can spend Halloween with us this year."

"Bryson, you shouldn't talk about his mother like that. It's rude."

"I'm sorry, Dad. I didn't mean to sound rude." Bryson bowed his head in shame.

"I know, son. I just want you to be mindful of the things you say. Especially when it pertains to women. They're delicate."

Here he goes again . . . twisting facts to paint the beautiful picture he wants to see. This ain't no trailer park, and she is certainly not in any shape to walk the entire neighborhood. Don't just sit here and let him soften the kid up even more. Evelyn ignored the silent pleas of her alter ego and nodded her head, as if her husband was right for correcting Bryson.

"Okay, Dad. I will. I promise."

"I think it would be a great idea for you to invite Domonic over for Halloween. We can order pizza for dinner. That way you two will be nice and full when it comes time to eat candy."

"Thanks, Dad! Can I go call him?"

Erick examined his son's plate. "Well, since you've devoured your lasagna, I guess so."

"Yes!" Bryson cheered, hopping up from his seat.

"Hey, buddy. Aren't you forgetting something?" Erick said, stopping Bryson before he could tear off toward his bedroom.

"Oh yeah. Thanks for dinner, Mama. It was better than ever." Bryson furnished his mother with a peck on the cheek.

His gesture of affection caught Evelyn by surprise. She grinned, her heart touched by her son's actions. "You're very welcome, bud. I'm glad you liked it."

Bryson stepped backward slowly. "I loved it."

"Tsk-tsk." Erick clicked his tongue against the roof of his mouth. "Your plate, son."

"I was gonna grab that." Bryson smiled, knowing all too well he was to clean his place before leaving the table.

The young boy did as was expected of him, then went on his way.

Chapter 31

Holiday Hellion

Across town, the Ravishes enjoyed dinner in front of the living-room flat-screen television. Everything had been going great that day, as far as Jocelyn was concerned. She'd successfully gotten Evelyn out of her husband's life, so it was just the two of them again. Although she had to take on the work denied Evelyn, for Jocelyn it was all worth it. The couple watched an episode of *Law & Order* as they quietly ate their meal.

Jocelyn stole peeks at her husband from the corner of her eye, wondering what it was that occupied his mind. Sure, his eyes were glued to the tube, yet Jocelyn couldn't help but wonder if it was the woman on the TV screen who looked almost identical to Evelyn that had his attention. More than anything, she wanted the paranoid, jealous woman she'd become to turn back into the woman she once was. Jocelyn hated feeling that she wasn't good enough, pretty enough and, most of all, capable enough to please her husband.

Colin had indeed noticed the striking resemblance the woman on the TV show had to Evelyn. He was so immersed in it, he'd begun fantasizing about their last steamy encounter. Colin couldn't help recalling the way Evelyn had straddled him on top of his four-wheeler. It was an encounter he'd been waiting for since the first day she'd ridden behind him. They'd moved from the ATV to the back seat of his truck, and even the porch swing had gotten a taste of their action that night. He remembered the way her silky bottom felt in his strong, capable hands. The thought of her made his member rise. Colin scooched his plate farther up his lap, hiding the erection, but he neglected to check his train of thought. Evelyn remained steadfast in his recollection.

Jocelyn couldn't take it anymore. She could feel Evelyn's aura invading her space, taking over her mind. The woman wasn't even there, yet Jocelyn felt as if she couldn't get away from her. "Wow. She looks a lot like Evelyn," Jocelyn observed, then waited anxiously for her husband's reply.

There's no way I'm falling into that trick bag, Colin thought. "I guess she kinda does. I hadn't noticed."

Jocelyn didn't believe a word he'd uttered. "How could you not? She literally looks just like her."

Colin could tell that his wife's annoyance was mounting. "Are you trying to start an argument?"

"Why would you say that?" Jocelyn frowned.

"You're snapping at me. The only time you ever snap at me is when you're agitated or hungry. And since you've inhaled your entire piece of salmon, it most certainly can't be the latter. Here, let's watch something else, something that doesn't have a dark-skinned black woman with curly hair in it." Colin grabbed the remote and flipped to a different channel—an action he hoped would spark guilt in his wife.

Jocelyn told Colin exactly what he wanted to hear. "I'm sorry. I guess I am overreacting."

"It's not a big deal, baby. We can watch something else."

"No. I'm not that woman, and I refuse to be. I'm not jealous and insecure." She snatched the remote from her husband and turned the channel back to *Law & Order*. "Besides, it's the season finale."

Colin grinned. "I knew you couldn't miss the season finale."

"Shut up." Jocelyn smiled back.

Jackson headed into a local diner, one he'd frequented in the past. The moment he came in the door, she noticed him. Janice, the formerly pregnant waitress, was pregnant no more. The twentysomething hippie with long red dreads had given birth to her son shortly after Jackson left Clarkston. Never forgetting the times he had sat and talked with her, she beamed when she caught sight of him there.

"Long time no see, stranger. Where have you been?" she called.

Jackson approached. "I moved out of state," he replied, taking a seat at the counter.

Janice thought his seating choice was odd. "You never sit at the counter. No booth today?"

"I don't think it matters tonight. You don't have any other customers."

Janice looked around at the empty restaurant. "I guess you're right. You always did like to rush in before closing time. Is that the key to getting me all alone?"

Jackson grinned. "Nah, I don't need to use tricks to get you alone. I'm sure you'd go out with me if I just asked."

"Well . . ." She waited, with a hand on her hip, for him to do just that.

"I'm at least ten years your senior," he revealed.

"I like a mature man. Besides, there's something about you that tells me I'd be safe with you. I bet you'd never let anyone harm a hair on my head."

Janice had assumed right. Jackson remembered the story she had told him about being raped by her child's father. *Maybe I could be his father.* Jackson mulled over that thought.

He hadn't seen his daughter, Mya, in months, and since he'd left his wife—because of the affair—Jackson missed family life. Moving around wasn't a problem for him. He had gotten used to traveling with the military before he was discharged. If he was going to strike up a relationship with Janice, he'd first have to make certain he couldn't be blamed for the deaths of Marcus, Mr. Sobieski, Randy, Deborah, and Jessica.

Evelyn was the only thing standing in his way. It would be only a matter of time before she could remember. Soon the police would be putting it all together, Jackson worried.

"How about I sit at a booth, and you come over and talk to me, like old times?"

"My shift ends soon. How about we eat dinner together?"

"Sounds good to me."

"What can we get started for you?" Janice inquired while filling the mug in front of him with freshly brewed coffee.

"I'll have the meat loaf and mashed potatoes, of course. Unless you've got some goulash back there?"

"I do! I was gonna have some goulash myself. How about some hot-water corn bread on the side?"

"You definitely know what I like." Jackson looked deep into her blue eyes.

Maybe I can come back and make a life here, after all, he thought, allowing hope to rein in his negative thoughts.

Domonic woke up at the crack of dawn the morning of All Hallows' Eve. Mrs. Danielson had made certain she got him the best costume her husband's insurance payout could buy from the local costume store. Naturally, he'd chosen a Tasmanian devil getup, which fit his rounded middle perfectly. The head, however, was a bit oversized, and so it was a bit crooked on him, and his eyes didn't line up perfectly with the eye holes. Regardless, Domonic had refused to choose an alternate getup. So, there he stood in front of the bathroom mirror, a Tasmanian devil with a crooked head. "At least I can see," he murmured, shrugging his shoulders, content enough with his decision.

Domonic wanted to make sure everything was ready for their first Halloween with his new friend. He darted back to his bedroom and snatched his book bag up from a corner, then emptied it onto his Looney Tunes bed comforter. Domonic peeked inside the empty book bag, judging its capacity. "This should work," he told himself before tearing back out of the room. Tasmanian devil head bobbing as he tackled the stairs to make it to the kitchen, the boy paused every so often to ensure that his mother remained in her deep slumber. There was no need for him to check her bedroom. Mrs. Danielson's snoring echoed through their house. The perfect opportunity for Domonic to make his move had come.

Acting fast, he made his way through the kitchen to the garage, where there was a fully stocked fridge prime for the picking. The trove of malt liquor before him when he opened the refrigerator door caused his eyes to beam with excitement. Without wasting another minute, he began filling his book bag with beers. At first, he loaded the bag with six beers for each of them; then, after examining the dent he'd made, Domonic decided to put half of them back.

"A six-pack should be a good time," he said, zipping the book bag shut.

Taking the bag of beer back into the house would be too risky. Instead, Domonic took the bag out back and hid it in their yard, beneath the porch deck. *She'll never look out here*, he decided as he shoved the bag under a pile of dead leaves.

Chapter 32

Territorial

Next door Evelyn baked cookies for the trick-or-treaters who would be knocking at their door on All Hallows' Eve. Apparently, Erick had reminded her of how she used to bake every year and give her cookies to the children, as opposed to handing out candy. She was not a fan of the way it caused children to bounce off the walls, so to speak. She wanted things to be as they always had been, for Bryson's sake.

"I hope all the kids like oatmeal-raisin." Evelyn slid another tray of cookies into the oven.

"Thank you so much for doing this, my love. I know you don't remember the activities you were accustomed to, and it's not easy jumping back into it as you have. I just want you to know that I see that you are trying."

This man is too extra, the voice in her head noted. *Does he realize you burned the last batch?*

Evelyn ignored the teasing by her own mind and continued to pack individual cookies into sandwich bags. "You're welcome. It's what Moms do, right?"

"Great ones . . ." Erick smacked her on the bottom while giving her a peck on the cheek.

No, a great mother drags a bitch for laying a finger on her kid, she was reminded by her alter ego.

Not in the mood for a debate, she allowed her better self to respond. "Anything for my Bryson."

Bryson sat up and stretched his well-rested muscles before climbing out of bed. He glanced up at the small analog anime clock on his wall and realized his parents had let him sleep until almost 11:00 a.m. The boy dashed over to the window to peer out his blinds, knowing all too well the fun would soon begin. Bryson took in the festive decorations in his neighbors' front yards. A house across the street stole his attention. He watched the homeowner, a petite, busty brunette, as she tested a Halloween coffin sitting in the center of her front lawn. Every time she walked past it, the coffin would open and out would pop a skeleton. The wilting bushes lining her walkway were covered in artificial spiderwebs. Pumpkins placed strategically along the edge of the porch looked as if they'd been carved professionally. It was clear the woman had outdone herself. She'd have a flickering light and a smoke machine by 3:00 p.m.

The woman turned just then and looked in his direction. For a second, he thought she noticed him spying on her; then, after taking a second glance, Bryson realized that his father, who had emerged from the house, was the one that had garnered her attention. His father continued to the mailbox, and the woman, giddy now from the sight of him, took the opportunity to cross the street and trap him there in conversation. She wanted Erick. A brilliant advertising executive, she was single and had no children. Her track record with the men in her life had not been without its challenges. The fact that she was a successful and independent woman made those of the opposite sex see her as more of a competitor than a lover. Melanie had become accustomed to dating men not on her level, mentally or financially, which tended to leave her heartbroken.

After years of celibacy, she had decided it was time for her to nullify her vow of purity. Unfortunately, she'd become smitten with Erick the day he had assisted one of the postal carriers with bringing an item into her house. Erick had no idea of the woman's admiration for him. He often didn't pay attention to those kinds of things, as he never gave himself enough credit when it came to the looks department. Erick was humble when it came to self-validation.

Melanie's plan was to get him to realize that she was smitten with him, without her uttering the words, considering he had a wife.

"Hey, Erick. How have you been?" She smiled as she approached him, and when she got close enough, she ran her hand down his bicep.

Erick blew the gesture off as endearing; however, not everyone who'd seen it felt as nonchalant about it.

This bitch. I know you saw that. Little Miss Hooters looks real comfortable with Erick, Evelyn's alter ego seethed.

Evelyn grunted, having caught sight of the scene through the window in the foyer. She took off her apron and dropped it to the floor on her way out the front door. "My love, my ass . . ."

Melanie had gotten in a couple more feels by the time she noticed Evelyn heading straight for them, big, black, curly Afro flying in the breeze. Melanie could tell she wasn't too happy.

So could Bryson as he peered in awe from his bedroom window. "Uh-oh." In just a couple of months, he had come to know his mother's temper.

"Heyyy!" Evelyn sang as she approached.

"Hello, Evelyn. I heard you were out of the hospital. I've been meaning to get you a plant or something. I'm glad to see you up and about. What happened to you was such a tragedy." Melanie shook her head, pouring it on thick.

Evelyn didn't bother mincing words. "Don't touch my husband."

Melanie frowned with worry, portraying an air of innocence. "Excuse me?" Her hand moved to cover her chest.

Oh, she's good, the voice in Evelyn's head admitted.

"Your hands," Evelyn clarified. "Keep them to yourself."

Erick's eyes closed. He feared what would come next, yet he remained silent. He knew better than to correct his wife in the presence of another female.

"I'm sorry—"

"Don't be sorry," Evelyn interrupted, leaving Melanie's mouth poised to speak. "Just don't do it. Ever again. Okay?"

By that time, Erick felt it was safe to look, as he had not heard any screaming.

"No problem," Melanie agreed.

"Good. Now, I have cookies baking, so I'll be inside, honey." Evelyn kissed Erick on the lips, then turned to leave.

After walking a few paces away, with Erick and Melanie still her rapt audience, she turned back to address Melanie a final time. "Oh, and, Melanie, I like hostas." Evelyn flashed a bright smile, then continued on her way.

Deep down she didn't feel good about giving Melanie a pass. *Why didn't you hit her?* her alter ego complained.

"Bryson is looking out the window. It'll ruin his Halloween," Evelyn whispered.

His mother's rational act warmed Bryson's heart. To see his mother not overreact gave him faith in the security of their foundation. He didn't want to lose his mother because of a hot temper. Sure, Bryson was only a kid. But that didn't make him oblivious as to how things worked. His parents had taught him those worldly lessons. Evelyn especially, given that he was a child of mixed race. She wanted her son to be aware of the dangers out there.

Ready to begin his day, Bryson jetted over to his closet, grabbed the plastic bag that housed his costume. He had it all there, everything he needed for his rendition of Alucard. But first, he had to solve the issue of his grumbling belly. The aroma of oatmeal-raisin cookies floating through the residence could have been the reason for its outcries. Either way, the young boy was famished.

At 3:00 p.m. a knock sounded at the Todds' door. "It's Domonic," Bryson yelled as he tore through the house, trying to make it to the door as fast as he could. "Mom, did you order pizza?" he inquired before answering the door.

From the kitchen, Evelyn called out, "It's on its way."

Flinging the door open to the sight of Domonic in his costume, Bryson cheered. "Yeah! Tasmanian devil!"

"Alucard!"

"Come on in. Let me show you my room."

Domonic seemed just as excited as Bryson to be hanging out together again. "Let's see it."

"How are you, Domonic?" Evelyn asked, standing in the kitchen doorway.

"Oh, hi, Mrs. Todd. I'm doing great. Thank you for letting me spend Halloween with you guys. Are you making dinner?"

"We're having pizza," she informed him.

"Yum. I love pizza," he admitted, his lopsided head bobbing.

"It'll be here before you know it. Bryson, your dad is picking it up now. I'm sure most of the parents around here are ordering pizza."

Bryson stood with a silly grin plastered on his face, happy she was playing nice. Little did he know, his dear mother had bigger grievances to settle.

"Come on, Domonic. Let's go. Last one is a rotten egg." Bryson tore up the hall.

Dominic chased after him. "Hey, that's not fair. You got a head start. Plus, I can barely see."

"Why'd you get the head part so big?"

Once he'd entered Bryson's bedroom, Domonic ripped off the Tasmanian devil head for a better view, along with some fresh air. "This is the size it came with." He placed the head down on Bryson's bed. "I brought you something."

"What is it?" Bryson could hardly wait to find out.

Domonic removed the book bag from his shoulder. "You should close the door."

Bryson shut the bedroom door, then closed the gap between himself and his pal. "It's shut. Now let's see what's in the bag."

Domonic unzipped it, then opened it wide for Bryson to see.

"Whoa." Bryson leaped back, mouth wide open.

"I told you I'd get us some. Where are we gonna drink it?"

"My tree house in the backyard. No one ever bothers me up there."

"I've never seen the tree house."

"That's because it's behind the pine tree row. Our property goes farther back."

"Cool. Well, what are we waiting for?" Domonic actually wanted to see the tree house more than he wanted to chug those few beers.

While she obsessed over Colin, Evelyn busied herself with decorating the cookies she was to present in just a couple of hours. *I wonder what he's doing*, she pondered. *Is he thinking about me? Does he even miss me?* Her questions posed remained unanswered, causing the jilted woman to become even more paranoid.

And now you're going to lose Erick too. Melanie probably moved in on him while you were laid up in the hospital. It's only a matter of time before Bryson will be calling her Mommy. the voice in her head said, goading her.

"Never. That'll never happen!" Evelyn blurted, springing up from her seat as if her alter ego were standing there in front of her.

It won't happen if you do something about it, the voice assured her.

Evelyn kept silent as the young duo wandered into the kitchen.

"We're headed to the tree house," Bryson informed his mother as he and Domonic passed by her on their way to the sliding glass door.

She was happy to see them go. "Run along," she murmured. With Erick having gone out to get pizza, the maleficent woman had a limited amount of time to do as she'd planned.

This time Evelyn kept her apron on. She traipsed out the front door to pay her neighbor Melanie a visit. As she neared her house, she noticed the front door was wide open. After walking right up to the front door, she crossed the threshold and entered the foyer, where bowls full of Hershey's Kisses sat on a side table. Her flats moved quietly across the gleaming cherrywood floor as her eyes combed over the interior. The home looked more like an office space than a house. Even the couches were square and hard.

Boring-ass bitch . . . , her alter ego muttered.

Evelyn strolled up the hall as if she owned the place, running her hands over crystal wall sconces, in search of Melanie. She was fueled by an eagerness to finish their conversation, you know . . . hash things out.

Out of nowhere, Evelyn heard her speak. "Ugh. I can't believe she's back home," Melanie complained, emerging from the bathroom on the left.

Evelyn dashed to the right, then hid behind the door to what she assumed was Melanie's home office. She listened in, hoping her neighbor would divulge her motives as she spoke to herself or to somebody on the phone.

"He can do so much better. I mean, she sorts mail for a living. He owns his own business. Fuck it. I need to get laid. I'm calling Robert. Hopefully, he'll whisper sweet nothings in my ear in his native tongue. I always did love Italians," Melanie mused.

Evelyn stood behind the door, fuming as calmly as she could, for a few moments. Then she stepped back out into the hallway before tiptoeing inside the bathroom Melanie had just exited. *What can we use?* the voice asked, prompting her to search for something useful. She opened a drawer, cracked a devilish grin when she realized she could use the first thing she saw. She snatched a bottle of melatonin pills from the drawer and set her plan into motion.

She could hear Melanie gossiping out on the front lawn. That was when she took her chance, stepping out into the hallway before making her way to the kitchen. A bottle of red wine sat breathing atop the granite center island. It was the perfect thing in which to dump the pills, Evelyn decided. She opened the bottle of sleep aids, then poured the pills into the wine bottle.

That should put her out for the night, her alter ego observed.

Satisfied with her actions thus far, Evelyn stuffed the bottle of melatonin in her apron, then snuck out through the kitchen sliding glass door. Before heading back across the street, she stuffed a coin into the lock hole, hoping to prevent the latch from securing.

Chapter 33

When No One Is Watching

Burp! Domonic and Bryson both let out long belches as they leaned back against the wall of the tree house.

"So, what do we do now?" Bryson inquired, now heavily under the influence of alcohol.

"Let's go get some candy. I'm hungry."

"What about the pizza?"

"Oh yeah, let's go get some."

"I've got a better idea." Bryson got up and tugged on one of two ropes above his head.

"What are you doing?"

"You see that box attached to the rope?" He pointed out the tree-house window.

Domonic shook his head in affirmation. "I see it."

"Well, this goes all the way to the house. Once it gets to the kitchen door, by the patio, my mom or dad will see it. They'll put pizza in the box for us, and then I'll pull it back."

"How will you know they put pizza inside?"

Bryson grabbed a small bell hanging from a string in a corner of the tree house. "When they tug on the rope, the bell will ring. That's how we'll know it's dinnertime."

"That's pretty cool."

"Yeah . . . My dad thought of it. He's really good at coming up with ideas out of nowhere."

"Not my dad," Domonic sadly revealed.

"Pizza's here!" Erick yelled upon entering the house, steaming boxes in hand. He looked around, searching the living room and great room before reaching the kitchen, but he found not a soul on his way. "Where is everybody?" he quietly questioned, placing the boxes atop the kitchen table.

They must be outside, he decided, moving over to the sliding glass door to peek out into the backyard. Erick didn't see anyone. As he looked around, his eyes fell upon something that clued him in to Bryson's whereabouts: a box hanging on the makeshift zipline.

"The boys must be hungry." The doting father grabbed one of the pepperoni pizzas and took it outside and placed it inside the contraption.

As Erick did that, Bryson told his friend, "We get the best candy around here. None of that trial-sized candy bar crap you see in other subdivisions. They pass out full-sized bars round these parts, my friend. Sometimes even king size." Bryson rambled on, schooling Domonic on their surrounding area, but then they heard a bell sound.

"The pizza is coming!" Domonic struggled to get to his feet.

"I told you they'd send it up."

The pair gawked from the tree-house window, watching the pizza box as it drew near.

Domonic rubbed his belly in anticipation of its deliciousness. "I hope it's got pepperoni."

"Pepperoni and lots of cheese," Bryson added.

After about two solid minutes of peering from the window, the box arrived at the tree house.

"Yum," they uttered in unison in response to the tantalizing aroma that was filling the tree house.

Bryson pulled down the pizza box and opened it to see eight slices of pepperoni pizza topped with pineapple. It was his favorite. "Yes! I love pineapple."

"I've never had pineapple on pizza before. We always get meat lover's."

"Here, try it. You'll love it." Bryson held the pizza box out for Domonic to take a slice.

Willing to entertain the idea of pineapple on pizza, and with his taste buds primed, Domonic snatched up a slice.

Across the street, Melanie's date pulled up in a red Corvette. You'd think by the look of his car he was over-compensating, but once you took a gander at his large hands, big feet, and lengthy body, that assumption quickly became void.

Melanie greeted the tall, olive-complected man with the long black mane braided into a ponytail that hung down his back. "Welcome to the party."

"Where is everybody?" He looked around but found only Melanie there in her kitty costume.

"It's a private party." Her brown eyes stared into his, as she intended to seduce him right there on the spot.

"All of this for me?"

She tugged at his black bohemian rhapsody T-shirt, pulling him farther into the residence, never breaking her stare. "All of this for us."

Robert was what you would call a bad boy. He had been with his fair share of women but hadn't found "the one." Melanie struck his fancy, as she was not only good looking but was accustomed to making her own money. Regardless of her shining attributes, however, he found her a bit too much of a workaholic for his taste. Her constant working for success made him feel inept at times. He preferred not to feel as if he was in competition with his mate. Not realizing his insecurities were blocking him from having a successful romantic relationship, Robert found himself a single man well into his forties, a fact that didn't bother him in the slightest. Until he could find "the one," Robert was quite satisfied with sampling goods. He had started his submarine sandwich shop at a young age and was doing rather well for himself. The way he saw it, he needed a woman for only one thing.

Pressing his hand to her cheek, Robert rubbed his thumb down her thin strawberry lips. "So, what did you have in mind, kitty kitty?"

Melanie purred. "Follow me." She took his hand and led him to the back of the house.

As they went, Robert enjoyed his view of her bottom as he imagined all that the frisky feline would do to him.

Meanwhile, contentment washed over the boys. "I'm so full," Domonic groaned, lying flat on his back in the tree house.

Lying right beside him, Bryson chimed in. "I'm full, and I'm sleepy."

"You can't go to sleep now. We still have to get candy."

Bryson sat up slowly. "We should get going, then. Besides, the early birds get all the good treats."

"I'm ready when you are, Alucard. Here . . ." Domonic pulled two pillowcases from his book bag and handed one over to Bryson. "We can fill these with candy."

"Thanks." Bryson accepted his pillowcase.

Domonic gathered his Tasmanian devil head and put it on so that he was in full costume. "Our mission is to fill these pillowcases, Alucard."

"Mission accepted." Bryson stood at attention.

Once the boys had climbed down out of the tree, they headed out to comb the neighborhood. Naturally, their street was the first they canvassed, and they pulled in plenty of chips, candy bars, and other snacks for their sweet tooth. When they came upon Melanie's house, the front door was open. She had it set up so that the kids could step inside the foyer to take a treat. The sign above the bowls of Hershey's Kisses read ONLY ONE. Domonic dug in and grabbed a handful of Kisses.

"It says to take only one," Bryson warned.

"One! What's one Hershey's Kiss gonna do for you? Whoever lives here sure is cheap." Domonic allowed his eyes to take in as much of the house's interior that he could see from the foyer. He saw no one. "I wonder where everybody is?" he inquired as Bryson dug into one of the bowls and took more than one chocolate.

"I'm not sure. The lady that lives here always has her door open for Halloween, but I never actually see her, unless she's in the yard, talking to my dad."

"We should check in back to see if she's okay." Domonic tiptoed toward the hallway.

"I wonder if she's even home." Bryson followed along, his better judgment impaired.

As they neared the staircase off the hall, they heard a series of giggles and moans coming from the second floor.

"Shhh . . ." Domonic pressed his paw to his mouth before gesturing for them to go up to check it out.

The boys crept up the staircase and tiptoed down the hallway until they arrived at the bedroom from whence came Melanie's cries of ecstasy. The door was open a crack, so Domonic nudged it open a little more. The boys peeked inside the room to find the neighbor's legs extended in the air and her date for the evening between them. Initially, they pulled their heads back, Bryson's mouth wide open in disbelief. He'd never seen a naked woman before, let alone two people having intercourse.

The boys took one more peek for clarity's sake and surmised, seemingly in unison, that the two people were definitely having sex, as Melanie had been overcome by orgasmic trembling. Bryson had seen enough. He tugged at Domonic's costume, letting him know the time for them to leave had come.

Domonic didn't want to cause a scene about leaving, fearing it would alert their neighbor as to their presence. So he complied, tiptoeing behind Bryson back down the hallway and the stairs, then out of Melanie's house.

"Oh my gosh! I can't believe we just saw that." Domonic ripped off his costume head as he walked up the street alongside an equally shocked Bryson.

"I've never seen that before."

"Seen what?" Domonic inquired.

"People having sex."

"You're telling me you've never walked in on your parents doing the nasty?"

Bryson's face wrinkled in disgust. "Ew. No."

"I have. Lots of times."

"That's gross, Domonic."

"It's not gross. How do you think you got here?"

"I know how I got here. That doesn't mean I want to see it happening. Besides, isn't it kinda weird to look at your parents naked?"

"That's probably why my mom always kept on her dress when they did it. Just in case I walked in . . ."

"When I walk in on my mom and dad in bed, they're always just cuddling. My dad loves to cuddle with my mom."

"Do they cuddle under the covers?"

Bryson shrugged his shoulders. "Sure. I guess."

"They're not cuddling. It's called spooning. That's what happens just before they start to do it."

"I don't want to talk about this anymore. It's giving me a headache," Bryson whined.

"Okay. Let's just concentrate on filling these pillow-cases."

Both boys trotted up the street, a bit wobbly on their feet.

Chapter 34

Deadly Insecurities

Back at the Todds', Evelyn and Erick finished their pizza in the living room as they waited for loads of children in costume to arrive on their doorstep.

"I wonder if the boys are done with their pizza. It's about time they started making their rounds," Erick remarked.

"They may have already started."

"Bryson knows not to leave without me."

"He has a new friend now. Maybe they decided to be big boys and go off on their own," Evelyn said.

"I don't think that's a good idea. It's getting dark, and they don't have on any reflectors."

"Do you want me to go out and check the tree house?"

"No. I'll go. You can stay here. The kids would much rather see your pretty smile." Erick made his way to the sliding glass door in the kitchen and headed out to find their boy.

By the time he made it to the tree house, a waxing crescent moon had risen. His foot caught the first wooden plank at the bottom of the tree; then up he went. Hand over hand, he made his way up to the big tree house. Erick poked his head in but found nothing but an empty pizza box. If only he looked inside Domonic's book bag, he would find the beers the boys had consumed.

However, Erick wasn't a nosy father. Furthermore, he trusted his son. Trust, however, didn't stop him from worrying. Finding his son was of the utmost importance. Erick worried that the absence of sidewalks in the neighborhood could become a problem at night with children roaming about. He already had had to watch his wife recover from being hit by a vehicle. The last thing he wanted was to watch his son fight for his life.

Erick climbed back down out of the tree house. "Bryson!" he yelled, hands cupped around his mouth. "Bryson!"

Since Erick had run off to find the boys, Evelyn thought it the perfect time to interrupt Melanie and Robert's evening. She left the house and crossed the street. All the lights were out over at Melanie's, to alert trick-or-treaters that the free ride had come to an end. She crept into the backyard, made her way across the brick pavers showcasing the patio furniture to get to the sliding glass door. The coin she had stuffed in the lock hole had done its job, keeping the glass door from locking securely. With gloved hands, she pulled the handle back, then walked right inside Melanie's house. The soft, smooth sounds of Barry White came from the record player in the living room. It had to be the most intriguing object in her home. The music was a plus for Evelyn. The louder the music, the less quiet she would have to be.

Where the hell are they? she thought, inching her way down the hall. Evelyn detoured up a set of stairs off the hall. The carpeted staircase made it even easier to muffle her footsteps. Once upstairs, she crept down the hallway until she noticed a flickering light coming from one of the rooms. Evelyn inched closer, then peeked her head in slowly, but she found no one in what turned out to be a bathroom. Three oversized pink candles had been placed around the bathtub, which was filled with bubbles, a sign that the couple's evening was quite romantic.

Evelyn eyed the door on the other side of the bathroom and assumed it led to Melanie's boudoir. But before going there, she needed to pick her poison, so to speak. As she opened the cabinet beneath the bathroom sink, it came to her, the perfect plan. Gathering the item her plan required, Evelyn stepped close to the bathroom's other door and poked her head inside the room beyond it. Her suspicions were confirmed.

There they were, lying naked on Melanie's canopy bed, apparently exhausted from what must have been an eventful evening, one complete with massages and all. Their bodies were greasy from the rubdowns they'd provided one another. She studied the tall, hairy, olive-complected Italian stallion lying sound asleep next to Melanie, his snores no longer drowned out by the sweet sounds of Barry White.

Melanie lay still on her canopy bed, her breasts and center covered by the white satin sheet. Evelyn had stood in the shadows of the room, but now she silently closed in on the pair. A wry grin formed on her face as she ran the straight razor down the prominent vein on Melanie's wrist.

"Looks like you didn't make the cut," Evelyn announced. Feeling some compassion for the woman, she'd decided to give her a peaceful death. Melanie would bleed out in silence, and the charlatan next to her would take the rap for it. She hoped he had a record. Judging by the skull tattoo on his neck and the inky dollar sign on his forearm, she assumed he'd had his run-ins with the law.

Blood poured from Melanie's wrist and soaked into the white sheets. The stream became a crimson flood as the blood ran down the edge of the mattress. *Let's give him a leg up*, Evelyn told herself, placing the razor in Melanie's opposite hand.

Yeah . . . maybe the police will think the sex was so bad she committed suicide, the voice teased.

Regardless of what her alter ego thought, Evelyn felt she'd done all she could to give Robert a fighting chance. In war there were casualties. Evelyn knew that fact well. She walked out of that room, satisfied she had successfully rectified at least one situation. There was no way she would allow Melanie to steal her husband from her, especially after she'd lost Colin.

Now that Evelyn had completed her mission, she could be bothered to deal with the next pressing issue. Where the hell were Bryson and Domonic?

The vengeful wife darted back across the street to join in the search effort. All she needed was her car keys, so that she could drive around, as opposed to searching on foot. The doting mother rushed inside the house, darted to the kitchen, and grabbed her keys from the kitchen counter. She hopped into the truck, the garage door rose, and then she started to back out. Just then Erick pulled in the driveway, his headlights illuminating the back of her Yukon.

"He found them," she whispered upon seeing Bryson hop out of Erick's back seat.

Chapter 35

Guilty Until Proven Innocent

The neighbor's rooster crowed, waking Robert at the crack of dawn. "One more round before I go," he muttered, turning to face Melanie's cold corpse. She didn't budge.

I must have really put in work, he thought, lifting her hand to give it a few pecks. "You're freezing."

That was when he noticed the razor blade that had fallen from the palm of her hand. "What the fuck?" Robert shot right up, startled by his discovery. "Melanie. Wake up, baby." He nudged her face in his direction, took note of the purple hue about her lips. Robert sprang up from the bed and walked around to her side for a more complete picture of what he was dealing with. Immediately, he noticed the crimson puddle that had soaked the sheets on her side of the bed. Her blood had run down onto the floor, staining the crème carpet. "Oh my God." Robert stood in fear of what would happen next.

Sirens blared, waking Erick and Evelyn from their slumber.

"What the hell is going on?" Erick muttered as he hopped out of bed. He rushed over to their bedroom window, peered out, and took in the chaotic scene. "The

police are at Melanie's house. Honey, look. Come see."
He urged Evelyn to come stand beside him. "Maybe we
should go over there."

She saw no need to rush. Evelyn knew exactly what
was going on. She also knew that showing her face at the
scene of the crime wouldn't be a good idea. They'd had
enough dealings with the authorities within the past few
months. Evelyn felt no need to add their names to the
list of witnesses. It would only further complicate things.
Melanie was dead, and Evelyn had washed her hands of
the entire situation.

"What happened?" Evelyn rolled over. "Did someone
toilet paper her house for being cheap and only giving out
Hershey's Kisses on Halloween?"

"Unfortunately not." He snickered, finding humor in
Evelyn's remark. But he grew deadly serious when he
added moments later, "It looks like they're arresting a
man. I think it's the Italian guy she's dating." Erick's
eyes bulged from shock. "Oh my God, Evelyn. They are
bringing out a body bag."

"Are you serious?" Evelyn played it off, then hopped
out of bed to watch the scene unfold.

At the same time, Bryson watched from his bedroom
window. "Oh no . . ." He grabbed his walkie-talkie.
"Tasmanian devil. It's Alucard. Do you copy?"

A yawning Domonic stretched his rested limbs. He'd
just woken up, surrounded by torn candy wrappers. He
fished through the wrappers and finally found the device
Bryson's voice was coming from. "This is Tasmanian
devil. What's up, Alucard?"

"You won't believe what's happening right now. Look
across the street at the naked lady's house."

Domonic climbed out of bed, still wearing the bottom
half of his costume. "Holy shit! Who's in the body bag?"

***

Later Barnes questioned a shaken Robert at the station. He was nervous not because Melanie was dead, but for fear he would be blamed for it.

"What is your relationship to the victim?"

"We were dating."

"How long had you been dating?"

"I don't know. A little over a year, maybe."

"So, you weren't the only one she was dating?" Barnes asked, fishing for a motive.

"I don't know who else she was dating."

"And how did that make you feel?"

"What are you trying to say? I didn't kill Melanie. I have plenty of women. There's no need for me to get jealous over one."

"So, you don't care that she's dead?"

"That's not what I said. Stop trying to twist my words around. I didn't kill Melanie, and I don't hurt women. Not physically, anyway."

"What's that supposed to mean?" Barnes asked, seeking clarification.

"I'm a lover, not a fighter."

"Well, Mr. Lover Boy, would you be willing to take a polygraph?"

"If that's what it's gonna take to clear my name."

"So, you expect me to believe you came over for a date and this woman killed herself while you were sleeping?"

"I don't care what you believe. That's what happened."

"Oh, I assure you, you better start caring about what it is I believe. Your life depends on it."

Evelyn couldn't help but remember Colin's birthday that day. Every time she opened the trunk of her Yukon, she saw the birthday gift she'd purchased for him. All day she had been home playing the doting wife and mother. Each time she tried to leave, Erick would jump in and offer to run whichever errand it was she claimed needed completing. Her frustration had mounted. Not only did she have to endure Erick's constant questioning as to her state of mind, but she had also had to answer questions from the police. The entire neighborhood had been paid a visit, in fact. The officers couldn't fathom how it was that the Todds hadn't seen anything suspicious, despite the fact that they lived right across the street and had a full view of Melanie's bedroom window. Both of them had assured the authorities they hadn't seen a thing. Evelyn just wanted to get out of there now and take Colin his birthday gift.

"Honey, I need to go out for a couple of hours. I promised Christian I would bring her my shirts for work at the retail counter since I won't be coming back anytime soon."

"I can drop them off for you, my love."

"No. It's fine. Christian was so happy to see me the other day. I'd hate to disappoint her. I don't want her to feel like I don't have time for her."

"I completely understand," Erick agreed before kissing Evelyn goodbye. "Just be careful, honey. I think it's going to storm."

"I'll drive like somebody's grandma. I promise."

Chapter 36

Lover's Quarrel

That was when Evelyn found herself leaning back in the black leather chair that sat behind the massive mahogany desk in Colin's corner office. Evelyn couldn't bring herself to leave the office until she'd completed the arduous task she had set out to accomplish. Though a lingering frigidness permeated the air outside, her view of the city of Detroit from the sixty-first floor of the Renaissance Center was breathtaking. A wave of passion overwhelmed Evelyn as she stared out at the star-riddled night sky, wondering if Colin was looking out at the sky at that very moment. Oh, how she missed him. The statuesque woman with the gleaming white teeth and mocha skin was utterly enamored with Colin—and was ready and willing to fulfill his every desire if he so beckoned.

Colin's chiseled physique complemented his kind smile, deep dimples, and intoxicating dark brown eyes, easily garnering him the attention of any woman in his vicinity. Sometimes, Evelyn couldn't manage to keep her focus, as thoughts of Colin would race through her mind. She would envision his strong, capable caramel hands coming at her from the rear, then traveling up her torso to meet at her breasts. He would hold them firmly while nibbling at the nape of her neck. At the thought of this now, Evelyn's heart raced. She began to sweat, and the scent of coconut escaped her pores. With her Ferragamo flats on, she was just tall enough for her ponytail to brush across his nostrils. In her mind, he breathed in deep the aroma of her curls as she closed her eyes, giving in to tingling she felt in her core. Evelyn's stockings grew damp between her thighs—the daydream feeling more real this time than it ever had.

The sound of a black Ferragamo tote bag hitting the mahogany desk startled Evelyn, ripping her from her daydream. Her eyes sprang open to the sight of Jocelyn. She was gorgeous. Her straight jet-black hair traveled down to the middle of her back, and her turquoise eyes matched the peacoat she was wearing. Jocelyn stood five feet, nine inches tall once she'd kicked off her heels. Evelyn was at a loss for words. She wasn't expecting to see Jocelyn there.

"What the fuck are you doing in my husband's office!" Jocelyn rested one hand on her hip.

"Calm down. I was going to go over the checks and balances for the audit. Plus, I wanted to drop off Colin's birthday gift."

"Bitch! You don't work here anymore. What about fired don't you understand? You're not even supposed to be in this building. How did you get up here, anyway?"

Before Evelyn could furnish a reply, Jocelyn added, "You know what? It doesn't matter. You need to leave. Now!" She snatched up the gift bag Evelyn had placed on the desk and slung it across the room. "Get your shit and get out."

Evelyn kept her cool as she rose from the chair to collect her belongings. "Fine. There's no need to get upset or call the police. I'll leave."

The smirk on Evelyn's face as she got up from the chair left a sick feeling in the pit of Jocelyn's stomach.

"I'll be seeing you around," Evelyn sang, gift bag and purse in hand, as she pranced by Jocelyn to exit the office. "Evelyn!"

Evelyn turned to see what Jocelyn wanted now. At that very moment, Jocelyn got a firm grip on the keyboard she had snatched up from the desktop then swung it at Evelyn. The keyboard cracked in half when it collided with Evelyn's face. The blow to the head caught her by surprise. Blood instantly began to leak from her nose, and it ran down her chin staining her silver blouse. The anger that simmered in her belly had reached its boiling point. In a jolt of fury, Evelyn lunged at Jocelyn, wrapping her hands around her throat. Evelyn's plans were to choke the life from her right then and there, but a swift kick to the abdomen sent her back across the room then onto her bottom.

Jocelyn grabbed a paperweight off the desk and headed straight for her nemesis. "I've been waiting to do this for far too long," she snarled as she closed in.

As Jocelyn approached, Evelyn grabbed a Taser from her purse, then zapped her in the leg before Jocelyn could exact her revenge. The surge of electricity brought Jocelyn to her knees. Evelyn didn't waste any time; she sat up all the way and jabbed the Taser into Jocelyn's side, delivering another jolt of electricity. Jocelyn's body jerked involuntarily. The five seconds it took for Evelyn to relent felt like hours to her debilitated opponent.

Finally, Evelyn stood, attempting to wipe the blood from her shirt with her hand, smearing it instead. Regardless, she refrained from losing the cool she'd regained upon getting the upper hand. It wasn't until she walked over and picked the gift bag up off the floor that her sanity waned. Hearing shattered pieces of what was once

Colin's birthday gift as they shifted around in the bag caused Evelyn to snap. Her eyes bulged. "Now look what you've done! It's broken! You selfish, spoiled little bitch. You're gonna pay for this." She released the bag from her clutches, allowing it to drop to the floor.

Chapter 37

One or the Other

Not a cricket could be heard chirping as Erick walked out his front door and headed toward the mailbox at the edge of his driveway. "Looks like it's gonna get nasty out here." He peered up at the passing clouds before glancing down at his wristwatch, worried that his wife wouldn't make it back home in time to miss the storm, which was fast approaching. "Come on, my love. It's about time you got home."

Erick wondered what could possibly be taking her so long. Every time he dialed her phone, the call went straight to voicemail. He didn't know if she'd left the post office or if she and Christian had decided to have dinner. *It may be best if I just wait here for her to come home,* he thought. A hard gust of wind carrying a trail of loose foliage up the road nearly blew from his grasp the manila envelope he had pulled out of the mailbox. "Whoa!" Erick shouted, maintaining his grip on the envelope, as he ran for shelter from the wind.

The moment he stepped foot into the foyer, he could hear Bryson's television blaring.

"You wanna fuck with me! Okay! You wanna play rough? Okay! Say hello to my little friend!" Tony Montana professed before a hail of bullets rang out.

Erick peeked into his son's room and shot him a scolding stare as the boy sat at the foot of his bed, eyes glued to the thirty-two-inch screen atop his dresser. "Bryson? You really shouldn't be watching that."

Although he hadn't turned to see the stern look on his father's face, Bryson had heard the harshness in his tone. So, he didn't waste time pushing the button on the remote, changing the station to something more suitable for a kid his age. "Sorry, Dad. I was just flipping through the channels."

"I think you can find something better suited for you."

"How about Pokémon?"

"Much better." Erick's face relaxed. Bryson was a good kid. Something that made his father very proud . . . He relished that, on top of the fact that Bryson, of all his children, was the only one who was ever there. His older siblings simply didn't need as much rearing.

"Hey, Dad, when do you think Mom will be home?" Bryson inquired, stopping his father from ducking out of the room.

Suddenly, a flash of lightning brightened their surroundings, pulling their attention to the bedroom window. A split second later a cacophonous crackling of thunder erupted. The torrential downpour that followed prompted Erick to spring into action. "I can't just sit here waiting. It's only going to get worse out there."

"Are you going to get Mom? Can I come with you, Dad?"

"Not this time, buddy. You stay here, just in case your mother shows up."

Erick darted off, in a hurry. He had wasted enough time waiting around for Evelyn to show up.

But his actions would do nothing to ease their young son's fears as he peered anxiously through the mini blinds. "Where are you, Mama?"

Walking the hall, Erick tore open the envelope from the mailbox and discovered a tape tucked inside, with a note attached to it. He detached the note and read it.

Erick, I just can't do this anymore. The lies, the unspoken distrust . . . I'm not the woman you think I am. And I can't bear lying to you anymore. There is no coming back from the things I've done. It all ends tonight. You have to know the truth before I'm gone forever, but I can't talk to you at home and risk one of the kids overhearing what I have to say. Meet me at the construction site. Please.

The odds were slim that Erick would not show up when the matter concerned his wife. Considering everything that had been going on, though, Erick thought it best that he brought along protection. There was no way in hell he was going to fail his family again.

With a plan to listen to the tape in the truck on the way to the construction site, Erick headed for the shed out back to retrieve the gun he had purchased after his wife nearly met her demise. At that moment, Erick feared history may be repeating itself. Either way, his picture-perfect life was in jeopardy.

Elsewhere, Colin exited through the doors of the Total Fitness building, flashing that handsome smile that had mesmerized Evelyn to the point of adultery. The woman privy to his pleasant stare smiled back, even bit down on her bottom lip to let him know if he just tried a bit harder, he could have her in his bed. Of course, the thought crossed his mind, as he'd become more brazen since his affair with Evelyn, but he had a more important woman to worry about today. Jocelyn had been waiting nearly all day for him to return home, and he hadn't even bothered to call or check his phone. On his birthday, of all days. He knew she had something planned, even though she'd canceled their trip abroad out of anger.

Colin finally took out his cell phone as he approached his vehicle. His eyes lit up when he realized he had more than a dozen missed calls from Jocelyn. "Damn it." He sulked over his mistake for a moment before returning her call. "Come on, baby. Pick up. Pick up." He tried willing her to answer, but to no avail. After several attempts, the furthest he'd gotten was Jocelyn's voicemail. She was at home, fuming, he assumed. "Looks like I've got some making up to do."

Colin opened his car door, then tossed his gym bag on the back seat. When he glanced up, a note attached to his windshield caught his eye. "What do we have here?" Colin wondered aloud, assuming some woman had left her number, hoping to receive a call back.

He carefully removed the note from the windshield and read it.

I know your secrets, and if you want to keep them a secret, you'll do exactly as I've instructed. Go to the construction site at the corner of Waldon and Sashabaw Road at eight o'clock tonight. Wait for me there. Remember, I'm watching you.
I'll be waiting . . .

To his surprise, the contents of the note revealed just how fragile his marriage had truly become. The sender threatened to expose every dirty secret unless he made an appearance that night. Only the sender didn't leave a signature. Instead, the note ended with the words *I'll be waiting*. That didn't matter. Colin had a good idea whom the note was from, and with a meeting location and an appointed time written there in black and white, he'd soon confirm his mystery correspondent's identity.

A blindsided Jocelyn opened her eyes and began kicking and screaming, only to realize her hands were bound with zip ties, while her mouth had been gagged by the designer scarf that earlier that night had decorated her neck. The tight pitch-black space in which she was confined smelled of pine. *I've been buried*, she thought, a current of fear traveling through her. *I'm going to take my last breath in a pine box, and my husband won't have any idea where I am. I can't die like this.*

She commanded herself to fight—to think past the pain that coursed through her body. Electric pulses sporadically shot through her neck and shoulders the more she fought to break free. It was a part of the sickness she was used to. But this wasn't the time to give in to her struggles. Repeatedly, she thrust her unbound feet against the wooden top of whatever confined her.

Evelyn's voice echoed from a dark corner in the open space. "She's got some fight in her," she admitted, not expecting the top to come flying off. Once it had, Jocelyn's head popped out of the box and her mascara-smeared eyes went wide with shock. Evelyn rushed over to regain the edge she stood to lose. "Get back down in the fucking box. You're such a nuisance." She shoved Jocelyn's head down to force her back inside the makeshift coffin.

The terrified woman thrashed from left to right, grabbing hold of Evelyn's wrist to hinder her from maintaining a steady grip on her head. As Evelyn fought to maintain the upper hand, Jocelyn saw her opportunity to turn the tables. She lifted her legs and folded her knees to her chest before kicking her intended target. Evelyn was catapulted across the room and landed on her bottom as Jocelyn climbed feetfirst out of the box. Years of Pilates helped her stand tall on her feet, at which point she darted for the door. Construction on the building was still underway, so locating an exit took no time at all. Getting to it, however, was a challenge. Just as Jocelyn reached the glowing red exit sign above the door, Evelyn snatched her by the hair and dragged her back across the sawdust-coated cement, toward the box from which she'd escaped.

"Let me go, you crazy bitch! You'll never have my husband. Ever!" Jocelyn screamed as loud as she possibly could. She began coughing from the dust she swallowed.

"*Never* have him?" Evelyn released her grip. "I have, in fact. On your basement sofa, on the sewing table, on your treadmill, on the porch swing, in his car . . . We even fucked in his office, on that beautiful mahogany desk. Would you like me to go on?"

Jocelyn cried silently, as hearing this list of her husband's transgressions shredded every bit of faith she had in their relationship. It was a gut-wrenching feeling. The tears that streamed from her eyes granted her not an ounce of sympathy from her captor.

Evelyn didn't let up. "He wanted me from the moment he laid eyes on me, and I wanted him too. It was only a matter of time before you would eventually find out. Now it's time for you to cut your losses."

Jocelyn's cries ceased instantly. "Cut my losses? Is that why you brought me here? To convince me to cut my losses? You're the loser here. Why else would you have to resort to such desperate measures? Colin doesn't want you. He toyed with you, and after he was done, he discarded you like the piece of garbage you are. My husband will never leave me, and you know it, Evelyn. So, try your best, bitch . . . You'll always come in second place."

Are you gonna let her talk to you like that? the voice in Evelyn's head asked, antagonizing her.

A vein pulsated down the center of her forehead as Evelyn tore toward Jocelyn, completely enraged by the truth she had uttered. A titanium wrench resting on the floor found its way into her clutches as she approached the tormented woman. "He's mine. He's mine. He's *mine!*" She smashed the heavy-duty wrench down against Jocelyn's skull. Evelyn's crazed rant was over in seconds, and silence set in. Her nemesis was out cold.

The only thing left to do is get rid of the body, the voice instructed.

"What do you mean, get rid of the body?" Evelyn blurted. "What's that?" She turned, on pins and needles, dropping the wrench down on the floor beside her. Something outside had caught her attention. She peered through the hole in the side of the concrete structure that was meant for a window. "Oh no. What is he doing here?" she whispered upon seeing Colin's vehicle pull up to the construction site.

He's here for the woman you just killed, the voice answered.

"She's not dead," Evelyn professed, walking back over to Jocelyn's limp body to prove it. "See?" She nudged her with her foot. "Oh, stop faking, you whore. Get up." One more kick to the abdomen for good measure proved her wrong. "She *is* dead." The realization increased Evelyn's panic.

You better get her into that box before hubby arrives, her alter ego warned.

Evelyn rushed back to the window to see if Colin had gotten out of his car, and at that moment, her heart sank into her stomach. There was Erick.

Are you gonna kill him too? the voice asked.

Just outside, thunder roared as two confused, angry husbands came face-to-face.

"You son of a bitch. You had the audacity to come console my wife in the hospital, knowing you were trying to break up my family!" Erick hurled his accusation at a fast-approaching Colin as the storm came down upon them.

"It wasn't like that. I swear to you. I never meant for any of this to happen," Colin replied, making an attempt to clear his name.

"I knew something was wrong with her. I could feel it. A real husband knows these things. And I saw you coming from a mile away, with your sly compassion. So, what now? You think you're her hero, her knight in shining armor? You think you're going to solve all her problems and save the day, huh? You have no idea what it takes to be a loyal husband, a doting father . . . I would do anything to save my marriage—to keep my wife. I'm not going to let you stand in the way of my happy family." Erick's watery red eyes burned.

"Man . . . so, what you wanna do? I said I'm sorry. There's nothing more I can say. I don't want your wife. I have my own. It's as simple as that." Colin turned to head into the building.

"So, you take advantage of my mentally impaired wife, and I'm just supposed to let it go? I wish I could, Colin." Erick rushed toward his wife's lover and tackled him to the ground from behind. "I won't let you ruin my life!" He crashed his fist into Colin's face. Every bit of agony he had experienced from his wife's betrayal was being absolved with each and every blow he inflicted on Colin. He gripped Colin's throat, threatening to choke the life from him.

"Die, you son of a bitch! Get the fuck out of my life. Get the fuck out of our lives." Erick squeezed until droplets of perspiration dripped from his forehead onto Colin's nearly purple face, signaling that his end was upon him. A sight that pleased Erick greatly. He wanted Colin gone forever. Only then would the slate be wiped clean.

At that point, Colin realized that brute force wouldn't give him the upper hand. Erick was too strong to overpower while he was looming over him. Colin's vision was blurred; his breathing was restricted. Then wasn't the time to choke. Instead, he grabbed a fistful of sand from the ground beneath them and chucked it into Erick's face.

"Ahhh!" Erick hollered, eyes stinging from the grains of sand. He released his grip on Colin's throat, attempted to rub his eyes free of debris.

Colin's chance had presented itself. He pushed Erick away, gaining the advantage. The minute Erick's back hit the sand, Colin took to pummeling him, just as Erick had done to him. By this point, the brutal battle had left both men bloody and panting for air. After an exhausting exchange of punches, Erick managed to push Colin off him, only to receive a crushing blow to his chest. Colin's foot had come down with so much force, it had fractured Erick's rib cage.

The jealous husband cried out in agony. Desperate to win at all costs, he saw no other choice but to draw his weapon. The moment he brandished the gun, Colin took off into the darkness. It was too little too late for Colin. Bullets traveled much faster than the panicked man ever could. After Colin entered the building under construction, Erick ran in and unloaded two rounds into the back of his cranium, not feeling the slightest tinge of regret. Not until his gaze moved from the smoking barrel to the horrified woman peering at him from a spot several yards down the dim cement corridor. "Evelyn, my love."

She had seen it all. Every terrifying bit of it. Her knees weakened, bringing her to the cement floor. Evelyn felt as if the wind had been knocked from her lungs. The man of her dreams was dead, and it was all her fault.

Now are you gonna kill him? the voice asked once more.

She looked up, eyes filled with hatred. Hatred aimed squarely at her doting husband. A drenched and exhausted Erick tore up the dimly lit cement corridor toward her as she rose to her feet.

"Evelyn!" he called out to her before being struck in the abdomen with the same titanium wrench she had used to murder Jocelyn. Erick fell to the floor and tried to catch his breath. "Honey, I'm not here to hurt you. I promise!"

She picked up his gun, which had slipped from his grasp, then pointed it in his direction. "Why did you do it? Why did you have to kill him?"

"Is that why you're pointing the gun at me? Because of him? You love him? Do I really mean *nothing* to you? Why can't you remember how perfect our life was? How much we loved each other? How much we loved our family? Why can't you *remember*, damn it!"

Evelyn held her tongue, unable to answer his questions. Questions she had often pondered herself.

"Just do it. Pull the trigger. I don't want to live if it's without you. You are the love of my life. You always will be. So, go ahead, Evelyn. End it all. Take me out of my misery."

With trembling hands, Evelyn squeezed the trigger, firing the gun, ending her life as she knew it. Pulling the trigger was all it took for her memories of Erick and the life they had shared to come flooding back. She remembered the look in his eyes when he lifted the veil to kiss her on their wedding day. Evelyn recalled the way it had felt when, together, they held their firstborn child. The day they met rushed into her mind, along with the moment she knew he would be the man she'd spend the rest of her life with.

"I remember. I remember everything." She dropped to her knees, in tears, thanking God that she had shot into the wall beside him.

The two of them kissed and shared a long-awaited embrace—one filled with their entire hearts.

"What have I done?" Evelyn whispered.

"What have *we* done?" Erick said.

"I don't want to go to prison, Erick."

"We have to get rid of the bodies," he replied, maintaining a calm exterior. "Who's that, by the way?" He pushed his chin out in the direction of Jocelyn's corpse, sprawled out across the floor.

"Colin's wife," Evelyn answered bashfully.

"My God, honey. You have been busy."

The Final Chapter

Full Circle

Jackson's plan to lure Colin and Erick to the construction site had come together perfectly for him. So far, the Todds were doing all the work. He watched the murderous couple through a pair of binoculars from the driver's seat of his vehicle as they dragged Jocelyn's body across the sandy soil and dumped her into a hole deep enough for her body to go undiscovered. Colin's body came next. Afterward, the husband and wife found themselves peering down into the hole, happy that the entire ordeal was almost over. It was then that Jackson crept from his vehicle and skittered across the ground.

"Look at you two. I don't know which one of you is more pathetic," Jackson blurted, catching them by surprise. The gun he held on them warned them not to move too hastily. "Now, what should I do with you?"

Evelyn's eyes narrowed. "You? It was you this entire time? I knew you were a psycho," she growled, her memories of Jackson surfacing.

"Oh, shut up, slut. You're out here reciting, 'Eeny, meeny, miny, moe, catch a husband by the penis.'"

"Funny you didn't seem to get tagged in. Is that why you're mad? Feeling not quite good enough?" she snarled.

"I should blow your fucking brains out."

"Or maybe I should blow yours out, mister. I'm not a perfect shot, but this red dot aimed at your head tells me my odds are looking pretty good," Bryson chimed in, having emerged from his hiding place in the back seat of his father's pickup truck. "I wouldn't make any sudden moves if I were you." Bryson used his free hand to support his wrist, stabilizing a wobbly trigger finger for a perfect aim.

Look who's not a pussy, after all, the voice in Evelyn's head proclaimed as she stood frozen in disbelief at the fact that her little boy was there and wielding a gun, no doubt.

"What are you doing, kid? You really shouldn't be here. Why don't you just drop the gun and run along?" The foreboding expression on Jackson's face conflicted with the softness in his tone. It frustrated him that he had to bargain with a child. But since he didn't abuse children, he saw no other way to persuade Bryson than by trying to reason with him.

"I promised my mother I would protect her. All I have in this world is my balls and my word, and I don't break them for no one. Now apologize, before I shoot you dead right here. Do it, chump!" Bryson snarled.

"Look, kid, I apologize for sullying your mother's good name. But if you want your parents to live, you should drop the gun."

"You first, asshole. Then we'll go our separate ways."

"I'm sorry, kid. I can't allow that to happen." Jackson took the risk, turning his gun on Bryson, but not before Erick pulled the nine-millimeter he had tucked into the back of his pants and unloaded it into Jackson.

Evelyn made a beeline for Bryson. "Bryson, are you okay? What a brave boy you are!" She hugged him tight for a moment, thanking God that she'd been blessed with a child as smart and brave as Bryson. "Give me the gun, honey." She removed the weapon from Bryson's clutches while he stood in amazement of his father's actions. "Where did you get a gun from? Is this fake?" She lifted it, testing its weight.

"Dad always gets me the best of the best."

"Aren't you a trickster!" She proudly ran her fingers through his curls before planting a tender kiss atop his head.

Erick knelt by the body to check for Jackson's pulse. He was dead. "Bryson, go back to the truck and wait for your mother and me there."

"Yes, Dad." Bryson did as instructed.

"What should we do with this one?" Erick said.

Add him to the pile in the hole, said the voice in Evelyn's head.

"I'm better now. I don't think I'll be needing your opinion anymore," Evelyn whispered.

Oh no, my dear. I'm a permanent fixture. The voice in her head cackled.

Still kneeling, Erick looked up at his wife, wondering what she was going on about so quietly. "Honey, did you say something?"

"Get his car keys. Then add him to the hole with the others," she said reluctantly, taking the advice of her alter ego. "We'll fill the hole with cement and then get rid of the rest of the evidence."

As the sun rose, Fackender stepped onto the sandy soil of the construction site. She was there to answer a noise complaint they'd received late the previous night. Erick was front and center, and he ended his conversation with one of his employees to greet her at the gate.

"How can I help you, Officer?"

"We meet again, Mr. Todd."

"Under better circumstances at least. I'm assuming . . ."

"I hope so. I'm here on more of an informal basis. There was a noise complaint that came in last night. Someone reported gunshots." Fackender looked around for signs of anything out of the ordinary.

"We've got several machines that may sound like gunshots, but we stop all construction by six p.m. My guys have to get home to their families, as do I. Not to mention there was a huge storm last night. Lots of thunder and lightning . . ."

"I'm aware of the storm. The incident was reported well after six p.m. So, you didn't notice anything strange when you got to work this morning?"

"Not a wrench out of place," Erick answered at the same time that he noticed a shell casing on the ground, right next to Fackender's boot. The sun beaming down on him started to feel much hotter than it was. *Don't panic*, he coached himself. "You're free to go inside and look around," he said and motioned toward the building's entrance.

Fackender removed her sunglasses and disregarded the glare, which caused her to squint. Assuming the look in her eyes demanded only the truth, she cross-examined the man before her. "Looks like you settled the disagreement." She alluded to the bandage above his eye, along with the shiner surrounding it.

Erick laughed off her assumption. "Nothing a good old boxing match can't solve."

"I guess so," Fackender remarked, unsure whether she believed him or not. Be that as it may, having no reason to distrust him, she focused on the task at hand. "I think I'll take a look. Just for the sake of being thorough."

He called over one of his employees, the new hire. "Hey, Harry! Would you mind giving this officer the tour?"

Harry rushed over, pushing his glasses up the bridge of his nose. "Sure thing, sir. Follow me, Officer."

Fackender shot Erick a suspicious look before tagging along behind Harry.

"Let me know if you need anything, Officer," Erick called when she was a few yards away. He smiled, confident there was nothing she was going to find. Especially since he had picked up that last shell casing and shoved it into a pocket of his jeans.

Erick remained confident his family's good name would go on unsullied. No one would ever notice that bloodstain upon their white picket fence.

The End